THE HOLLOW WITCH

MARY BORSELLINO

Clan Destine
PRESS

First published by Clan Destine Press in 2024

Clan Destine Press
PO Box 121, Bittern
Victoria, 3918 Australia

National Library of Australia Cataloguing-In-Publication data:

Borsellino, Mary

THE HOLLOW WITCH

ISBN: 9781922904881 (paperback)
       9781922904904 (eBook)

Cover illustration by AkirouArt
Cover Design by Willsin Rowe
Design & Typesetting by Clan Destine Press

Clan Destine
P R E S S

FOR ERIS

"Beautiful and macabre, Borsellino weaves a darkly spellbinding tale of sapphic love in a world where the dead aren't always gone. The Hollow Witch will keep you turning the pages deep into the night."

C.S. Pacat

New York Times
bestselling author of *Dark Rise*

"This is a wild, magical, powerful story; a force to be reckoned with. Our queer disabled heroine may live in a world of zombies and witches but, like our own, it's also rife with corruption, oppression and violence. Can love, friendship and hope survive in such a place? The Hollow Witch dares us to imagine what ending we'd choose for this story, and perhaps even our own world... red fan, or white?"

Jess Walton
author of *Stars in Their Eyes*

THE
HOLLOW
WITCH

1. SILVIE

'THERE ARE TOO MANY GHOULS IN THE FOREST. WE NEED YOU,' SAID Kolya.

The poor kid was exhausted and pale, his usually sharp gaze dulled with tiredness. Silvie gave him a second fruit bun. There was no harm in a little petty crime and the buns weren't selling anyway. If she was leaving the bakery today, it hardly mattered whether she was giving away free samples.

'I'm not due back at the barracks for another week,' she reminded him.

'Bd hr d–' Kolya swallowed his mouthful before trying again. 'But you're the best, and we need you.'

Silvie shook her head, smiling. 'I'm not the best, I'm just the closest. The others went further away for better work. Don't try to butter me up.'

'I'm not buttering you up! You're the best,' Kolya said, absolutely buttering her up. He was good at turning on the charm when he wanted to. 'And you have to help. Please? It's going to be dark soon. The ghouls get hungrier then.'

'No, they don't. That's superstition.' Silvie didn't bother to correct him on "ghouls". Sentries weren't allowed to use "upir", like the villagers did, and although she used the official "cadaveri" readily enough while working, she baulked at adopting it into her own vocabulary. "Ghouls" was a compromise she was willing to overlook.

She argued with Kolya for another few minutes, but they both knew how the debate would end. After saying goodbye and thank you to the owner of the bakery where she had worked this leave-break, Silvie went upstairs to collect the sentry cloak she'd stored out of sight weeks earlier.

She held it in her hands for a few moments before putting it on, rubbing one thumb idly against the mustard-yellow fabric. Silvie was used to the weight of the wool on her shoulders. It was one of the most familiar sensations in her life.

When she'd first worn it, the hem had reached her ankles. Now it was high on her calves. As sentries went, Silvie was tall.

Leave was a routine part of a sentry's life, a chance to recover from the strain of the work they did. Not from all work, of course – while they were away from the barracks, they had to earn their own living. Silvie was used to it; she'd never known anything else.

'I hate being in the village,' Kolya complained as they walked through its outskirts towards the barracks. He kicked at a pebble on the path. 'On my way to see you, some boys threw snowballs soaked in piss at me. Yellow snow for the yellowcloak.'

Silvie spent a few uncharitable seconds imagining how helpless and terrified those boys would be if ghouls overran their safe little world. But she was older than Kolya, so she had to set a good example.

'We should feel sorry for them,' she told him. 'They'll never be anything other than human.'

'Well, I don't,' he retorted. 'I hate them.'

'Don't let anyone hear you say that. It'll only make things worse.'

'I know, I know. I still wish they'd all drop dead.'

Kolya hadn't been turned over to the sentries until he was seven and, for all its bullying and restrictions, his new life in a yellow cloak was a reprieve from what had come before. He'd learned how to be a child eventually, but he was always brittle and blank in how he dealt with others, as if something fundamental had been stolen from him. Silvie didn't have a name for it, or even know how to define it beyond its absence.

'Then we'd all get reassigned to other parts of the kingdom. If they all dropped dead, I mean,' Silvie pointed out, humouring him. 'No point in having sentries if there's nobody left to protect.'

'Doesn't sound so bad,' sniffed Kolya stubbornly, refusing to relent on his daydreams of murder. 'Maybe we'd be sent to Gemelli, and have cherry cheesecake for every meal.'

'I don't think they have it for every meal, even in Gemelli.' Silvie couldn't help but give a merry laugh at Kolya's resulting pout.

No matter how much she resented having her leave cut short, Silvie felt a familiar thrill as she settled into her seat in the sentry-house, drawing in a deep breath and sending herself out into the wolf waiting at the forest's edge.

Once upon a time, the sentry-houses had tried to raise the wolves with the same strictness as they raised the sentries themselves, but it hadn't worked – only the truly wild, unfettered wolves that lived freely in the forest had minds open enough to link with. Domestic animals were too human.

Silvie had first connected with her current wolf four years ago, when he was scarcely more than a cub and she was younger than Kolya was now. He wasn't her first wolf, but he was the closest bond she'd felt, her mind slipping in easily to overlap and blend with him as he paced.

Connecting to wolves was a learned ability, and a hard-learned one at that. Silvie was glad of the skill, but looked back on her earliest years with an echo of remembered pain. Sentries did not have childhoods, they had a very specific and very difficult education.

There was no way to know how aware the wolves were of being controlled, but they didn't seem to mind it. Silvie was glad. She would have felt bereft without the freedom she felt when she was a wolf. It was the one truly bright thing in her life.

She was off! Senses alight with a thousand things at once as she ran, Silvie thrilled at the sheer pleasure of being a creature utterly at home in its environment, powerful and strong and adept. Every petty cruelty of her life as a sentry was worth this.

A scent that came when the snow melted into the dark soil made her wolf-mouth water as much as the quicksilver living aroma of small prey between the trees did. To the wolf's keen senses, that cold-smell was the language of home, nuanced and subtle as a poem.

The twigs and bracken were cold and rough under her wolf-paw. Magic crackled wild and weird in the air all around, another symptom of whatever imbalance was stirring up more ghouls than usual.

Distantly, she was aware of her arms prickling to gooseflesh, but Silvie dismissed the irrelevant sensations of her human body and concentrated on the world around her wolf-self. There was a dank, dense feeling in the air, the ominous atmosphere that often came when the ghouls were out in numbers.

Silvie could tell that one was nearby already, the scent of it like a falling ribbon in the dark, bright and twisting in the air. The whole forest pulsed with life, making the un-life she was tracking stand out even more. She could taste her victory already, the rend of her claws and the snarl of her mouth as she rendered dead flesh inert and eliminated the threat.

But she didn't hear the one on her left. It didn't have the pungent reek of the one she tracked, it was too old – more desiccated bone and sinew than corpse. After the skull-crushing snap forward of its upper jaw, there was no time for comprehension or pain to dawn. It was as instant and simple as the breaking of a twig: one moment she lived and the next…

A window was wide open, letting in the din of heavy rain and of bells. Stirred by the deluge, the air carried with it the stench of decay, a dank rot thicker than the prey-scent Silvie had chased as she rode the wolf's mind.

She'd died as she'd always expected to. Most sentries didn't live long enough for their yellow cloaks to become as short on them as hers had. She should consider herself lucky. She'd grown old enough to become tall: a small victory.

So what now? Was she a ghost? If so, why was she haunting this unfamiliar place? What connection did she have to this room, and why was that link strong enough for her last seconds to fling her consciousness here, so much further than the distance to a wolf?

Two girls were huddled together beneath the open window, oblivious to the rain. One comforted the other, rubbing her back and whispering inaudible sympathies into her ear. Other people were in this strange, sumptuous room as well, but they were a blur to Silvie.

She moved closer. That was the only way she could think of it, even as she understood that direction and dimension didn't mean much to her anymore. Her wolf was gone, like a thousand wolves before it; and, like a thousand other sentries, Silvie was gone as well, like a sailor caught in the rigging of a sinking ship, drowning as it descended. This strange scene was some final flare of magic before she vanished, her story over.

The older girl, about seventeen, Silvie's age, raised her head. Unlike the younger one in her arms, she wasn't crying. She had an unnervingly beautiful face: wide, seafoam-green eyes, lashes as black and bold as stitches. Heavy dark curls framed her grief-drained face.

'What's going to happen to Lena?' the beautiful girl asked, arms curling closer around the other girl, who was probably no older than fourteen years. Her face was buried in her hands and her form swallowed by the heavy pink velvet of the skirt puddled around her. What little of her skin was visible in that position was the porcelain tone some women attained by magic, but this girl was far too young for that.

'What's going to happen to her?' the beautiful girl asked again, her voice sharper and more demanding. 'You can't send her away. You can't.'

Silvie shifted focus, turning the world to see who the girl was speaking to.

A handsome man in his prime lay in the middle of a huge bed, his patrician form still and diminished in the particular way that told Silvie he was dead. Distantly, she realised that her own body must look that way now, as well. Empty.

Another man, this one younger and very much alive, stood by the body. He cast a brief, numb glance in the direction of the demand. 'Nothing.'

'Nothing?'

'I have no intention of taking a queen. The tower is hers.'

One of the other figures came into focus as they approached the man. 'Your Majesty, you must see to the christallo immediately; the cadaveri are rampant throughout the city.'

The living man turned away from the dead one and from the girls, setting his shoulders with a deep inhale. Most of the other people followed him as he strode from the room.

The beautiful girl's shoulders dropped with relief, her face softening from fear to calm. Silvie felt a small sting of regret that she'd never know anything more about her.

As if on cue, the world gave a sickening lurch and Silvie thought *I wish* and everything went black.

The first sensation of her new life was vertigo, her whole self reeling and spinning, a sense of falling that didn't stop despite the bed beneath her.

The second was the sound of bells, ringing and ringing, barely quieter than they'd been in that other place she'd gone to. Her head, already aching, could hardly bear the sound.

Even more unbearable than the clang of bells were the voices, a dozen of them all layered on top of one another like a deck of shuffled cards, no single thread of conversation distinct from any other. Silvie's senses all felt dull and clumsy, like when she was a child and first learning how to ride a wolf's mind. Nothing was as vivid as it should be. Everything was a little too slow. It was as if she was trying to ride her own mind but didn't know the trick of it.

'Silvie! Silvie, can you hear me?'

'Kolya?' she managed to reply, opening her eyes and then slamming them shut again an instant later. Everything was too bright, like the world was made from sunlight on water. Her head throbbed, spinning and spinning. 'How am I alive?'

'We saved you. We…' He trailed off. Silvie thought he might be crying. 'Anyway, it doesn't matter. All that matters is that it worked.'

He was deflecting, and clumsily at that. She thought she'd taught him to speak with more cunning. But maybe the scolding could wait for a little while. Until the spinning stopped.

Silvie drew in a slow, steadying breath, trying to quell her nausea. It didn't work.

Another peal of bells made her wince. Everything was so loud, like the whole world was happening right beside her pillow.

'Why are the church bells ringing?'

'We know why there were so many extra ghouls, now.' Kolya squeezed her hand again, as if to reassure himself that she was warm and present. 'The beacons caught fire an hour ago.'

'The beacons?' Muddled, she tried to make sense of his words.

'The signal beacons, from Arteria,' he told her. 'The King is dead.'

2. AZURA

One year later

'—EASE DISMEMBER OR OTHERWISE DESTROY ANY HUMAN CORPSES lying in state.'

The warning ripped Azura out of sleep. The corridor outside the apartment was alive with footsteps and voices. The amplified announcement rang out again, cutting sharply through all other sounds, as if the magic it required wasn't making the whole situation even worse. More magic in use meant more ghouls rising, a simple and horrific equation.

'Attention please. Attention please. One of the Stregoni has died. Please remain in your homes until the all-clear is given. Do not approach any cadaveri unless you are armed. Please dismember or otherwise destroy any human corpses lying in state.'

Azura checked the clock on her wall. Just after four. She considered making the trek to check on Lena, but decided against it – if Lena had slept through the warnings, Azura didn't want to disturb her; and if Lena was on her way to the servants' wing then Azura didn't want to risk them missing one another in the palace's labyrinthine hallways. Her best option was to stay where she was, no matter how frustrating that might be.

The amplified voice repeated and repeated. Azura felt a shiver of deja vu from the scenes of a year earlier; the only thing she'd ever heard as loud as the voice, was the cacophony of mourning bells that had rung for the King.

Azura's weekly languages lesson was due later in the morning and a few hours of lost sleep wouldn't be a valid excuse if she did poorly. Sometimes she felt like nothing was a valid excuse. Either she did as she was told and excelled at it, or she was a failure.

She pulled her pillow from under her head and tried to use it to muffle the sound, but all that did was give her thoughts a chance to become louder inside her skull, and her thoughts were no more comforting than the din she was trying to drown out.

She imagined King Dante's preserved body breaking free of its glass coffin, the shattered shards splintering further under his blindly groping hands and lurching feet. The idea made the skin between her shoulder blades crawl.

The mourning hall, where the King's body was displayed, was too far away from anyone's living quarters for his rising to be any real danger, but rationality and sensible facts were poor weapons against fear. Azura learned long ago that what terrified her in the night felt silly and insubstantial by the light of day, but that knowledge wasn't much good when night held sway and the dark seemed endless.

She was well aware that it was a good ten minutes' walk from the servants' wing to the mourning hall, and that she was absolutely safe even if the King rose, but logic didn't help with the way her heart hammered.

'Attention please. Attention please...' the words began again. Then the confident rhythm faltered and trailed off.

'If you can't bring yourself to sever the head, please seal all exits to the room and wait until someone is able to attend to the situation. Ensure that you and the other occupants of your home are safe.'

These new instructions lacked the measured placidity of the standard alert, and Azura felt a flare of hot guilt for worrying about her lessons and imaginary threats when real cadaveri were rising and causing havoc in the world beyond her comfortable room.

Turning her thoughts away from the King, dead a year already, she wondered instead which of the Stregoni had died and caused this new chaos. There were six of them, all pretty ancient, and their careful balancing act kept the country's magic running smoothly. With one of them gone, the whole system was thrown off, and the result was an increase in cadaveri.

Not that it made much difference in the end who had died. This night of frantic panic and the earnest debates about raising the tariffs on magic would go the same way regardless. People would object, King Claudio would placate them and promise no increases, and then eventually a new Stregone would be appointed to replace the old one and everything would go back to normal. Even the most frightening elements of the process were predictable.

The arguments about magic prices would put Azura's father in a bad mood, and the palace would increase the number of cadaveri drills, which would put Azura in a bad mood, so things were probably going to be miserable at home for a while.

After the King's death, the riots – and what happened to the rioters – were frightening enough that Azura took the drills very seriously. At first, anyway. Anything that promised to enforce order onto the chaos, even a little bit, felt like salvation. She'd gratefully thrown herself into the minutiae of the emergency procedures, because that way she wasn't stuck with her head under a pillow with nothing to distract her from her fear.

She'd had a lot of nightmares about cadaveri in those first few months. But the nightmares faded, and the drills went on, becoming tedious, the small comfort they offered worn down by the way they interfered with her life.

Now they would be even more frequent, more tedious, right as her studies were especially difficult. Now her worries would be twofold: a renewed fear of cadaveri to keep her awake at night, and never-ending drills to interrupt her day.

The repeated drone of the warnings – back to their standard script now – was giving her a headache. Azura put the pillow over her head again and pressed it hard against her ears. She hoped Lena's tower had better soundproofing than the servants' wing.

Azura's imagination, ever helpful, spilled over with memories of the night King Dante had died. She and Lena had watched from the tower window, the world blurred and dark through the storm, as the soldiers worked to hold back the crowd in front of the palace gates.

Lena had given an almost soundless gasp, her slim fingers tightening to fists where they lay on the sill, when the first casualty fell to an officer's sword. The blade was dark with blood for a moment before the rain sluiced down and diluted the red. Even a year later, Azura sometimes found herself thinking of that tiny gasp, of the rain washing the colour away.

The bodies hardly had a chance to hit the cobblestones before they rose again as cadaveri, launching their gaping mouths at soldiers and citizens alike. Even from their high vantage point, even through the dark, Azura and Lena were able to see how utterly changed the figures were – eyes glassy and fixed, or rolled back half-closed with only a sliver of milky grey visible.

They didn't move like humans, because humans constantly calibrated themselves to their surroundings in tiny ways: shifting their posture, blinking against wind or grit, breathing air. Cadaveri did none of those things. If they stumbled on uneven ground, there was no staggering to regain their balance; they just fell and then hauled themselves forward. There was no awareness of their own existence or of the world around them. Nothing but driving, devouring hunger, the need to bite and destroy.

Azura knew those ghastly scenes of a year ago wouldn't repeat this time, though. This wasn't the death of a monarch, just a spell-caster. Spell-casters were replaceable, no matter how important they made themselves out to be.

Kings were replaceable too, but Azura had seen firsthand how much messier that process was.

The alarm was again growing more urgent and anguished, the instructions becoming pleas. Another shudder crawled up Azura's back. She gripped the pillow tighter.

It took her a long time to fall back to sleep.

Her father was already at the table when Azura stumbled out for breakfast later in the morning, absorbed in the thick stack of correspondence that always awaited him with his tea and toast.

Azura's father was tall and wiry, but Azura was small and short like her mother. Azura wished she'd known her better. There was so much she wanted to ask about, but there was nobody to ask, really. Her father would get sad and quiet, and that made Azura feel guilty as well as desperately curious.

Maybe that's why she and Lena had become so close so quickly as young children, despite the difference in their status. Two girls in a castle of men.

Their suite of rooms in the servants' wing was a holdover from earlier times more than a reflection of rank. Doctor Antonio Corsetti was the royal record-keeper and alchemist, and the comfortable clutter of the living space provided for him and his daughter reflected the prestige of the role: not nobility by any means, but respected and compensated fairly. They could have moved to a more convenient part of the palace, but Azura's father declined any such offers, saying that these well-appointed rooms had been good enough for his father and they were good enough for him. Azura suspected he just didn't want to go through the hassle of moving.

His work kept him busy every waking hour of his day, including meal times. When Azura was younger and needier, she'd resented that, especially after the loss of her mother. Over time, she'd done her best to make peace with it. She took what little of her father's attention could be spared for her, and told herself that it was enough.

'Did the alarms wake you last night?' he asked as Azura poured herself a cup of tea.

'Yeah.'

'Eugenio passed away. I've been asked to conduct the autopsy, in my capacity as alchemist.'

Azura's eyebrows went up in surprise. 'He was poisoned?' She remembered Lena telling her that Eugenio was one of the better-natured of the Stregoni, looking the other way whenever Lena smuggled novels into long, dull ceremonies. 'Who would poison somebody nice?'

'I doubt anyone suspects foul play,' Azura's father clarified, attention still on the morning's messages. 'It could have been a poorly made batch of chemical wedding–'

Azura coughed pointedly. She hadn't even finished her first cup of tea, which meant it was way, way too early in the morning to hear her father talk about drugs and sex.

'I'll go to the palazzo for dinner, then, if you're busy.'

'Nope.' He shook his head. 'There'll still be a heightened cadaveri risk for a day or two. You're staying in the palace grounds.'

Azura scowled, but knew from experience that there was no point in trying to argue. She thought she'd spent less time annoyed at her dad when she was younger, but that might have been the rosy patina of nostalgia.

'These magic tariffs are absurd,' her father muttered, his scowl a mirror of her own as he read the next memo in his stack. 'We need to use less magic. The cadaveri wouldn't be an issue if people relied on it less.'

Azura, who felt the thrum of magic around and through her at all times, thought it would probably be easier to stop breathing than to stop using it.

'I'm going to lead by doing,' her father declared. 'I'll get an apprentice, and I'll get one that doesn't use magic.'

'Out of all the people in Arteria, I'm pretty sure the royal alchemist and record-keeper has the most justifiable reasons for using magic, Dad.'

'That's why I should set the example by cutting back, don't you see?'

'No, not really.' Azura slurped her tea.

Most of the population, close to four out of five people, had a minimal amount of magic. The efforts of the Stregoni and the King then channelled the raw power through a christallo – a dense quartz that boosted untethered potential into something useful. At least three people at a time worked its magic, with the King taking more shifts than anyone else. The exact workings of the christallo were kept secret to a select few. No matter how much Azura wheedled and begged, her father was never forthcoming.

She'd heard all the rumours about what being in close contact with the christallo was like – the way it messed with people's heads, the way it seemed to speak right to them. It frightened her to think of it.

The remaining percentage of the population was split fairly evenly between true magic users, like Azura and the Stregoni, who had significant innate ability, and those without any magic at all – voids or hollows, pitied by the general public.

'By "doesn't use magic", do you mean someone who can but mostly doesn't, or someone who really can't?'

'Someone who really can't. A void.'

Of course he meant a void. Azura somehow refrained from rolling her eyes.

'That'll make your life much harder than it needs to be, and will have minimal benefit for anyone,' she pointed out. 'Seems kind of stupid.'

Her father shook his head. 'It'll be fine. I know what I'm doing.' He shuffled through the stack of papers beside his plate, distracted again. 'Finish up your breakfast quickly and go to the study. Lena and your morning tutor will be arriving soon.'

The study had the same furniture and knick-knacks in it that Azura's grandfather had put there when he'd been the record keeper. After his son – Azura's father – had inherited the title, the study had fallen into disuse, with Doctor Corsetti choosing to spend his time in the records library instead of secluded on the other side of the palace grounds.

Now Azura and Lena used it for their lessons, but Azura was reluctant to change anything. It didn't feel right for a couple of young students, no matter how incongruously highly-ranked one of those students might be, to overhaul a room that had remained static for generations. Maybe when she inherited it herself she'd feel differently about it, and change the decor to suit her personal preferences. But Azura didn't want to think about that future.

And so the room remained as it always had. A large and beautifully-painted globe of the world sat in one corner, and there was an overstuffed dark leather couch and a couple of rattan chairs with crisp white cushions.

A glass and wood display case was mounted on one wall, filled with neatly pinned butterflies. Lena loved it, so Azura couldn't have removed it even if she'd wanted to. She wasn't sure whether she did want to, in fact, so it was a relief to have the decision out of her hands.

The two girls were in absolute agreement about making one change on their first day using the room, though. When Azura's grandfather was alive, the bare polished boards of the study floor were covered by a tiger-skin rug. He'd killed the tiger himself. Azura and Lena put it inside a chest in the corner of the room.

Azura felt slightly guilty about that, as if they'd rendered the poor animal's death meaningless by storing it out of sight, but she couldn't stand the thought of leaving it in the open. Even touching it for the few seconds it had taken them to put it in the chest had made her flesh crawl.

Azura fiddled with her grandfather's antique letter-opener, embossed in gold with his initials and kept because it matched the names of subsequent owners. A.C: Amadeo Corsetti, Antonio Corsetti, Azura Corsetti.

Azura's mouth curled into a momentary smile, her heart full of fondness for her humble, clever family. Then she remembered her father's plans to take on a new apprentice, and her mood plummeted to irritation, though she wasn't sure why.

As if to provide her with a justification, her glasses started pinching the side of her head. They were too small, but trying to get a new pair would end in disapproval and disappointment from her father. The prospect was exhausting.

It had been obvious from her earliest years that Azura couldn't see well. She couldn't remember a time before her first pair of glasses. Sight-correcting magic was common among adults, and very occasionally administered to teenagers, but the risk of permanent damage was too high if the patient was too young. Ten years was the absolute legal age minimum, and so the sight of children wearing glasses wasn't uncommon among those who could afford them.

Azura had never thought much about getting sight magic done someday, and didn't mind wearing glasses. She didn't actually like having any kind of magic performed on her, choosing to endure sunburns and scraped knees rather than have them tended to by spells, as other children of means did.

As soon as Azura turned ten, however, King Dante had magnanimously offered Azura's father the opportunity to have the girl's eyes fixed without cost. The King hated imperfection anywhere in his palace, and considered Azura's eyes a problem, and problems demanded solutions. That attitude had made him a diligent, engaged leader when it came to the business of ruling a country, but a benign tyrant when it came to the world within his palace. Although the offer was generous, in her secret heart of hearts Azura could never forgive him for forcing her to get her eyes fixed.

Two weeks after the King's death, Azura had gone out and bought a pair of glasses. The lenses were clear glass with no curve to bend the light, since her magically improved eyesight had no need of their help. She wore the glasses whenever she could get away with it. With the King gone, it was her choice to make again – and so she did, even if it was no longer necessary.

Her father disapproved of the glasses, of course, so Azura often didn't bother with them. The arguments and comments were exhausting. But she wished she had the strength to stand up to her father's remarks, to wear them all the time. Even after so many years of perfect vision, she felt more like herself when she was wearing glasses. They were a shield she could hide behind, a mask to help her face the world.

Azura didn't know whether Lena missed the things King Dante had changed about her. When Azura was ten and having her eyes fixed, Lena was seven. Well below the minimum age, she'd nevertheless had her skin lightened to a delicate porcelain and her eyes given the double lids of Arterian-born beauties.

A few weeks later the incident with the canal happened, after which Myles had become Lena's constant shadow and protector. His thirteen years had seemed very grown up to Azura. She could still remember how tongue-tied and shy she'd been around this real teenager acting as the Queen's new bodyguard.

What she couldn't remember, no matter how she concentrated, was whether the King had ordered anything about Myles to be fixed when the boy was hired.

Maybe it didn't matter. King Dante was dead now, still and silent in his glass coffin. His opinions didn't count for anything anymore.

3. SILVIE

Being out under an open sky always gave Silvie a feeling of deep calm. As the last twelve months had dragged on, she was in increasingly desperate need of it, and sought it out in whatever small moments she could snatch from her life.

Her wolf's mind had been woven with her own when the ghoul's teeth sank into it, and so the parts of the wolf's brain that were sliced and torn had died inside Silvie's head too. Half her stability and half her hearing were wrenched away by the jagged bite. The other sentries had used their magic to sever the tether before death could take Silvie along with the wolf, but her own magic had died in her place.

Over the past year of recovery and rehabilitation, Silvie often wondered whether that wasn't almost the same thing as dying. Magic had always been an integral part of her, more than her height or her name or her blood. She had started small, then grown tall over time; her name held no more meaning than being the next choice in the crèche's book for new arrivals; and her blood spilled easily and without consequence. But her magic…

Her magic had been her own.

Silvie knew with utter certainty she'd never forget the moment after waking when she reached for it and found it missing. When she'd no longer felt the energy and freedom that made everything else in her life bearable. Now she was stuck. And so small.

And the world, stripped of magic, was such a disappointment.

The loss of it was so monumental that it seemed impossible Silvie had any self pity left over to notice the other losses. But one misery didn't cancel out the capacity for other miseries. The deafness on her left side was a far greater blow than the need for a cane to steady her. Hearing loss destabilised her more than vertigo. It skewed her whole life sideways, not just her balance.

Seeing the last glimmer of the night's stars made Silvie's terror at her own smallness a little more manageable. It helped her put into perspective that everything else was small, too.

Even plaited back tight enough to hurt her scalp, Silvie's hair always stank of smoke by morning. It was the cheap tobacco kind that slithered into every corner and crack of air throughout the tavern, including Silvie's part of the kitchen.

She'd worked there before, years ago, when she was Kolya's age. Back then she'd scented her hairbrush with rosewater to drive off the stink each morning, but these days she didn't bother. Perhaps she'd chop her hair short, like girls in the city did, since the barracks were unlikely to care about whether she kept it the minimum length anymore.

Cooking tavern meals wasn't as fun as baking pastries, but neither the owners nor the customers cared if her dishes were very good, which was good because Silvie didn't care either.

She looked down at her hands, lacing the sore knife-nicked fingers together. On the thin inner skin of one wrist she had a small tattoo, the paw-print of a wolf. Kolya had done it for her a few months ago, with a pot of ink and a needle from a sewing kit.

'You'll regret this when you're old,' he'd warned, but helped her all the same. 'Maybe sooner. You know the villagers will be cruel about it.'

But Silvie knew she'd never regret it. Accidents, diseases, freckles, time – one way or another, bodies changed. She just had to hold her cane, note the silence at her side, or feel the lack of her magic to know that. At least the tattoo was a change within her control, a small reclamation of a body that would never be completely hers again.

She wished the villagers with their scoffing looks understood that, but at the same time there was no way she was going to explain it to them. They didn't deserve to know her like that. They didn't deserve her patience.

It was almost dawn, the sky beginning its slow creep through grey and back to colours, the stars vanishing in the growing light. The ground outside the tavern's front door was scattered with the usual detritus of customers, and Silvie scuffed lines through the mess with the toe of her boot.

'Morning.' Kolya's face was thinner and paler every time she saw him these days, but he always had a smile for her.

'You're up early,' Silvie replied, attempting a smile and half-way managing it.

'No, I worked late too,' he answered, leaning on the wall beside her. His breath painted mist in the air as he looked up at the dishwater sky. 'We're still rationed on how many wolves we can send out, so the shifts are running longer. A Stregone died a week ago, so it's been a bad few nights.'

Silvie fumbled in her pocket before pulling out a small bundle of cheesecloth. 'Here, eat that.'

Kolya unwrapped the cloth, exposing the portion of sausage inside. 'I'll split it with you.'

'No, I'm okay,' Silvie assured him. She didn't want to admit that food was all ash on her tongue, because that would just worry him.

He crammed the chunk of meat into his mouth, closing his eyes in contentment as he chewed. She couldn't help but smile at the sight.

'Come on,' he said, when he'd swallowed the mouthful, nodding his head towards the slowly waking world. 'Let's go for a walk.'

Silvie retrieved her cane from against the wall beside her and they fell into step, Kolya slowing his gait to keep pace with her.

'I like this time of day,' he commented.

Silvie nodded in understanding. The earliest moments of the morning were the best time to be in the village, because there weren't many people around to make them feel like they didn't belong. She wasn't surprised when their seemingly aimless walk brought them to the playground, the shapes still and eerie in the silvery light.

'Remember when I first came to the barracks?' Kolya asked her, 'and I didn't know how to play?'

Silvie's memory was he hadn't known how to do much of anything: his face grubby and tearstained until she'd taught him how to wash it; his hand a clumsy fist around the handle of his fork before she'd guided it into a more nimble shape.

'I did my best to teach you, but it's not like sentries learn much about being children either,' she said. 'I guess we did our best.'

'I wanted to repay you for that. I still do.'

She reached out with the hand that wasn't braced on her cane and lightly cuffed the back of his head. 'You don't have to repay me for anything, don't be stupid.'

'That's why I wanted to bring you here, after...' he trailed off and sighed, breath misting. 'After. If I'd thought about it, I'd have realised you wouldn't be able to because you get vertigo now.'

'No more swings for me,' Silvie agreed. She wanted to say more, to thank him for the kindness of even trying, but sorrow made her shy and stopped her tongue. She hoped he understood anyway.

'No swings for anybody,' Kolya replied. 'Not with them iced over like that. But summer will come again.'

Not for me, she wanted to remind him, but held her words back. If she couldn't manage to voice kindness, the least she could do was soften cruelty.

He took her hand, squeezing it gently.

She'd never been a true spellcaster, only an ordinary girl with a little ability, no different to hundreds upon hundreds of others, except for the bad luck of being left at the barracks door. Now she wasn't even that. She was a hollow, a void, a rare being with no connection to the thrumming currents that ran through everything.

In people like Silvie, innate magical talent was amplified by the christallo, kept in its palace far away in Arteria. And the more magic it amplified, the more ghouls rose.

Whether they were a fair price to pay for magic was a debate that had raged for decades, but that fight had been won hundreds of years ago. Nobody really talked about it anymore. What was there to say? Nobody liked ghouls, but for most people – city people, comfortable people – they weren't much of a hassle. The dead were never buried near towns. Sentry stations stood between civilisation and the old battlefields or ancient forests where unquiet bones lay waiting.

It wasn't a perfect system, but it didn't need to be. Nobody in the cities had to pay attention to the imperfect parts of it, and the sentries were supposed to be grateful for the food and shelter they were given in exchange for their service.

That was Silvie's very first lesson in life: she was supposed to be glad. She was meant to thank her lucky stars she had a little magical talent and could therefore become a sentry. Foundling children and changelings who were born without enough magic to make them useful became soldiers, and soldiers died even younger than sentries.

Silvie had certainly tracked and downed her share of tiny corpses, crawling sightlessly through the forest in the remnants of small scarlet infantry coats.

Foundlings were a drain on national resources, a blight. Ordinary children were taught to mock them, to throw piss-soaked snowballs at their yellow cloaks and red jackets.

The way people talked about sentries and soldiers, it was like they hated them more than the ghouls.

The sun slowly bled colour back into the world as it rose, lending everything life for a new day. Silvie and Kolya watched the transformation in silence, reluctant to break the peace of the moment. When this bubble of quiet ended they'd have to go back to their ordinary routines, face the miseries they'd momentarily escaped.

Their respite ended before they'd prepared themselves, a yellow-cloaked figure approaching them out of the hazy dark. It was little eight-year-old Anya.

'Silvie, you've been sent for,' she told them, giving a brief glance of longing to the unoccupied, unusable swing. 'I'm to bring you back with me.'

Kolya and Silvie were surprised at the instruction. Silvie was still a sentry, of course – but everyone knew that was just a formality. Without magic, she couldn't play the role. Her leave was indefinite on paper, permanent in practicality.

The younger sentries looked to her for direction, though she had the least sense of what to do next out of all of them. She drew in a breath, air cold and sharp.

'Come on, let's go, then.'

Kolya was still working when Silvie's meeting ended. She didn't like hanging around the barracks, but waited for him anyway. She still hadn't slept since finishing her own work the night before, but exhaustion had been her way of life for so long that she thought of it as a character trait by now: Silvie: tall, broken, always tired.

Kolya's face broadened into a rare smile when he saw her. 'What did they want? They can't possibly expect you to come back, not when–'

'No,' Silvie cut him off. 'They're sending me to Arteria.'

4. AZURA

THE DAYS CLATTERED PAST ONE AFTER THE OTHER, LIKE A LINE OF CARTS making their way along Arteria's narrow cobbled roads, and with each day came new lessons.

Azura loved learning, as long as the subject was interesting, but the constant pressing anxiety that she wasn't learning fast enough, that being behind was as bad as total failure, took away any happiness from the whole enterprise. She shared most of her lessons with Lena, despite being a few years her senior.

'Is it hard? Keeping up with lessons, I mean. I know you're smart, but I have a tough enough time with this stuff, and you've got so much else going on as well.'

Lena's only answer was a mildly baffled look. As often happened, Myles was the one who supplied an actual reply. 'Lena's good at meeting expectations, even inordinately high ones.'

Their tutor was late again, leaving them to their own devices. Some of the canals had been closed off since Eugenio's death weeks before, in order to concentrate the flow of magical energy created by the city's telluric currents towards the christallo. The closures threw the boat traffic into chaos, making everyone late for everything.

In those circumstances, Azura and Lena were supposed to spend the time in quiet independent study. Instead, the desk between them was covered with paperwork related to Lena's upcoming sixteenth birthday celebration.

'Bright pink sealing wax on official court invitations, really?' Azura asked in a nonplussed tone, picking one up between thumb and forefinger.

'Don't be boring. It looks cute,' Lena replied, snatching the letter back.

'I'm not being boring. I just don't know how Arterian nobility at large is going to react to the royal seal in bright pink on their official court correspondence.'

Myles, standing in his usual attentive spot at Lena's side, offered a shrug. 'They're birthday invitations. I figured it was harmless.'

'Everything's going to be amazing,' Lena enthused, giving Azura one of her rare quicksilver grins, which were nothing at all like the polished royal smiles she wore in public. 'I'm giving out dozens of honours and knighthoods and the cake will be a croquembouche and there'll be singers and acrobats and a ballet performance.'

'Sixteen's old enough that you can officially wear heels to a public function, too, isn't it?'

'Hm.' Lena shook her head dismissively. 'I don't think I will. My deerskin slippers are so pretty, they deserve the spotlight. I feel like a dancer in them.'

'Did you say you're giving knighthoods?' Azura's mouth twitched in a smile. 'I think I trust you more with sealing wax than with a sword.'

Myles laughed. 'Don't worry, the blade's blunted. Strictly ceremonial.'

'The sword's being made specially. It's inlaid with pezzottaite and pearls. I've seen the design sketches and it's going to be–'

'Pezzottaite? The smiths are forging you a ceremonial blade encrusted with bright pink gems?' Azura snorted. 'Very regal.'

'Last year was so dour it didn't really count,' Lena said, ignoring Azura's aside and pressing the weighty signet ring on her thumb into another blob of the bright wax. 'But this year will be different. I'm going to make it count.'

A still, unreadable expression smoothed her features for a moment, making her doll-pretty face as cold and hard as porcelain. Then it passed, animation brightening her once more. 'I'm giving out so many patronages, the whole city's going to end up blanketed in art and music and colour.'

Her fifteenth birthday was marked with a banquet but, coming so soon after King Dante's death, it hadn't been much of a party. A year later, the only remnant of those mourning days was Lena's own small form, dressed in black silk with a small jet brooch in the shape of a butterfly at her throat, her dark hair bound up in an intricate coil of braids at the nape of her neck.

Myles was as polished as Lena, the soldier-doll made to match her queen-doll. He wore black from head to toe as well: a crisp shirt, trousers, and a waistcoat, all of it impeccably tailored. The one exception was the infantry scarlet of his coat that marked him out as bodyguard as well as butler. The vivid red clashed violently with the deep violet colour of his hair, making it even more noticeable.

The unnatural shade proved Myles was a changeling, and nobody was likely to forget it with his aberration so clearly on display. An outcast of society, wrong in a fundamental and visible way, fit for nothing save sentry and soldier work.

'This one might be a slight problem,' Myles warned Lena as he handed the next parchment to her. 'I checked the palace guidelines, and – due to the balanced scale laws forbidding gender discrimination – the wording simply specifies that each guest may bring a partner, with no stipulation about the mix of people involved. As far as I could tell from the records, though, that's always meant that men bring along women, and women bring along men. This particular actor you're giving a patronage to though, well, he's known to live with another man, one I imagine he'd like to bring along.'

Lena tapped one smooth fingernail against the old leather of the desktop for a moment. 'Add a note making it clear that he's welcome to do so. I'll insist to Claudio that consorts to my party can be whomever my guests see fit to bring.'

'He'll object.'

She gave a small hum of acknowledgement. 'Probably. I don't really care. He can't say no to a birthday request without seeming like a tyrant, and most of the reason why I get to throw a party this lavish is because it makes him look like a generous stepson. He wants to improve his image, not damage it.'

Their tutor arrived, wearing the slightly frazzled, unkempt cast that had become his habitual state as the weeks of prolonged commutes and the worry of keeping the queen waiting took their toll.

'We'll finish this lot tonight,' Lena told Myles, gesturing to the remaining invitations.

'You'll be at Visconte Salvadore's tonight, I'm afraid.'

Lena made a small grumbling noise. 'He only knows three jokes and he always laughs uproariously after telling them. And his candles are always smoky and make my hair stink afterward.'

'You can come back to the apartment after it's finished, and Dad or I can do a cleaning spell for you,' Azura offered. 'I'm always up late.' Her shoulders slumped with sudden realisation. 'Dad might get funny about it, though. His new apprentice starts today, and he made a big fuss about recruiting a hollow so he can "set an example" by not relying on magic as much. Something like that. I don't really understand it, but it might mean you get told off if you ask him to get smoke out of your hair.'

Their tutor cleared his throat quietly to get their attention. He was too timid to be more pointed about it, though, so Lena and Azura pretended not to hear. At least he wasn't trying to tap Azura on the shoulder, like some in the past had when she was ignoring them. Azura didn't like to be touched, and would flinch away from most attempts. Her father thought it was rude of her, but she couldn't help it.

'Why get some strange boy from the outside when you're right here? Doesn't he believe in the balanced scale laws?' Lena asked, puzzled. 'He was always supportive of equality measures to me. It's one of the reasons I like him.'

'I don't think it's that.' Azura shook her head. 'I've never wanted to inherit the role, and he's learned not to offer it.'

Lena was thoughtful. 'If he's concerned about excessive magic consumption, maybe I should curb some of my celebration plans.'

As she spoke, the door opened again. Their tutor's shoulders slumped in defeat, interrupted before the lesson could even belatedly begin.

Azura's father entered, smiling at the girls and nodding to Myles. 'I'm on my way out again, but I wanted to stop in and say hello, in case I'm not home until after you've gone to bed tonight.'

He dropped a kiss on the crown of Azura's head, and then another on the back of one of Lena's dainty hands. 'As to what you were saying, Lena, you should make your party as extravagant as you like. That's an entirely different set of circumstances.'

Azura raised her eyebrows. 'What happened to "being an example"?'

'Birthdays are special exceptions,' he insisted with a grin. 'Anyway, as I was saying, I'll be back late. Please give my sincere apologies to the Visconte for declining his generous invitation to dinner tonight, Myles, but I'll be training my new apprentice and can't make it.'

Lena made an outraged little huffing noise. 'That's not fair.'

'It's perfectly fair. Just because you envy me doesn't make it unfair.'

She scowled. 'You'll probably conjure an excuse to avoid my birthday.'

Azura's father put his hand over his chest. 'I promise I won't miss it for the world, dear heart.'

Lena ducked her head, hiding her expression. 'I mean...it would be all right if you did.'

Myles patted her on the shoulder, as if to reassure. The two of them shared one of their wordless, opaque looks. Then Lena was back to her ordinary self, smiling at both Azura and her father.

'Neither of you are allowed to miss the party. Nobody is. That's a royal decree.'

Another knock interrupted them, and if Azura hadn't been in a constant state of antagonism against her tutor she might have felt genuine sympathy at the look of despair on his face. Myles opened the door, revealing a chambermaid with wispy brown hair and nervous, darting eyes.

'I've a note for Doctor Corsetti, sir,' she explained in a voice so soft it was almost a whisper.

'Oh, he's not a sir, he's just Myles,' Lena corrected cheerfully. 'Are you new? I don't think we've met. I love your hair.'

The girl blushed almost as scarlet as Myles' coat. 'Thank you, ma'am. I mean your Royal Highness... I mean–'

'You can go, Kate,' Myles excused the girl, who gave him a grateful look and fled the room. 'Lena, stop traumatising your staff.'

Lena frowned. 'I was trying to be nice. She's the same age as me. Is it so awful that I want a friend once in a while?'

Myles handed the note over to Azura's father, offering Lena a rueful smile. 'Of course it's not awful that you want that, but you can't expect people to react normally when the Little Magdalena suddenly pops up and wants a chat.'

Lena sighed, posture deflating as much as her impeccable deportment allowed. 'I know, I know.'

Azura's father read the message, already making for the door as he did. 'The devil's work is never done, as they say. See you later, girls.'

Finally devoid of interruptions, the tutor cleared his throat again.

'Maybe it's good,' Lena mused to Azura, 'that your father's getting an apprentice. He works too hard. This might turn out to be a good thing after all.'

5. SILVIE

THE SMELL GOT WORSE AS THE BOAT DREW CLOSER TO THE CITY, but Silvie felt it was a small price to pay for all the other sensations that came with it. After a lifetime of the dense horrors of the forest, the narrow utilitarian lines of the barracks, and the humble huddle of the village architecture, the bright wild sprawl of the skyline was like a vision from another world. The noise and temperature and texture of the bay winds against the skin of her cheeks made her laugh out loud.

She knew she should feel more nervous, maybe frightened, but the only negative emotion she could conjure was the discomfort of seasickness. She didn't care if Doctor Corsetti turned out to be cruel; she knew how to survive cruelty.

The truth that had made her numb for the past year now made her fearless: the worst had happened already, so now nothing could hurt her. She could do anything.

As soon as she alighted from the boat onto comfortingly stable dry land, Silvie set off for the palace. Arteria's street signs and shopfronts were all labelled in the southern language, rather than the northern tongue, but Silvie knew both. She'd been taught to read and speak with southern, as was standard for barracks throughout the country; and she'd picked up northern on visits to the village and from reading the few storybooks that made their way into her life.

Upir was northern, cadaveri southern, though frankly Silvie didn't see why it made a difference what you called them. Ghouls were ghouls.

Compared to the one and two-storey cottages and cabins of the village, the city loomed impossibly high in a riot of domed steeples, stretching brick walls and thin, spindly adornments atop church towers. It was a whirlwind of shapes and textures, and Silvie knew she was gaping like the country bumpkin she was as her attention was drawn in every direction.

The day was warm, and she felt even warmer as she walked. She hadn't bothered to pack the sturdy brown civilian coat she'd worn away from the barracks, during the months she spent in the bakery or other odd jobs, while her magic recovered from the gruelling work of riding the mind of a wolf. She'd given that coat to Kolya, making him promise he'd live long enough to grow into it so that she got her money's worth.

Instead, she'd brought her yellow sentry cloak, although she didn't have any claim to it anymore. But now, so far from home, the cloak felt like a badge of honour.

The damp air of Arteria smelled of decay and of the dense life of a city, all the mess and humanity a large population entailed.

Silvie had half convinced herself that the vision she'd seen during her brush with death was only her imagination, but those lofty, rational thoughts were stripped to nothing as soon as the wind of the bay changed direction and she got a gust of rot up her nostrils. There was no denying the familiarity of the scent. She'd been to Arteria before, on the strangest and worst night of her life.

She'd been taught about the city as a child, the same lines everyone learned: if sentry outposts like hers were the country's sword and shield, then Arteria was its pulsing heart. The extensive canal system had been designed centuries earlier to charge the telluric currents with constant flowing energy, which the King's spell-casters then channelled through a large crystal of quartz, graphite and marble called the christallo. The christallo filtered the raw energy into a form usable on a mass scale.

The more magic the King and his Stregoni marshalled into being from the raw chaos of the world, the more ghouls rose, as if chaos was determined to keep pace with human hubris no matter how grand the scale grew.

A sprawling, colourful palazzo outside the palace's portcullis gate was full of vendors and stalls and noise and movement. Silvie sat on a bench that bordered the wide open space as she attempted to regain a little steadiness. She was exhausted already, and the true heart of her day hadn't even begun.

Even after a year, the feel of her cane against her palm wasn't habitual, but it was at least familiar in such unfamiliar surroundings. She gave it a brief squeeze, for once grateful for its necessary presence.

As she watched the bustle in the palazzo, she was aware these were the last moments of her in-between, the limbo she'd been caught in while travelling here. Although, in truth, she'd been in a rootless limbo the whole year, since she'd woken to the sound of bells, without any purpose to tether her.

As soon as she reported to Doctor Corsetti, Silvie would have a role again, a duty that defined who she was. So this was the last moment where she was nobody but herself. The freedom offered by that selfhood was terrifying, and also dizzying in its power.

Though exhausted, her desire to explore outweighed her need to rest. Silvie plunged headlong into the crowd and the bright promise of the stalls displaying their wares. She marvelled at the heavy bolts of vivid cloth and the jewel-like sweets in jars and the perfect otherworldly tableaus of blown glass globes filled with confetti snow.

Those snow globes caught her interest and held it – no small feat when the whole world was a distraction, everything around her making her laugh in awe. But the globes were tiny fairytale versions of the dark forests of the north. Almost nobody in Arteria would ever see the real place, and so they could project their daydreams of it onto the miniature replicas, could imagine fir trees dusted with snow and delicate glittering flakes drifting through the air. They didn't have to think about sludge underfoot, or of a cold so deep it made children's lips bleed when they breathed it.

Silvie had a little southern money after exchanging her meagre savings for local currency with one of the sailors on the ship. Without pausing to second guess herself, she spent nearly all she had on the smallest of the globes, the only one she could afford. Among the whirling flakes of a fantasy winter was a figure caught in limbo, caught in a memory, her black cloak a bit like how her yellow one had looked when the light was very low.

The snow globe could stay suspended in a single moment forever, but Silvie's frozen bubble of time was over. She took a deep breath, set her shoulders back, and made her way to the palace gate.

Doctor Corsetti was tall and lanky, with thick chestnut hair and green eyes with deep crow's feet at their corners, as if he had spent many years smiling often.

'I'd love to give you a tour, but something urgent's come up, so I'm going to have to leave you to do filing for your first day. I'm dreadfully sorry, but it can't be helped,' he told her almost immediately. He sounded genuinely apologetic, too. Silvie was rather baffled by that.

'Come on, it's this way,' Doctor Corsetti went on, setting off at a rapid pace down one high-ceilinged corridor before pulling himself up abruptly, waiting for Silvie to catch up. She wondered if it annoyed him to have to slow down so much when he was in a hurry, but could tell – despite having just met the man – that he'd never admit to anything as uncharitable as annoyance at someone's infirmity.

'We met once, years ago, up north. I doubt you remember a random official dropping in for a day or two,' he told her as they walked. He was right; she didn't remember. 'I noticed you because of your name and how old you were – you're about the same age as my daughter. I almost called her Sylvia, so to see a nine-year-old trainee sentry named Silvie felt like seeing a different world, you know? Two children whose fates were so opposite.' He chuckled.

Despite herself, Silvie softened at his words. Not because of any asinine fantasies he had about the parallel lives of his lucky daughter and an unlucky sentry, but because he'd thought of the two little girls of long ago as belonging to the same species at all, comparable in any way. Trainee sentries were very rarely referred to as children, especially not by the officials overseeing their progress.

Doctor Corsetti's office was a chaotic rabbit warren of a library. Shelves and archiving drawers bulged with files and books of every height and thickness; sturdy dark wood shelves doing their best to stay reliable under groaning weights of information. Light spilled in from generous windows, but simply served to highlight how wildly haphazard the interior of untamed forest of paper and ink was.

'There's this, and then the alchemy workshop – don't worry, I keep that in better order than this place,' he told Silvie as they ventured inside. 'That's for the practical side of my duties, but as you can probably tell, the majority of my time is taken up with paperwork. Not quite as glamorous as being a sentry, I'm afraid.'

Silvie wanted to reply that being a sentry was hard and cruel, not the stuff of adventure, but the memory of her wolf stayed the acid on her tongue. She could never deny the thrill of that part of her old life, never betray the memory for the sake of scoring some caustic pity-point now.

Doctor Corsetti handed her a thick sheaf of documents that was heavier than she could comfortably manage with one hand. 'To start with, it would be ideal if you could file these. They're going to keep gathering dust on my desk if they aren't taken care of.'

Silvie glanced at the neat handwriting on the topmost page. 'That won't be a problem. I can read southern.'

Doctor Corsetti looked surprised, as if it had never occurred to him that he should verify this. 'Right. Good. They need to be sorted into provisional, soldier, and sentry. The cabinets are over there.'

Silvie spent her first hour of work dividing and alphabetising the files of foundling babies, children removed from unsuitable homes, and the newly orphaned. She envied the names of those who found their place in the sentry section.

After that she had to update the records of sentries and soldiers who were on official time off from their training or duties, noting down where they were working and making sure that the breaks were the right length for maximum efficiency counterbalanced against lowest loss of life.

When Silvie went back to ask Doctor Corsetti for the next lot of files to organise, his amiable face wore a brief hesitant frown.

'Here.' He handed her a single sheet, a list of names. 'You'll need to pull these files from the sentry and infantry sections and put them in the retired section.'

'Is it divided into deaths and injuries, or all together?' Silvie asked. He shouldn't have worried about giving her the list. She didn't feel anything at all as she looked at the names.

'All together. I saw your name on this list, actually.' His frown brightened a little, animation returning to his face. 'They were longer than usual, in the period following the king's death. Cadaveri activity was less predictable while King Claudio learned the art of controlling the christallo, so I checked the lists with special care. Making sure that everything was kept running to code and all that.

'I recognised your name, and decided you'd be ideal for what I wanted in an apprentice. I figured you must have been clever and disciplined to reach such an age as a sentry.'

'Thank you,' Silvie said, more because she knew it was expected of her than any genuine gratitude. 'If you don't mind my asking, what happens to the retired files when they're full? You couldn't possibly keep all the records here, they'd fill the room in no time.'

Doctor Corsetti nodded. 'You aren't wrong. After a while they're sent to an island in the bay, an old quarantine spot. All they do there is get mouldy and turn into pulp, but protocol is protocol, and they're not especially useful as reference materials. I suppose you could call it a graveyard of sorts.'

Silvie was surprised at that. She hadn't realised anybody in Arteria was so aware that soldiers and sentries lived at all, much less conceptualised a memorial to their loss. She found herself warming to her new master.

The work wasn't challenging by any means, but proved gruelling after the pressures of her journey. Silvie spent hour after hour learning the quirks of the records, which drawers stuck on their runners and which were overfull.

'It's getting close to dinner time,' Doctor Corsetti said as twilight slipped towards night. 'Why don't you come back to my apartments for the meal? It isn't far from your quarters, so I can show you to them after.'

'Oh, I couldn't possibly–'

'Of course you could. Come on.'

6. AZURA

HOURS OF STARING AT PAGES OF SMALL PRINT AND DRY LANGUAGE LEFT Azura feeling seedy and wrung out, her eyes aching. Even with the improvements to her weak eyesight when she was young, her vision still became strained if she had to focus on text for too long. Now she had the beginnings of a headache.

She'd been waiting to eat dinner until her father got home from his work, so that they could catch up over the meal, but now it was late enough that she was considering simply going to bed. Missing a meal once in a while wasn't that bad for her, was it? Lena avoided eating all the time and it didn't seem to have any adverse effects on her.

The new apprentice had started that day, Azura knew, but she hoped her father wouldn't talk about him too much. Azura still felt weird about the whole thing.

She closed her book with an exhausted sigh, dragged herself to her feet, left the study and headed for the kitchen to get a drink of water before going to bed.

The door opened as she was finishing her drink. Her father stepped inside with a second person following him.

'Oh, Azura! Excellent. I was worried I'd have to track you down. We stopped by the kitchens and got some food for the three of us. This is Silvie, my new apprentice. Silvie, this is my daughter, Azura.'

The girl standing with Azura's father seemed as surprised as Azura was, and looked at her almost with recognition. That meant that Azura's dad had been boasting about her, or complaining about her. Azura was used to both, and couldn't decide which she disliked more.

Silvie was tall, especially compared to Azura's smallness. Her face was more angular and defined than the curved smoothness of Azura's Arterian features. She was spare and pale, like something built to live in winter. Her hair was a reddish blonde, streaked with white near the front, the long weight of it tied back in a braid. Her lips were a vivid pink, as if she'd been nervously chewing them until only a moment earlier.

Her walking cane had the same hard spareness as its owner, a length of old gnarled wood polished smooth through constant use.

'That's really cool,' Azura said, nodding towards the cane. 'I've never seen one like it.'

Silvie gave her a flicker of a smile, a moment of gratitude showing on her closed-off face.

'Sit, sit,' Azura's father ordered. Silvie looked uncomfortable at the prospect of being waited on but followed the instruction, obedience winning out over hesitation.

Azura's dad brought over dishes piled with food, and crockery and cutlery for each of them. He handed the serving utensils to Silvie first.

'Creamed cod mousse on grilled white polenta with basil and garlic.'

Silvie's eyes widened as she took her first bite. Azura thought she'd probably be embarrassed to be watched while she ate, but it was endearing to see. Food on the ship to Arteria had likely been pretty mediocre, so it must've been a while since she'd had a proper meal.

Azura's father offered her the serving utensils next, whereon Silvie looked mortified, as if she'd realised she should've waited for all of them to be served before eating. Probably dinners in her old life had been more jolly and noisy than poky family meals around a little table. Azura wondered if Silvie missed them.

'Come on, Azura, hurry up,' her dad prompted her.

Azura shook her head. 'You know I don't eat meat.'

He didn't bat an eyelash 'It's not meat, it's fish.'

'Dad. I'm not eating it.'

'Well, you have to eat something.'

Azura grabbed one of the extra slices of polenta and dipped it into the dish of olive oil by her plate.

'There. Eating. Happy?'

'You have to eat something with protein in it as well. Are eggs all right, or are they out of bounds now too?' The question dripped with sarcasm.

'No, eggs are okay. But Lena wants to lose weight before her birthday party, and I said I'd diet along with her in solidarity, so I probably shouldn't have any.'

'If Lena jumped off a bridge – wait, what am I saying, that literally happened when you were children,' Azura's dad replied drily. 'She's got no need to lose weight, anyway. She's becoming a beautiful young woman.'

'There's always gossip. She hears more than she lets on.' Azura picked at the polenta, hardly eating it.

'Well, it's nonsense. She's growing. You're growing. Have some eggs.'

Silvie cleared her throat quietly.

'I can put some eggs on to boil, if you want.'

Azura scowled, feeling like they were ganged up.

'Thanks, Silvie.' Azura's dad smiled. 'They're in the pantry. Pots are in the cupboard to the right of the water tap.'

Silvie nodded, her cleared plate in one hand and her cane in the other as she rose from the table.

Azura felt like a fool for assuming that her father's apprentice would be a boy. Of course it was a girl. He'd never liked Azura spending time in male company, and the only reason Myles was granted exemption was because Azura's dad seemed to consider foundlings another race of people entirely. Silvie was a foundling, and lame, and a girl – three times safe and sexless in his eyes.

'I wish you hadn't brought up her walking stick like that, you know,' he said, interrupting her thoughts while Silvie was in the pantry. 'I was mortified.'

'Huh?'

'It's not polite to mention things like that.'

'Why not? Did she tell you that?'

'No, because I wasn't rude enough to say anything about it to her!'

'I don't see what the big deal is. I just said it was cool.'

'I wonder if it would bother her if I offered to glamour off the white streaks in her hair.'

'If she wanted them glamoured off she'd have them glamoured off already, Dad. Stop fussing about how other people look all the time.'

'She can't glamour them off, though. She doesn't have magic.'

'Yeah, yeah, I know, she's a hollow, that's why she's here. But she could have asked another sentry or someone to do it, right? Her friends would have magic.'

'I suppose. If she asks you for help, please indulge her, don't go off on one of your strange little crusades about…whatever it is you meant about me fussing how other people look.'

Azura rolled her eyes. 'It would be totally different if she was the one asking. That's, like, the opposite of you offering, don't you get it?'

'Sweetheart,' her father said fondly. 'I "get" almost nothing about you these days.'

Strangely, Azura was flattered by that. She liked the idea she was so complex she was difficult to understand. Although she also knew the truth was that she was perfectly comprehensible, her father was being deliberately obtuse.

'I keep telling Claudio that he'll find it smoother sailing with Lena when she grows up and leaves behind this teenage tumult, but he despairs of it.'

Azura bristled. 'So one second you say that you get almost nothing about me, and the next it's just a phase you understand well enough to be giving advice about?'

Her father didn't rise to the prickle in her tone. 'I'm supposed to be one of his chief advisors. It's my job.'

'Ugh, you're impossible,' Azura said, pretty despairing herself.

7. SILVIE

THE RARE TIMES SILVIE HAD SLEPT ALONE HAD ALWAYS BEEN IN familiar surroundings: a quiet corner of the barracks library, when her eyes wouldn't stay open no matter how she tried; or in the attic bedroom of the bakery, while the girls she'd shared with had been out.

She'd never had to rest somewhere so new and quiet on her own like this before. She set down her comb and the little snowglobe on a table, while bristling at the solitude. It added uncomfortably to the silence which was already an oppressive presence at her side. The terrible absence of sound blanketed half her world and jumbled the rest.

Lying in her new, quiet, solitary room, the dead spot inside her skull expanded to fill the universe. Her whole life had been spent in the barracks, in cheap, over-booked boarding houses, or in shared servants' quarters. Silvie had expected her new life in Arteria to be an extended version of those enforced down-time months she'd spent behind the counters of village shops and bakeries, or working as an errand girl for wealthy merchants. She'd imagined that she'd share a room with a handful of other servant girls of similar age and status – not always friends, but at least comrades. But no, apparently working as Doctor Corsetti's apprentice was prestigious enough to warrant a room all of her own.

Trying to sleep without the familiar sounds of other people breathing and shifting nearby was unsettling. Though she rarely let herself feel lonely, the absence of other bodies close by made her skin feel too bare, too exposed.

After a while she realised it wasn't completely silent. Faint sounds came from the city beyond her half-open window: the lap of water against the sides of the canal, faint rattles of cartwheels over cobblestones. The corridor outside her door provided other quiet noises – the soft comings and goings of other servants, conversations and footsteps. They weren't enough, but would have to do.

It occurred to her that sentiment – "it would have to do" – was the story of her life back home.

Home.

She sighed. Home, where the northern air was thin and sharp and cold not damp and thick and mild like it was here.

An enormous ache welled in Silvie's chest, which didn't make any sense because she'd never in her life thought of the barracks or outposts or attics or flophouses as home. She was angry at her own sentimentality.

Her nose started to sting, prickling her eyes and making her breath ragged. Her self-directed fury grew. She was far too old for this; practically a grown-up now. And growing up meant growing sharp, as sharp as winter air, and abandoning whatever softness she'd held onto to safeguard her younger years.

After all, Silvie had nearly died. Shouldn't that alone afford her a toughness against pain, an extra layer of thickness to her skin? And she'd survived the gruelling, numbing year since, the months of grey fog inside her chest as she struggled to find a reason to keep going, to learn how to live in this new body with these new limits. Accepting this unfamiliar version of herself was a hard-won victory.

So crying over an unfamiliar empty room was the height of absurdity.

Silvie swallowed back the first sob with a deep breath. She managed to stifle the second one, as well. But the third one slipped out, a great broken gulp of air and sound. She buried her face into the too-soft, too-clean pillow.

Perhaps she was just tired. It was exhaustion, and having to meet all those new people, and the humidity, and…

Silvie had always thought that people crying themselves to sleep only happened in books.

The architecture of the palace was neither intuitive nor efficient, having been cobbled together over centuries of additions and demolitions, things built atop what was there before instead of ever being taken apart and put back together from scratch in a more logical design. In Silvie's opinion, the place was a pretty apt metaphor for how the whole country operated.

On her second day in the records library, she stayed absorbed in her tasks until after the sun had gone and the room began to chill. Her vision swam with lists of the dead, and lists of those who'd be dead before much longer. Her head ached.

'You should get yourself some dinner, Silvie,' Doctor Corsetti told her. 'You shouldn't be a workaholic just because I am.'

His smile was kind enough, but Silvie knew better than to trust smiles too much. Still, she knew she shouldn't disobey him so she nodded, put away her work and left the library.

In truth, the dining hall held no attraction for her. Silvie was anxious at the thought of chattering crowds. Noise was always a problem now, a cacophony of sounds tangling together into a single roar, flattened by her deafness. And, no doubt, the other palace staff would try to be social with her, which would be exhausting. Or worse, nobody would try to be social with her, and she'd be lonely.

She'd skipped breakfast, still full from the previous night's meal, and the midday meal had entailed an attendant bringing a tray of pastries to the library for the pair of them. Silvie had felt weird about taking one, even though Doctor Corsetti had told her to do so. Didn't he understand she was there to help him, not to be served by others? It had all been too much.

What Silvie really wanted right now was peace and freedom, a moment away from this alien world of plenty. Perhaps a walk would clear her head.

She couldn't stare at the stars as much as she wanted, as her concentration and eyesight were preoccupied with not stumbling on the scrubbed grey cobblestones. Not that there were many stars to see, with the light pollution generated by Arteria's lamps and torches. The footpaths near the docks were all cramped and muddy, but around the palace the spaces were open and wide, with lots of room for foot traffic between the buildings on one side and the canal on the other.

Silvie walked on and on, losing track of time, pushing herself to her physical limits. The air was cooler than the night before and she'd worn her cloak for the walk, as much for the familiar weight as for the warmth.

'Look at this, then. A bright little yellow bird. You a canary? Wanna sing for us?'

Two dark figures loomed in front of her, blocking her path. They radiated menace like heat from a stone.

'I'd heard that sentries had a sweet, easy life, and I guess this here's the proof of it. Having a holiday in town, are we? Lording around in that cloak of yours while decent people work hard and still go to bed hungry?'

'What's the use of you, anyway?' the second man added, lip curled in a sneer. 'We still get cadaveri here in the city regardless. My sister's kid was up all night with those alarms, terrified out of his little wits. What good were you then?'

Silvie trembled.

'She gonna do some magic on us, you reckon?' A mean laugh.

'Oooh, I'm scared, the little witch is gonna get me.'

'Nah, she ain't tough. Anyone can fight a cadaveri, all you need's a blade or a torch. This magic bullshit's just a rort.'

Silvie kept her eyes down and her breathing even. They'd get sick of trying to get a response out of her eventually, wouldn't they?

'You reckon witches are the same as ordinary girls? I don't much like the idea of getting surprised while I'm having my fun.'

'Aw, I dunno about sticking it in a sentry, mate. There might be wolf teeth down there.'

The laughter drew closer, became crueller. Their breath on her cheek made her flinch.

'Better see if she floats, instead.'

Silvie didn't even have time to properly process the threat before a fist slammed into the side of her head, turning the whole world to jagged black and white stars.

Something foul and bitter was in her mouth. Silvie spluttered and gagged, desperate to cough it out.

'Here.' A little wineskin was shoved into her hands. 'Don't tell my father I have that.'

Silvie took a swallow of merlot and immediately puked it back up, along with more canal water. Her stomach heaved, her throat burned.

'Good. That's good. Get it all out.'

Silvie blinked hard, bringing the speaker into focus. Azura Corsetti. She was as soaked as Silvie, both of them dripping brown-grey water from their hair. Silvie sneezed.

'Ah, crap. Let me—'

Their clothes were instantly dry, still filthy but no longer chilly or wet. The spell made Azura's hand glow with a faint peachy light.

When she'd been a sentry, Silvie's clothes were neat and crisp every day. The familiar texture stabbed her heart, but she shoved the feeling down. She had far more immediate reasons to feel miserable, there was no need to dip into nostalgia.

She struggled to stand. Azura offered a hand. The whole world reeled around Silvie dizzyingly, and she almost went back down again.

'Easy, easy.' Azura counterbalanced the stumble. 'Do you feel like you can walk?'

'I don't need your pity,' Silvie mumbled.

In all honesty she wasn't at all sure she could walk, but the thought of showing weakness in front of someone she hardly knew was enough to make her grit her teeth in determination.

'Oh, no need to thank me, I love jumping into revolting canals to save people who can't swim,' Azura snarked. 'Your stick didn't go in, luckily. Here.'

'I can swim.' Under the grime, Silvie's face burned with embarrassment as she took her cane back. 'If I'd been conscious, I would have been fine. Even with my balance gone, I've still got muscle memory.'

'No muscle memory for manners, though, apparently,' replied Azura breezily. 'So I guess it's true that people with no magic can't float, then. Most people have at least a tiny bit, so it's not exactly easy to test.'

'I've got no idea about that,' Silvie admitted, forcing herself to keep up with the gentle pace Azura had set. 'It's so hard to find out anything about what methods the witch trials really used. We were banned from talking about it at the barracks.'

'My tutors have never taught me anything about the trials, either. Maybe it was your clothes weighing you down. That cloak's pretty hefty.'

'Thank you for saving it.' Silvie found it much easier to offer gratitude for that than for her rescue. She didn't want to even think about losing her cloak. 'It's lucky that you were close by.'

Azura gave a snort. 'I wouldn't say your luck's all that good, considering that we're covered in canal filth right now. I heard commotion and followed the sound, that's all.'

Silvie was no longer able to tell where different sounds were coming from, the same way that somebody with one eye lost depth perception. If their positions had been reversed, she wouldn't have been able to help Azura at all – no chance of following the direction of the sound, no chance of running. Silvie felt useless and ashamed.

'And no, I didn't do it out of pity.' Azura's voice lost its cheerful edge. 'I did it because sometimes being a girl sucks. We have to look out for each other when things like that happen.'

Silvie threw up twice more before they made it back within the palace grounds. They made a beeline for Doctor Corsetti's professional chambers, heading to the alchemy workshop next door to the records library. The comparative familiarity of the set of rooms was a relief for Silvie.

Azura leaned against the doorframe while Silvie went to prod at the embers still glowing in the room's pot-belly stove.

'I think this'll be hot enough. I'll make us a curative.'

Azura nodded. 'Dad would be furious at me if he found out what happened. I've had… problems with canals in the past.'

Silvie unhooked a copper pot from overhead, filled it with water from the barrel in the corner, and then placed it on the stove. She collected elderberry, garlic, zinc, wormwood root, and ginger from the abundant reagent shelves, pulling their cork stoppers free and dumping a liberal dose of finely ground powder from each into a mug. 'I'll try it first, to make sure it's not a disaster.'

When the water was hot enough, she ladled some into the mug, stirred it with one of the thin glass mixing rods, and then gulped the concoction down before she could lose heart.

'That good, huh?' Azura asked in a dry voice.

Silvie held out the mug in one hand, the other grasping desperately at thin air.

'Wineskin,' she choked. 'Please.'

Azura handed it over and Silvie swilled a mouthful quickly, desperate to wash away the dregs of the potion. Then she handed it back, so that Azura could have the potion and the wine.

Her good ear seemed to be all right, but she couldn't afford to lose even a little bit of its hearing. She hated how fragile she was, how vulnerable.

'If we each have another dose of that in an hour or two, and hot baths when we go back to the servant's wing, we should be able to stave off getting sick,' Silvie told Azura, pulling two chairs over to the warm halo of the stove. 'Here, you sit. I'll make us tea.'

Silvie put more water on to heat and spooned loose leaves into a pot. If it had been for herself, she would have added them straight into a mug, but suspected Azura was used to a slightly less crude level of tea preparation.

Should she have heated the mugs beforehand, with a little hot water? Fancy people did that, didn't they? Silvie remembered reading that in books.

'Your father's library is amazing, and his workshop is maybe even more wonderful,' Silvie said, trying to stave off any further silent panic.

'He's not here, you know. You don't have to try to be nice about it.' Azura leaned back lazily, her chair giving a worn little squeak at the movement.

'What? No, I'm being honest. It's remarkable.'

Azura looked around, as if she'd never really noticed the workshop interior one way or the other. 'I guess it's okay. And I guess you have to butter my father up by complimenting it, since you're working for him.'

Silvie frowned. 'I told you, I'm being honest. I've never seen stores this extensive. You really think I'd need to lie about being impressed by what's literally the royal standard?'

That startled a chuckle out of Azura. 'Okay, fair point.' She looked around the room again. 'Dad really does love this place. Which is pretty ironic, considering how much he hates regular cooking and baking.'

Silvie handed one of the mugs of tea to Azura. 'Sorry, do you mind moving to the other chair?' she asked, ducking her head. 'I'm deaf in one ear, so I have to sit on the side where I can hear you.'

She curled her shoulders forward a little as well, an automatic tic whenever she needed to ask someone for something. She'd had the habit since her early teens, when her first growth spurt hit and she was suddenly taller than most of the other sentries. Ducking her head, slouching, staying near the back, keeping small to avoid unnecessary attention, especially in moments when she needed to speak up, became part of how she moved through the world.

Now that she was damaged, no amount of postural self-defence was enough to save her from being the centre of attention. Her walking stick might as well have been a pennant or a flag held over her head, drawing everyone's eyes to her as soon as she entered a room. And if that wasn't bad enough, there were a thousand tiny things she needed help with now, things like asking Azura to shift to the other chair so they'd both be able to hear each other.

Silvie, self-sufficient since she'd been old enough to understand that she had a self at all, prickled at the humiliation. Her whole life tasted bitter now, no matter how she tried to swallow it down.

Azura blinked in puzzlement, shifting to the other seat. 'Why would you say sorry for that?'

Silvie shrugged. 'I just do.'

In the red-gold dancing shadows of the firelight, Azura's features shifted, clever and complex one moment, naive and sweet the next. In all the changing guises, she was beautiful.

Silvie wondered what it would be like to be her. To be naturally smart, rather than cunning by necessity; loved and coddled enough that apologising for a simple request was not instinctive.

The chill they'd brought back from the canal faded, heat seeping into their bones. Silvie hadn't even noticed her head was aching until the pain began to ebb away.

'Good thing I didn't have my glasses with me,' Azura commented, taking a slurp of her tea. 'They'd've ended up broken or lost, and I don't think Dad would tolerate it if I bought another pair. He hates that I wear them.'

Silvie couldn't properly follow the logic of what Azura was saying, but the warmth was making her slow and comfortable enough that she didn't bother to ask for an explanation.

'I'll have to replace the elderberry we used,' she told Azura, turning her mug between her palms. 'There's still a lot left of the other ingredients I put in the potion, but the elderberry's basically gone.'

'Driade Island always has heaps of elderberry, if you know where to look. That's out in the bay. I can take you there and show you. I like it out there. Don't tell my dad, though. Or Lena. She'll want to come, and Myles is such a pushover of a bodyguard that he'll let her, and then we'll all be in trouble with her advisors for letting her skip her schedule.'

Azura put down her mug and stretched, catlike, not bothering to hide her yawn. Then she gave Silvie a sheepish look. 'Sorry, that wasn't ladylike of me.'

Silvie decided she didn't want to hear Azura say sorry for anything ever again. The idea that someone was protected and loved enough that shame was alien to them was an appealing fantasy.

'A bodyguard who's a pushover sounds a little ridiculous,' she commented instead.

'He's not a bodyguard, exactly. He's sort of there to save Lena from herself. It's hard to explain. I don't know if it really worked out like Dad intended.'

Azura settled into her chair. 'Lena jumped off everything when she was a kid. Really really high things. She always had bruises all over, and would have to wear long-sleeved gowns in summer. And this one time when we were kids, she talked me into jumping off the portcullis gate into the canal beside the palace grounds, and I was too much of a reckless dummy to tell her no.

'Being in the canal was even more horrible that day than it was for us tonight, because the telluric currents were especially strong. There was a so much ice in the water. We both got incredibly sick from it. My magic was severely affected – before then I never tended to fire magic, especially, but now that's my natural skew. The chill I got that day never went away completely. I always feel like I'm still just out of the ice.'

Azura slurped her drink, the warmth of it making her close her eyes momentarily. 'Lena doesn't have enough magic to have ended up hurt the same way I was. I don't even know how much magic she has, since she's never been assessed.

'But even though Lena didn't get magic-sick, she still got canal-sick. Badly. The King was so terrified she'd die that he was a wreck. I never saw him like that, because I was recovering in bed, but my father talked about it. How King Dante would tear his hair and pace the halls in front of her sickroom. She was like a daughter to him. They were very close.'

'His wife was like a daughter?'

'She was two years old when they were married, so it's not as if she was like a wife to him,' Azura clarified. 'He had several political unions before her, as well. I think his first marriage was a real marriage – she was Claudio's mother. But after she died, he made alliance matches; Lena was the third of those. By then I guess he was way too old to have any kind of new bride, and she was much too young to be one, but treaties are treaties. He loved her though, and I think she loved him.' She cleared her throat, pausing briefly.

'Anyway, after the canal happened, Dad knew letting me and Lena spend time together on our own was bad, because I wasn't stopping her from doing risky things, and her ideas were getting wilder and more dangerous all the time. Because I was useless, Myles got recruited to be there, to take care of her. To make sure she didn't do things that would put her in danger.'

Ignoring the little whirl of vertigo the action gave her, Silvie leaned over to nudge shoulders with her.

'You weren't useless tonight. Thank you.'

Azura gave a quiet hum of reply, distracted, gaze resting on the glow behind the grille of the stove. Silvie wondered if Azura could feel the fire's energy, the inherent natural magic of it, as well as the comforting warmth.

The heat went some way to dry out the humidity of the Arterian air, restraining most of the damp atmosphere that permeated the city. That, combined with the scents of ingredients and potion-making, the gleam of instruments and wall of labelled containers, filled Silvie with a blunt, terrifying homesickness like a physical weight inside her, a gnarled and knotted organ sitting heavy where other people had a heart.

'Driade Island is just beyond the boundaries of Arteria, out in the lagoon,' Azura said, the sound of her voice so unexpected in the quiet that it pushed away the worst of the ache. Silvie felt helplessly grateful for that small mercy.

'I wish I'd been able to pay more attention to the bay while I was arriving,' she told Azura. 'I was seasick. I'd never been on a boat before.'

Azura looked surprised, as if she'd never even considered the thought that there were people in the world who'd never been on a boat. Of all the enormous ways their life experiences were different, that small surprise was enough to make Silvie grin.

'What's funny?'

'Nothing. Doesn't matter. What's the island like?' Silvie asked.

'Pretty. Tranquil. Nobody lives there now. People who die in the city are shipped over there to be interred, so they won't pose a threat to anyone if they rise again. The corpse shipments are pretty thorough, from what I hear. The bodies are laid to rest face-down with bricks between their jaws.'

'Sounds like they're as close to at peace as any dead can be,' Silvie remarked. Azura nodded.

'Yeah. The island's right on the edge of the city limits, so people feel like their loved ones aren't being sent away somewhere out of the way. They're right on the margin. I think that's why I like it on the island, because it's away from the centre. Things feel more alive there.'

'That's what being a sentry is like,' Silvie told her. 'You live on that edge. And I was a sentry almost my whole life, so I guess I don't really know what it's like to be in the middle in the first place.'

'It's not a good or a bad thing, exactly. I guess it's just…different. Weird.' Azura gave a helpless shrug. 'Sorry, I'm being dumb.'

'It's fine,' Silvie assured her. 'I know what you mean. We've got weirdness in common, I think.'

That made Azura give a little huff of laughter. 'Yeah. That's something, I guess.'

8. AZURA

DESPITE SILVIE'S BEST EFFORTS WITH THE HERBAL TONIC, AZURA woke next morning groggy and feverish. The canal could have done a lot worse to her, but she still felt like garbage.

Lena and Myles were in the kitchen, as they often were when Lena's schedule permitted the detour. They looked impeccable, of course. Azura fumbled for the teapot, too lethargic to object when Myles got there first and handed her a cup.

Her father, absorbed in early work as always, gave her a brief smile before becoming distracted once again.

'Azura, look, I learned a new trick.' Lena held out her palm, tiny swirls of frost gleaming on her fingertips for a moment. 'Try your tea now. You too, Myles.'

Myles, styled and tailored and lean, had gone to stand by the window. Azura missed the freckles he'd had across his nose when they were younger but as Lena rarely spent much time outside these days, neither did her bodyguard. The freckles had faded.

The way he looked now, after years of shadowing Lena as she navigated labyrinthine palace protocol, had its own austere beauty. But Azura couldn't help feeling a little sad that the scrappy, emotive boy he'd been when he'd arrived had been honed and tempered so dramatically.

He sipped his tea again. 'Oh, good. Chilled. Just the way I like it,' he deadpanned. 'Thanks. Not gross at all.'

Azura gave Lena a withering glare. 'I need tea to function, you gremlin. How dare you deprive me?'

Lena cackled with delight, her refinement breaking in her mirth. Myles' mouth twitched in a smile.

'Don't worry, I'll make a fresh pot,' he assured Azura, putting the kettle on again.

Azura's father huffed in frustration.

'Morning to you too, Dad. What's up?'

'Conspiracy theorists are convinced Eugenio's death was an assassination.'

'Seriously?'

'Mm-hm. They're saying the true circumstances around his death are being kept off the public record, and that–'

'Well, they're not wrong,' Lena interrupted, voice droll. 'That's why I have to suffer through a bunch of public appearances with Claudio today. Misdirection away from the rumours.'

'Ye…es,' Azura conceded hesitantly. 'But I feel like there's a difference between a secret shadowy conspiracy and, you know, trying to avoid someone's death being tainted by an embarrassing sex scandal.'

'The supposed conspiracies aren't about how he died, actually,' Azura's father told them. 'The whole thing is centred on the shipping schedule for taking bodies out to Driade Island. Eugenio died on the night of the year when, statistically, there were the lowest number of corpses within the city limits.'

Azura pursed her lips. 'So they think if it *was* an assassination, it was motivated by politics, not cruelty, and so the killer aimed to cause minimal collateral damage by having the smallest number of potential cadaveri occur when the christallo was destabilised?'

'That's how you know the conspiracy theorists are delusional,' Lena chimed in cheerfully. 'Because they think anyone in politics cares about whether or not ordinary people are hurt.'

Myles, returning with the fresh tea, made a soft scoffing noise in the back of his throat. 'Careful you don't cut yourself on the edge of that cynicism there, Lena.'

She ignored him, swallowing a bite of toast before replying. 'I bet you anything that Claudio appoints Salvadore as the new Stregone, even though he's not that good a wizard. Claudio wants better trade terms for the coal from Salvadore's land holdings so, as far as he's concerned, it doesn't matter if a weaker spell-caster in the Stregoni means less magic and more cadaveri.'

Myles gave a disapproving hum. 'You don't have to sound quite so cavalier when you're talking about life and death, you know. Azura, tea?'

'Yes, and don't let it anywhere near the ice princess here.' Azura sneezed. 'See, look, now I've got a chill.'

'Ice *queen*, thank you very much. And don't worry, I don't have enough magic to do the trick twice so soon.' Lena buttered another slice of toast. 'And I'm not being cavalier about life and death. I'm being cavalier about politics.'

'Probably not all that smart to be cavalier about that either,' Myles said dryly.

Lena gave a sharp little laugh. 'What's Claudio going to do, have me assassinated? I won't be old enough to quietly do away with for another year or two. As long as I'm tiny and tragic and sweet and distracting, I'm functionally immortal.'

'Lena.'

His tone was hard now, a frown accompanying the chastisement. Lena sighed. 'Sorry. I just hate having to do things with Claudio.'

The front door of the apartment opened, then closed again a few seconds later.

'Silvie?' Azura's father called, looking up from his pile of palace department missives. 'Come through, we're at the table. You're here at the perfect time; Myles has boiled the kettle again if you'd like coffee or tea.'

'I had to make new cups for myself and Azura, thanks to Lena,' Myles explained as Silvie came into view.

The same neatly-mended yellow cloak that had caused so much trouble the night before was draped over her arm, the rest of her clothes simple and worn but carefully kept. Azura wondered if Silvie would eventually have to wear a uniform, like most of the palace staff did, or if she'd remain exempt, like Azura's father.

Silvie looked a little drained, the same as Azura felt, but even dulled by exhaustion she had a striking energy in her gaze. Her hair was tied back from her face, and the style gave a slightly severe cast to her already spare features.

'Silvie, this is Myles and Lena. Myles and Lena, this is Silvie, my new apprentice.' Azura's father waved his hand between them but barely looked up from his work.

Silvie's eyes widened. 'The Little Magdalena,' she said softly to herself, transfixed. Then, remembering where she was, her gaze dropped to her cane. 'Your Majesty. I'd kneel if I could, but—'

Lena shook her head, giving a dismissive wave of her hand. 'Please, please, stop worrying,' she said. 'When I'm here I'm just Lena. No kneeling required.'

Silvie looked doubtful. Azura was ready to give her a smile, help her feel at ease, but Silvie's gaze flickered to Myles.

Azura felt a weird little tinge of hurt at being passed over for comfort, though she could see how it made sense: even though Azura had come to her rescue the night before, the two of them had little common ground. By contrast, Myles' coat marked him out obviously and immediately as a foundling and a soldier. Silvie had been a sentry, which meant she was a foundling too. They were two of a kind, with Azura now the odd one out.

Unlike Myles' hair, nothing about Silvie's appearance marked her out as a changeling, but the signs weren't always visible: she might have been born with a full set of teeth, or webbed toes, or as a twin.

Not all foundlings were changelings, either. Sometimes families just couldn't afford to feed another mouth.

Myles noticed Silvie's glance towards him and he smiled broadly at her. 'You're fine, I promise. Tea?'

'Oh, um. Yes. Thank you.' Silvie eased into an empty seat at the table as Myles poured her a cup.

'Lena and I have lessons together some days,' Azura explained, oddly determined to reinsert herself into the conversation. 'So she and Myles come here for breakfast when they're able. Myles is sort of a bodyguard, like I explained, but he's kind of a butler, too. Just think of him as Myles, it saves confusion.'

'Or as Azura's future husband,' Lena said playfully.

'Cut it out with that stuff, it's so creepy,' Myles protested.

'What? It's not creepy, it's romantic. I'm trying to steer the course of fate to make you both happy.'

'Yeah, and it's creepy,' Myles repeated.

Silvie sneezed.

'Feeling all right?' Azura's father asked.

'Oh, yes,' Silvie assured him. 'I'm fine. It's only a cold.'

Then Azura sneezed.

Lena gave Azura a sharp glance, then Silvie. 'It's probably all thanks to me,' she informed them airily. 'I'm probably carrying all kinds of exotic maladies, after meeting with so many different dignitaries and diplomats coming to pay their respects to Eugenio. There'll be even more today, and over the next few days. I'll probably wind up with all kinds of gross bugs. Just you wait. I'll be the sickest of any of you.'

'I could make you a batch of remedies and preventatives, if you like,'

Azura's father said, only paying mild attention to the conversation as he scribbled replies to important messages. 'I recently fine-tuned a distillation that'll be a good health booster. Not certain about the taste, though.'

Lena swerved the topic away from her own health as abruptly as she'd introduced it. 'Myles, let's skip studies today. We should head back to my tower, so I can get ready for my appearances with – ugh – Claudio.'

'We should get going too, Silvie,' Azura's father chimed in.

Azura drank the remainder of her tea. 'I'll get some study done before today's tutors, then.'

She spent the morning at her grandfather's old desk, forcing herself to pay attention to the history work the tutor wanted her to cover in her own time.

The double-page spread in the textbook was a selection of newspaper comics and postcards, their publication dates stretching across recent decades. The only real change over the span of eras was the art style; the content remained almost exactly the same.

In each strip, an underdog husband was beleaguered by a nagging wife. Then when she died, he was finally able to breathe a sigh of relief. The punchline was always his moment of surprise and terror when she came back as a cadaveri.

Azura knew her tutor intended for her to write about how the older examples tended to have expository dialogue and guiding captions, while the newer ones assumed their meaning would be conveyed by the images alone. Or maybe she was supposed to write about how the postcards used a broader, more caricature-like style compared to the newspaper cartoons.

Even though the answers were obvious to her, she couldn't muster the motivation to put pen to paper. She still felt feverish and sickly from the canal, and had less than no desire to spend any time on the assigned task. She turned the page without bothering to write a response.

She winced at a sudden sting, the sharp slice of a paper cut. Azura stuck the wounded index finger in her mouth, the metallic tang of blood hitting her tongue a moment later and making her general illness and discomfort even worse. She'd become a vegetarian for ethical, rather than aesthetic reasons – she'd rather liked the taste of meat, back when she'd eaten it. But her tastebuds had grown unused to the flavours, making the little cut far more repellent than it otherwise might have been.

The reproductions of postcards on the next page were even more upsetting and unsettling, making Azura's stomach roil in disgust. The largest image showed a loose circle of young men holding machetes as a cadaveri, tethered by rope to a stake, lunged at them. One of its arms was already a twitching mass on the ground. The caption read:

Sports such as cadaveri baiting have been largely driven underground, as safety concerns for the participants have become a more foregrounded concern. Ephemera such as this gives us insight into an earlier perspective.

Azura felt like an overfull kettle coming to boil, about to spill burning steam in all directions. How did everybody accept all this so easily? How were the cadaveri – these nightmares made of human remains – an acceptable price to pay for magic?

People could get used to anything, if they had to. They could make jokes about it, and devise cruel games. Even the worst things could become normal, given time.

Azura wished the whole world would collapse into a pile of stinking rubble. It already felt like that to her, so why hold on to the illusion of civilisation? Let it crumble. Let it be as savage and heartless as it obviously was under the thin veneer of society. At least then it would be honest.

She wished the christallo would shatter into gleaming dust, scattering its cruel costs and balances into the wind. She wished the dead would be allowed to rest where they lay – away from machetes wielded for sport, away from stupid sexist ugly jokes. She hated it all so much it felt like a physical presence inside her, a knotted little organ full of bitter bile.

She turned the page. Her finger, still bleeding and slick with spit, left a watery smear of blood on the page as she flipped it over. She didn't go back to clean it off. With any luck the pages would dry stuck together, and anyone trying to get them apart would ruin them completely, destroy the pictures forever.

When her study was done, Azura slipped out and made her way to the palazzo, arriving in time to see the King and Lena still waving and smiling at the gathered crowds. They were giving out shiny coins to those closest. Azura pushed her way through the throng until she got close enough to stick out her hand.

When he reached her, Claudio's smile broadened with recognition. He lightly smacked her palm and shook his head. 'Your father would scold us both if I gave you money meant for the needy, Azura.'

'Only if he found out,' she replied with a smile before he moved on to the next subject waiting for his attention.

Azura glanced over, but it didn't seem that Lena had noticed the interaction. That was probably for the best – she'd likely consider Azura to have been fraternising with the enemy. Lena's dislike of her stepson was common knowledge among the few people who truly knew her, despite the perfect manners she put on in public.

Why Lena disliked Claudio so much was something Azura had never been able to work out, or get out of her. Then again, Lena had always seemed fond of King Dante, while Azura had been afraid and resentful of him by turns. So maybe it was the same kind of thing. Just because Azura thought Claudio was nice enough didn't mean Lena had to feel the same way.

'It's a pity he hasn't a queen,' a voice behind Azura remarked. She turned to see a woman about her father's age, speaking to a friend. 'I like it when there's all that fuss, marriages and queens and that. The last one was forever needing new queens. Those girls he married were so frail – none of them lasted long.'

'Well, we've still got the Little Magdalena, don't we? So it ain't important if this King hasn't chosen one yet.'

'It'd still be nice though, wouldn't it?' the first speaker insisted. 'I hope he takes a queen of his own soon.' Her voice turned arch. 'Maybe he's already got one in mind. After all, the Little Magdalena won't be little forever, will she?'

9. SILVIE

THE CHAOTIC LOGIC OF THE RECORDS ROOM WAS SLOWLY becoming familiar, to the point where Silvie now knew instinctually where to correctly place the teetering sheafs of paper that Doctor Corsetti left haphazardly on any spare surface.

It was dull, repetitive work, but Silvie was pleased to be efficient at it, to earn her place. And it was better than cooking greasy tavern meals.

The rhythm of her task was broken in the late afternoon by a light knocking at the door. She didn't have a chance to open it, or even to call out in response, before the knocker opened the door and stepped inside with a query of 'Antonio? Are you in here?'

Portraits of the King were not as common in the village as portraits of the Little Magdalena were, an adult man making for less striking iconography than a widowed child-queen, but those that did exist were accurate enough that Silvie recognised him immediately.

King Claudio was every inch the noble, beautiful young ruler. He couldn't have looked more suited to it if he'd been designed for the role, with a tumble of golden-brown curls and bright blue eyes surrounded by thick lashes. His jaw was strong and well-shaped, and his generous mouth widened into a smile at the sight of Silvie. 'Hello, you must be his new apprentice. Charmed to meet you.'

Silvie noticed, to her great puzzlement, that Claudio was much more attractive in real life than he'd been in the vision she'd had the night of his father's death. It was as if her view then had been filtered through the perception of someone who disliked him.

It was another inexplicable aspect of a mystery Silvie suspected she'd never fully understand.

Claudio held out a hand for her to shake, which Silvie did after a moment's hesitation. Such casual familiarity with the King of the realm was extremely unnerving, but who was she to deny him the terms he wanted to greet her on?

As their hands met he pressed a heavy coin against her palm, grinning at her visible surprise.

'Azura tried to get one off me when I was handing them out in the square, but you may have one if you like,' the King explained, still smiling cheerfully. 'I know Antonio well enough to know he thinks of you and his daughter as two of a kind. He has many sterling qualities, but about some things he's painfully naïve. He and Azura have the luxury of living largely unaware of the hierarchies which bind most of us in our places.'

Silvie took the proffered coin. She disliked accepting charity, but she wasn't proud to the point of idiocy. She also knew that being trapped by hierarchy wasn't the same for the one at the top as for the one at the bottom, but making such an observation to a King was less than wise.

Claudio's smile managed to broaden further. 'I suppose I'm worse than Antonio, really, aren't I? Presuming to call the pair of us two of a kind, when there's even greater difference between us than there is between you and Azura. It's a failing of mine, looking for common ground with those I meet. Being monarch is lonely work at times. It's why I never moved into the tower quarters traditionally held by the king. I would have felt too isolated from the rest of the world.'

'It did cross my mind that our experience of hierarchies is unlikely to be similar,' Silvie conceded. His friendliness seemed genuine enough – what political gain would there be in chatting to an underling like her, after all?

He nodded. 'My remarks were thoughtless. I hope you forgive me for them. I should leave you to your work and find Antonio, before my guards catch up to tell me off for going place to place without their protection.' Another grin lit up his handsome face. 'Come and find me if you ever want another coin or two. I usually have some on me.'

Claudio closed the door as he left, leaving Silvie alone again. She turned the coin over in her hand a few times, admiring the newly-minted shine of it, before placing it in the pocket of her skirt and returning to her work.

Silvie had no illusions about the temporary nature of her position in the palace. Everyone used the word "apprentice", but she was an assistant, not a pupil. Nobody expected her to take up the role of record-keeper and alchemist as her own someday. Not when she was a void. Not when Azura Corsetti existed, naturally talented in all the right ways and the direct descendent of those who'd taken up the duties in the past.

Silvie was merely a convenient spare, filling in until the rightful heir could be convinced to take her place. One day, Azura would realise that inheriting her father's position was the best possible path to take to a comfortable future, and that would be the day when Silvie's life would lurch underfoot yet again. Silvie just had to be ready for whenever it happened.

Sometimes when there was too much quiet, her deaf ear gave little rings of nothing-sound, like the aura left behind after the peal of a bell. Then that weird absence would be matched and counterpointed by the overworked strain of her functional ear, hallucinating noises in the effort to prove it could still hear.

The silence and the noise were equally oppressive. Her half-deafness wasn't chronic pain but was something like it – a chronic unmet expectation, a chronic sorrow. A chronic frustration, one she wasn't sure she'd ever learn how to live with; not without peevish anger bubbling below the surface of every mood.

She was so tired of being angry.

As she did so often, that night Silvie dreamt of the death she'd been wrenched away from. Cold rough bracken and twigs underfoot, the occasional small animal or bird sound somewhere distant through the trees, the scent of death bright and twisting through the air before her.

There was no time for pain, not even for understanding of what was happening. There was just existence one moment and then–

Silvie jerked awake, momentarily disoriented to find herself human-shaped. Then reality came back to her: this was the only shape she'd ever be from now on. Her wolf days were gone. The cold night air, the scent ribbons, the satisfaction of understanding her whole world with a perfect clarity that she'd never feel as a human, all gone.

What was worse, she didn't even feel like a human anymore. She was an in-between thing, like the ghouls, a creature that human hubris had snatched back after she'd fallen over the lip of the dark.

She fumbled at the wall beside her bed for where the cane rested and leaned on it as she made her way carefully to the bathroom. She dipped her hands into the barrel and lapped at the water collected in her palms, still too caught up in the echo of her lost wolf to want to use a cup.

Straightening up, she looked at herself in the mirror's antiseptic reflection. The harsh white of the palace's magical indoor illumination put a sickly cast over her features, or maybe the nightmare was to blame. Her tattoo was stark against her skin, an inkblot over the tracery of veins lining the inside of her wrist.

She'd tried writing to Kolya several times, desperate to believe their bond could survive this distance. But it was difficult to know what to say, how to mimic their old easy everyday interactions. Now that they weren't every day, they didn't feel easy either.

Sometimes Silvie thought she probably wasn't a very good person. She didn't like other people enough to be kind or generous in her heart. Trusting strangers was a mug's game.

And, while Azura was all right, Myles and Lena were interesting, Doctor Corsetti had given her a role when she'd none, and even the King's kindness seemed genuine, if trifling, Silvie missed the camaraderie she'd had with the other sentries. Maybe after spending such a significant portion of her life as a wolf, she'd become more of a pack animal than she liked to admit.

She didn't like people, but she didn't like being alone either. Yet again, she was stuck somewhere in-between.

Allowing herself one more little sigh, she shuffled slowly back to bed.

Morning brought a nasty reminder of everything Silvie had lost, as if she needed another. It wasn't the first time she'd experienced this weird little hangover of the magical triage that saved her life.

Some days, one of Silvie's eyes would be a ghostly pale colour, like her wolf's had been, the iris a milky grey instead of her usual hazel. On those days, Silvie found it nearly impossible to meet her own gaze for long enough to properly inspect the change.

She didn't know if the grey in her hair was another echo of the wolf she'd died with, or if it had turned that shade from the overall trauma of the experience. There was so much she didn't understand about her body now. She was a stranger in her own skin.

Her lingering ill health from the misadventure in the canal was compounded by her usual vertigo, as it compounded any mild sickness. It wasn't exactly like seasickness, though it was similar. Some days she felt strong enough she could largely ignore it, but there were times when Silvie felt so sick and worn down from the endless struggles of her changed body that doing anything more than surviving seemed impossible.

Usually, she tried to get as much done as she could, no matter how she felt when she woke up, because there was no point in waiting until her energy and strength were at a comfortable level. She'd be waiting forever and, even more pressing than that, the thought of having nothing to do was almost more frightening than death.

If she didn't force herself to work, even when she had no vitality or motivation, she'd lose her role as an apprentice very quickly.

This morning's task was relatively easy: painting magically-treated eggs with coloured wash in the apartment kitchen, while Doctor Corsetti did other tasks in the workshop proper.

Azura and Lena lingered nearby, watching her and procrastinating their own tasks in the process. Myles kept to the background, an unobtrusive presence on the margin of the tableau.

'I used to love painting eggs when I was a kid,' Azura said, glancing over at Lena. 'Remember? We'd beg Dad to let us help him.'

Lena nodded. 'He let us, but Dante found out and forbade me from doing it again. He said it was unseemly for his queen to do such a lowly task.'

Azura gave a sad little smile. 'Yeah. It wasn't as fun after that. I stopped asking Dad if I could help.'

Lena suddenly became fascinated by her own fingernails, addressing Silvie without looking up. 'Why do you paint the eggs with different colours, if they're already enchanted?'

'Presentation matters as much as the magic,' Silvie answered. 'Not just for nobles, either. Even in my village, if you give a customer an ordinary egg and say it'll improve their chances of conceiving, they'll get annoyed at you for trying to sell them nonsense. But paint it up prettily, and they'll trust it without hesitation.'

Azura gave a sudden laugh. It was a warm, throaty chuckle, without the sarcastic catch that her speaking voice often had to it.

'I spilled egg over the floor once, when I was a kid. In the workshop,' she explained. 'I scrubbed it up as best I could, but I didn't tell Dad because I was scared of getting into trouble. Sprigs of moss and stuff started growing up through the cracks between the bricks of the floor, and then mice ate it – can you even imagine what a nightmare it is when mice eat a virility and vitality potion?' She laughed again.

'Speaking of the workshop,' Silvie said, concentrating on keeping the coloured wash even as she spoke. 'I'd still like to collect elderberry supplies sometime soon, if possible.'

'Oh, from Driade Island. I can take you. It's easy enough to row there.'

'I want to come too!' Lena interjected.

'Isn't your schedule absurdly full at the moment?' Azura reminded her. Lena made a noise of disgust.

'I'll plead with Myles. Sometimes he manages to get me a bit of freedom, if I've been especially well behaved.'

'Hey,' Azura interrupted. She stared at Silvie. 'One of your eyes is different.'

'Oh yeah, it gets like that sometimes. I don't know why. Side-effect of becoming a hollow, I suppose. Sorry it's so strange.'

Azura gazed at it for a long second and then looked away abruptly, cheeks going pink like she'd just realised she'd been staring.

'That's... that's pretty cool,' she managed to say, giving a cough.

Silvie's own cheeks heated up too, though she wasn't sure why. 'It reminds me of the Doll's Eye plant,' she said, trying to salvage the moment from its sudden awkwardness.

'I know the one. That's called white baneberry here.'

Silvie kept her eyes fixed on the neat row of eggs spread out on the towel in front of her. 'I know. I've been studying witchcraft since I was a child, you know. Just because I'm from the middle of nowhere doesn't mean I don't know anything.'

Witchcraft, unlike magic, could be done by anyone, provided they had the reagents required. It was the study of theory as much as it was a practice.

Magic, however, needed latent ability in the caster. People with magic ability could perform more powerful witchcraft than those without; in its most potent form it was dubbed alchemy.

Azura, more visibly flustered than Silvie had seen her before, began to stammer. 'I didn't... I didn't mean it like that. I didn't mean it like anything. I was just saying, in case you didn't know.'

Lena, whose own lifelong training was in smoothing over awkward social situations, stepped in to save them both. 'Why is the plant called a Doll's Eye?'

'Let me show you.' Azura left the room, returning a minute later with a hefty hardcover book of botanical illustrations. 'Here.' She showed the open page to Lena.

Lena grimaced. 'Well, that's disgusting.'

The Doll's Eye plant had a thick red stalk with stems branching off it, each ending in a little grey-white berry with a black spot, like the pupil of an eye. Silvie had always rather liked them, for exactly the same reason Lena was repulsed: they had an incredibly macabre look to them, gory and medical and unnerving.

'Be careful if you come across it in the wild,' Silvie warned. 'They slow the heart to the point of death if eaten. They're extremely poisonous.'

Lena's doll-mouth widened into a grin. 'Cool.'

Azura rolled her eyes, putting the book aside. 'Don't worry about Lena. She might be the highest seat in the land after the king, but frankly she's kind of a bloodthirsty little creep sometimes.'

Lena gave a derisive laugh. 'If there are plants called Doll's Eye that look like bloodied nerve stalks and kill anyone who tries to eat them, then being bloodthirsty is a fairly reasonable reaction to living in the world.'

'Dad's away checking outpost facilities tomorrow. Are you going with him, Silvie?' Azura said, changing the subject completely.

Silvie shook her head. 'Tomorrow's my first afternoon off. Do you think he'll want me there, though? I can offer to go along if you think that's more appropriate.'

'What? No! Have your break, silly.'

Lena's eyes lit up with sudden enthusiasm. 'I'm attending a ballet tomorrow. Something more fun than diplomacy, for a change. You two should come as well!'

Silvie's private heart sank. She didn't let it show; she knew better than to protest the whims of those with power over her, no matter how in need of a rest she might feel.

'I don't really have the attire for that,' she offered instead. 'It wouldn't be appropriate.'

'Wear your cloak. Military officials wear their uniforms to performances all the time; this is the same. Oh, and I can help with–' Lena gestured to Silvie's cane. 'I broke my ankle once when I was younger. I can't remember how, probably jumping off something much too high. I have a propensity for that. Anyway, my mother and father had a cane sent to me. It was much, much too long, because they'd had to guess how tall I was. I don't think they even tried to guess, frankly. They just told someone to send a cane and left it at that. It might be a bit short for you, but I think it should be all right. We'll be back in a little while, wait here.'

Silvie wasn't sure whether or not to be surprised that Lena set off on her own errand, with Myles tailing like a brilliantly-hued shadow to her black-frocked form. The little queen acknowledged and ignored protocol depending on her whim, constantly in motion.

Silvie hoped Myles would be at the ballet as well. It would be easier if he was there. Azura's family apartment might be in the servants' wing, but Azura had far more in common with the patrons of the theatre, counts and lords and duchesses in their finery, than Silvie did.

Soon enough, Lena and Myles returned, presenting Silvie with the cane in question. It had clearly been selected for the queen on the basis of how expensive and ornate it was rather than for any kind of functionality. Even ignoring the fact that it was far too large for a child – it was almost the right height for Silvie to use, and she was tall and near adulthood – it was heavy and poorly-balanced. It didn't feel sturdy at all as Silvie tried to lean her weight on it.

The shaft was glossy ebony wood and the handle-piece was silver, shaped like the head of a bird with a long narrow beak.

'It's... very elegant.' Silvie said, as diplomatically as possible.

'It's okay, you can say it's useless,' Lena assured her. 'I mean, I assume it's useless. My parents excel at useless gifts. But it's nice of them to make an attempt, I suppose. Considering they don't know me, they're doing their best.'

Silvie wondered if Lena had the same echoing, wistful feeling that she did – not missing her parents, exactly, because you couldn't miss what you'd never had, but knowing that something was absent. A kind of undefined emptiness.

Her days were the limit of what her patchy stamina could handle, but no matter how exhausted Silvie was by the time she fell onto her bed, sleep refused to come easily.

She lay in the dark, hating the quiet and hating the emptiness of the room, wishing desperately that she could stop thinking until morning arrived.

The sound of knocking made her sit up so quickly her vertigo lurched, but she ignored it. 'Hang on a moment!'

She grabbed her walking stick and made her way over to the door.

Myles stood on the other side, still dressed in his uniform. 'I thought you'd be awake. The quiet, right?'

Myles had been a soldier. Of course he understood. Silvie nodded, mouth pulling up into a crooked little grin.

'Yeah. It's different.'

She was wearing her usual sleeping clothes: an extremely old dress, made up more of mendings and patches than the original fabric, the hemline so short it left her knees bare. Briefly, Silvie realised that she should feel self-conscious about being seen in her nightgown, especially by somebody as impeccably turned out as Myles, but the idea of being ashamed of it was vaguely ridiculous to her.

He held up a green glass bottle filled with liquid and stoppered with a cork. 'Honey wine. I don't know if it's exactly the same kind they drink up where you're from, but it was this or the orange-peel liquor that King Claudio stocks the cellars with. I thought this was a better bet. Want to come have a drink?' He smiled.

'Let me get my cloak,' Silvie said, offering a smile of her own in reply.

Myles led her up several flights of stairs to the long, flat roof of the servant's wing. 'If we climb those steps over there, we can get to the beacon tower, but that might be a lot for you to handle with your cane.'

Silvie thought about it, then shook her head. 'No, let's give it a try. If it ends up being too much, more fool me.'

It wasn't easy, but when they reached the top of the tower Silvie decided it was well worth it. There were two lit torches at the ready to set the prepared bonfire aflame if needed, but there was no guard on duty. Just open air above and the glittering sprawl of Arteria all around them below.

'It's prettier from up here than down on street level, isn't it?' Myles observed, helping Silvie sit on the ground. 'You don't have to see the grubby parts.'

'The smell's better, too,' Silvie noted. She watched as Myles pried the cork out of the bottle with his pocketknife. He offered the drink to her, and she took a swallow. The wine in Azura's little skin was grape-based, foreign, but this was the familiar mead that Silvie had grown up with.

'Quite a few of the other servants come to the roof of the wing to drink from time to time, if you're looking for a way to strike up first conversations with them,' Myles told her. 'I found that easier than the dining hall. I still have trouble with the dining hall.'

'Maybe I'll try that. It might be nice to get to know some people.' Better than lying awake for hours, anyway. 'I wouldn't have thought you'd get much chance to go to the dining hall, since you have to wait on the queen at mealtimes.'

Myles nodded. 'Not very often, no. Not since she was widowed. When the old king was alive, though, I wasn't allowed to attend to Lena if she was dining with him. I'd come up here then.'

He pointed to one of the palace's other towers, even higher than the one they were on. 'That's the queen's tower there, where Lena is currently theoretically asleep, but in practice probably reading a romance novel. She has a bell she can ring if she needs me, charmed so I'll hear it no matter where I am in the palace.'

Silvie stared over at the queen's tower, thinking about the night she'd almost died. That night was never especially far from her thoughts, but for once she wasn't thinking about the forest, about the bite she'd never seen coming.

Instead, Silvie thought back to the strange hallucination she'd had, in the moments before she'd been wrenched back into herself. The vision of Azura and Lena, of Claudio and Dante.

Projection like that, consciousness moving through the world without any tether to an animal familiar, was practically unheard of. It took an incredible amount of magical strength, far more than Silvie had ever possessed. No amount of disruption or imbalance from the King's death could account for what had happened to her.

She shivered. Silvie preferred to shove the mystery of her vision to the back of her thoughts whenever possible. The misery of all the things she'd lost was an ordinary, solid kind of unhappiness, without any haunting questions or strangeness adding to it.

Myles offered her the bottle again, and Silvie took another drink. She knew he was trying to get a read on her, to evaluate whether she posed any threat to Lena. Silvie didn't feel offended by the ulterior motive, since it was proof that Myles was dedicated to his role as the queen's protector. Offers of company and wine usually had some kind of hidden agenda, and wanting to ensure that a child was safe spending time in someone's presence was a fairly straightforward motive.

Myles gestured to Silvie's cloak. 'I always envied the sentries when I was a kid, before I came to work in the palace.'

Silvie wasn't surprised. The life of a sentry was brief and hard, but the life of a soldier was even worse.

'I used to feel so angry that my hair had ruined my life by being so obviously magical,' he said. 'But then I had almost no magical ability of my own to speak of. It seemed like an especially cruel joke.'

The wind wasn't biting-sharp but was cold enough to make her glad of her cloak. She handed the wine back to Myles. 'I feel that way when I see how my eye looks sometimes,' Silvie agreed. 'It...' She laughed, knowing Myles would understand the not-quite-joke. 'It doesn't seem fair.'

As if fairness had anything at all to do with the lives they'd been given.

'What you've done, coming to Arteria to be an apprentice to Doctor Corsetti like this, it's pretty brave, you know.'

'I assure you, there's nothing brave about me.' She took the wine back from him, swallowing a long gulp. 'I've spent my whole life doing what I was told. I just found someone else to do the telling.'

'That was the hardest thing to get used to, about living in the palace.' Myles chuckled. 'Even if I'm following orders, nothing's straightforward and simple the way it was when I was a soldier. There's all these unspoken social cues and things nobody talks about. I miss the simplicity of being cannon fodder. Nobody had a hidden agenda; they were quite clear about their intentions to make use of you until you wound up dead.'

The grin on his face fell away, and he looked serious again. 'Not that I'd ever give up this life for anything, mind you.'

'It seems like you love looking after Lena,' Silvie agreed. 'When I see you together, it never looks as if you're simply carrying out your duties.'

Myles nodded, the torchlight dancing over the calm set of his features. 'It's, it feels like a kind of grace. Everything that's ever happened to me, even the worst things, feel like they were worth going through, because they brought me to this life I have now. That probably sounds stupid. But I would walk through fire for her. I'd–'

He cut himself off, staring out at the city below. Silvie didn't press him. They drank in silence until, eventually, he sighed and stood up. 'I should go back to the tower. Have to make sure Lena gets a few hours of sleep.'

Silvie nodded, letting him help her back to her feet, dreading the empty room that awaited her.

It wasn't just her role as sentry that Silvie lost when her magic was taken from her. Her whole life had been sliced away. Afterwards, during those horrible, numb months when she'd been trying to learn how to be someone new, Silvie had continued to sleep in the barracks with everyone else. Those nights had been the only time everything felt all right. When everyone was asleep around her she could forget she didn't belong with them anymore. She could pretend, even if only for a moment, that life was just as it always had been.

Now there was nobody. Just Silvie and the night, and pretending didn't work anymore.

She and Myles made their way carefully back down the stairs to the servant's wing. 'Do you sleep here, or over in the queen's wing?'

'I sleep in the tower. The only person who does, other than Lena herself. I sleep by her door on a bedroll.'

'Doesn't sound very comfortable.'

He made a noncommittal sound. 'There are worse places.'

The fountain in the courtyard outside the Royal Opera Hall arced and danced in ways impossible to accomplish without magic, its verdigris-coloured stonework and cascades of water interweaving in shifting coils and patterns. It was a marvel of technical design and a work of art, and Silvie barely stopped herself from gasping slack-jawed at its beauty.

She wished Kolya could see it. She wished all the sentries could: this immense accomplishment made possible by their work and sacrifice. It wasn't fair that none of them save for her got a chance to bear witness to it.

Silvie touched her fingertips to the edge of her cloak, and thought of distant snow.

The ceiling inside the theatre was lavishly painted with a mural of a sky at sunrise, delicate pinks and blues and peaches breaking joyously from behind the clouds. The walls were decorated with an abundance of gilt carvings, winged figures spilling from every corner of the architecture. Enormous velvet curtains obscured the stage.

The queen's box was even more sumptuously appointed, and included silver-domed dishes piled with local seafood appetisers that Silvie didn't know the name for, and glistening fruits arranged as beautifully as a still life. The audience, still in the process of taking their seats below, applauded Lena's arrival with thunderous enthusiasm.

'Oh, it's *Under the Fig Tree*. I love this one. I cried for days the first time I saw it, it's devastating,' Lena told Silvie with incongruous cheerfulness.

'It's only devastating if the red fans win out,' Azura reminded her.

'Red fans?' Silvie asked.

'It's a branching river ballet. The style's been in vogue recently, probably because I love it so much. Companies can ensure my patronage if they stage them,' Lena explained.

'The story divides near the end,' Myles said. Silvie turned to hear him properly. 'When the performance reaches that split in the flow, the audience votes on which branch to follow – the white or the red – by holding up one of two fans. But when Lena's in attendance, she's the one who decides, no voting needed. The queen's decision on the ending trumps all else. Typically, the red is the more dramatic ending, while the white is happier.'

The production began. It was an adventure story, and a love story, about a sweet boy and a thorny girl, two sentries working as farmhands in their fallow months. A terrible rock slide isolated the farm, leaving the large, young family there in danger from approaching cadaveri and forcing the central pair to hold the line alone.

The deft dancers playing the horde of ghouls were aptly menacing, nightmarish, but it was the safe kind of menacing – like the thrill of dark fairytales around the fire.

It was one of the strangest experiences of Silvie's life, which had never lacked for strangeness. Seeing even the tiniest sliver of who she was reflected by the story played out in front of her was indescribable. People in stories had never been anything like her before.

As the second act reached its climax, everything froze between one moment and the next, suspended between two ticks of the clock. The lead dancers, caught in the final moments of a staggeringly beautiful pas de deux, turned their faces towards the queen's box.

'Silvie, which should I choose?' Lena asked, holding out two fans in her hands. Without hesitation, Silvie tapped the red one, and Lena held it up.

Motion resumed, as smoothly as if it had never been still. The story moved forward, with the couple splitting up to defend the children from opposite sides of the property. They succeeded, holding back the ghouls until reinforcements arrived.

Then, a dissonant chord ringing from the orchestra pit, an unexpected aftershock of the tremor that caused the rock slide, a second cascade. The lighting gels illuminating the stage shifted, dyeing the girl sentry's yellow cloak black with blood as she was buried. There was no reunion, no chance for the pair to be together even one last time.

It was beautiful and sad. Silvie wasn't sure it would be beautiful without the sadness, what the ending of the white fan might have offered. But the story was over now, no chance to go back and change it.

It was strange, leaving the heightened world of the ballet and going back to the ordinary one, watching the other audience members as they shed their borrowed sorrows and began talking of supper and sociability.

Azura's tear-stains didn't vanish as easily as those of the people around them. 'Occasionally it would be nice to leave a performance without my face blotchy from crying. Just occasionally. I don't know why you even own a white fan; I've never seen you hold it up,' she complained to Lena.

'The sad endings feel like the truer endings.'

'Suffering isn't more authentic than joy,' Azura countered hotly.

Lena chuckled. 'Really, it's embarrassing that you haven't outgrown your need for happy endings.'

'It's more accurate if at least one of them dies,' Silvie pointed out gently. 'At their age, it would be unreasonable otherwise.'

10. AZURA

THE DAY AFTER THE BALLET SAW AZURA BACK TO HER ROUTINES. HER morning tutoring session was lonely and dull, with Lena absent due to other commitments, and Azura felt increasingly grumpy as the time crawled by. When the lessons were done, she made her way back to the kitchen, intending to make herself a pot of tea in an attempt to clear her head a little.

Silvie was standing against the counter, decorating another batch of charmed eggs. The sight gave Azura a surprising lift. Watching Silvie add colourful washes and swirling designs to the shells should have been at most a mild distraction, but instead Azura found it genuinely fascinating to observe.

'Mind if I watch?'

'Not at all,' Silvie answered, not looking up from her careful work. Her face and posture were statue-still with a concentration that bordered on reverence, and there wasn't the slightest tremble in her hands as she swept the brush across the eggshells, creating bold strokes and delicate flourishes.

Despite the loss of her inherent ability, Silvie still trusted herself completely around magic. She could only have it second-hand, but her confidence with it remained unwavering.

Azura lost track of time, caught up in the meditative act of observing Silvie at work, so she wasn't sure when Lena and Myles joined them. The pair had managed more unscheduled visits to the Corsetti home than usual in recent weeks, probably because the loss of a Stregone had caused massive upheaval in the palace schedule. Azura was a little sad at the thought of losing that frequency when things settled down again. It was nice to have company.

Silvie's face brightened at the sight of Myles, which darkened Azura's tranquil mood. She knew it was awful to envy Silvie and Myles for having similarly horrible childhoods, but she couldn't help but hate being the odd one out.

Lena's poised posture slumped ever so slightly as the pair joined Silvie and Azura in the kitchen, her formal manners giving way to her genuine mood. Her crankiness made Azura feel better – if someone else was feeling rotten too, then her dumb jealousy wasn't such a crime.

'What's up?' Azura asked her. Lena groaned in melodramatic dismay.

'Dinners. So many dinners. Today I had one at ten in the morning! How is that a dinner?! Especially considering there's another one tonight.'

'Two more, actually,' Myles corrected. Lena groaned again.

'How've they been?' Azura asked. 'I mean, assuming "terrible" is a given. Are people genuinely sad about Eugenio, or is it mostly lip service?' She knew politics was a game that never ended, but it was sad to think that nobody really mourned the man they celebrated.

Lena gave a careless, loose-jointed shrug. 'I guess they've been genuinely sad, but it's not like that changes anything either way. The dinners have been the same as dinners always are. Exhausting. Complicated food that you have to think up polite compliments about, insufferable people you have to pretend to listen to intently. Everyone acting as if we don't already know that the position of Stregone is going to one of the boring old friends that Claudio inherited from Dante.'

She thought for a moment before continuing. 'Although, now that I think about it, he might have been King for long enough by now that he has boring young friends of his own that he owes favours to, instead of just the ones left over from when his father was in charge. The Stregoni themselves are the worst of all of them. You don't strive for power like that without part of your heart being dead. Either they killed it themselves, or someone killed it for them. It hardly matters, the result's the same.'

Silvie set the last of the eggs aside on a towel to dry, then washed her hands. 'Do you think Doctor Corsetti would mind if I did some baking? I've finished my tasks for the afternoon, and I want to repay his kindness in making me feel so welcome. I worked at a bakery, so I'm not bad at it.'

'Ooo, can we help?' Lena asked excitedly, bad mood forgotten with typical mercurial swiftness.

'You really don't have to suck up to Dad this much, especially when he's not even here to hear it,' Azura reminded Silvie playfully. She thought it was funny how Silvie was austere to the point of being prickly in how she spoke to people, but underneath she was actually desperate for those around her to like her.

Silvie ignored the teasing. 'I was thinking I'd make pies, since there's so many apples in the fruit bowl.' She turned to Azura. 'I haven't made them without magic before, so I might need your help.'

'Sure, of course.'

Lena grinned. 'I've got magic too! A little bit, anyway. All I really know how to do is tricks like making people's tea go cold.'

Azura scoffed sharply in disgust. She could see Silvie attempting to hold in a grin at the reaction, and felt a warm curl of satisfaction in her chest.

'It's not proper for royalty to do magic, except for the King's part in controlling the christallo,' Lena went on. 'That's why my magic levels are officially listed as "unknown", but I know I have at least a bit. Nothing like what Azura has.'

'In that case, you can prepare the apples.' Silvie took a few out of the fruit bowl and started to peel one. 'It doesn't need to be very precise, so don't worry if it's more than you can handle.'

'What about me, what can I do?' Myles chimed in.

'You can do the non-magical parts with me,' Silvie answered. Azura felt another prickle of jealousy and forced herself to shove it aside.

The four of them got to work. It was fun creating something together. Azura didn't get many opportunities to do things like that; her studies were increasingly solitary tasks, designed for her tutor to check when she was finished. Even when Lena was there, they worked alone, side by side.

So it was nice, to stand and watch as Lena – tongue-tip peeking out of her mouth in concentration – used her magic to chop the apples into small pieces between her palms. Silvie was having fun too, a pink-cheeked smile softening her face. She looked the prettiest that Azura had seen her so far.

'I'm glad we're doing this,' Silvie remarked as they worked. 'It's nice to make new memories. Whenever I thought about baking, I'd remember the good things I don't have anymore, and that always made me sad. But now it can remind me of this.' She shook herself, like loss was a dust that could be knocked off the skin. 'It's fun to create something that didn't exist before, through transforming the ingredients. Maybe, if I'd been a different kind of person, I could have managed to run away from the barracks and start a new life as a baker. I would have been good at it, I think.'

She took a deep breath, blinked hard, then nodded her chin at their work. 'Now the dough needs to mix and rise, then mix and rise again. Even with the specialised equipment at the bakery, it was always tedious. I tended to cheat and use magic, so I'll need your help now. Sorry.'

Azura waved her hand dismissively. 'Please. This barely even counts as using magic, since I don't have to concentrate or think or anything.'

Silvie looked surprised. 'Really? You don't even need to think about it when you do this kind of spell?'

'Not really. Not any more than I have to think about yawning or flexing my fingers or anything.' Azura's face went hot at the admission. It wasn't like she'd asked to have strong magical talent, it had just happened.

'But you don't want to take over your father's work. Not even the alchemist side of it.'

Silvie's quiet tone was flat, neutral, but Azura bristled at the words. 'So? I shouldn't be obligated to do something just because I'm good at it.'

'For some people, that's exactly what it means. Choice is a luxury.'

Silvie's words were quiet, but there was a quaver of anger to them. Feeling pretty ruffled herself, Azura decided that it would be better if she stayed silent, rather than risk an argument.

When the dough and the apples were both ready, Silvie guided the others in shaping the pastry into circles, adding sugar and apple to each, and pinching them closed. 'Now we glaze them with egg.'

'We should use one of the alchemy-treated eggs,' Lena suggested with a smirk. 'Make them magic pies.'

'Certainly,' Silvie agreed, her voice recovering a little of the playfulness it had lost in the discussion with Azura. 'If you want to be the one to explain to Doctor Corsetti why the stocks are short of what they should be. We need to heat up oil in a pan.'

Lena's eyes gleamed. 'Can I do it?'

Myles shook his head. 'Let me take that task, eh? I haven't been pulling my weight in this operation compared to you three.'

'But,' Lena protested in dismay, 'queens in novels get to cook people in boiling oil all the time. It's not fair if I don't even get to cook pies.'

'It's really hard to turn a blind eye to the kind of novels you read when you outright tell me about the terrible things in them, you know,' Myles replied drily.

The conversation startled a laugh out of Silvie. Azura hadn't heard a laugh like that from anyone before. There was a lightness and freedom in the sound, even after everything Silvie had gone through. Azura had never met anyone else who allowed themselves such unrestrained joy.

Azura looked at each of them in turn. Myles had stowed his scarlet coat, and in the warmth of the kitchen Silvie wasn't wearing her sentry cloak. Lena's delicate black voile overskirt was protected by a kitchen apron, voluminous on her small form. And it occurred to her that Silvie and Myles could shed their yellow and red, and Lena could cover up the fragile trappings of her station, but she was always stuck as Azura.

The life expected of her – the one she could defer and deny as much as she liked but which sat, placid and waiting and patient and inevitable in her future – wasn't a uniform she could cover up or put aside for a little while. It gnawed at the back of her mind every hour of every day, reminding her how trapped she was. Fate and circumstance had brought Lena, Myles and Silvie to their roles in the life of the palace, but Azura was born there. She'd never existed in any other place, any other context.

This was all she was, and she hated herself.

Her father worked late again that night, so Azura took the opportunity to slip out of the palace and into Arteria. He didn't like it when she did that, but sometimes she felt like she couldn't breathe, like she'd go crazy if she had to stay inside the palace for a moment longer.

Walking beside the canals always calmed her down. Azura could sense the thrum of the telluric currents carried on the flow of the water like a living thing beside her. Magic was so woven into the shape of her life that she couldn't imagine who she'd be without it.

She didn't feel sorry for Silvie – mostly because she could tell that Silvie would be furious at the idea of anyone pitying her. But the thought of suffering the same loss, of being left bereft, terrified Azura. She didn't want the future laid out before her, but the thought of it being snatched away completely was equally undesirable.

Tonight even the familiar flow of the canals didn't help her mood, so Azura made her way back to the palace and to Lena's tower.

The procedure for visiting the queen's tower was complicated, since nobody was allowed inside without Lena's express permission. Usually, Azura had to ring the bell beside the doorway at the bottom, and Myles would let her in to climb the long flight of stairs to Lena's rooms.

On this occasion, however, there was no need for all that. Lena was standing inside the doorway, with Myles a somewhat anxious-looking shadow behind her. In front of the door, as close to the tower as protocol allowed without an invitation, was King Claudio.

'Half of your birthday demands are just trouble for trouble's sake, don't think I can't tell,' he said, his even tone frayed with frustration. 'I don't understand why you insist on being so wilful and contrary.'

'I don't think there was anything wrong with my requests,' Lena replied, puzzled.

Azura didn't buy that for a second – Lena always knew exactly how much she could get away with, where the line between custom and laws hovered.

'You have all the wealth and luxury anyone could want in life, and all life asks in return is that you obey the laws of your station. All you need to do is behave, and you can't even do that. You're as shifting and impossible as a snake.'

Lena gave a mean little laugh. 'I'll take that as a compliment, Your Majesty.'

'You can be such a child sometimes–'

'Yes, that's the point. I am a child. Whatever defects are present in my character are there because of those who raised me.'

Claudio's sigh was one of defeat, of old arguments played out endlessly in circles. 'You can't blame me for my father forever, Magdalena.'

'Oh, I don't. Don't worry, the things I hate you for are entirely your own doing.'

Abruptly, Lena turned to address Azura, her mood flitting immediately to a smile. 'Come upstairs, we'll play chess.'

It was chilling, how quickly she could shift from venom to sweetness, but Azura was used to Lena's capriciousness.

Claudio, understanding he'd been dismissed, turned to walk away. A frown clouded his habitually sunny expression. Azura tried to catch his eye, to exchange a comforting smile – don't take it personally, you know what she's like – but he was gone before she could.

'Behave,' Lena spat dismissively as they climbed the tower staircase. 'He thinks we owe the kingdom something, that in return for our lives here in the palace we should be grateful, and...' She trailed off with a noise of frustration. 'He knows nothing.'

'It doesn't matter,' Myles soothed, voice calm and even. 'Your birthday will go ahead just as we've planned it.'

11. Silvie

The brilliant, unnatural colour of Myles' hair was an obvious example, but even smaller kinds of strangeness were enough to mark out a baby as a changeling, not fit to be raised in ordinary society. They were dumped on church stoops, or deposited directly at the doors of sentry posts.

At least, that's what Silvie had always been taught. More and more often as she grew up, she'd begun to wonder. There were children in the village whose hair was shorn so short that the colour was hard to tell. She'd shared rooms with maids and shop-girls who never took their socks off in the presence of others, not even to bathe, or who'd been injured in early childhood and lost a hand or an eye.

Had their parents wanted a child so badly that they'd ignored the marks, disguised the imperfection in whatever way necessary?

There was no way to know, and Silvie had never heard anybody speak of it. As far as the official version went, all changelings were abandoned without exception.

The changelings were left at church steps or sentry posts but never, ever at infantry settlements. Even as they turned their babies over to an unknown future, every parent held out a hope that their child would show magical talent, would grow up to be a sentry rather than a soldier. Both died young, but soldiers died younger.

The list of things that marked out a changeling grew longer every year. Strange hair, strange eyes, favouring the left hand over the right for writing, too many or too few toes, skin too pale or too dark, more than one baby to a birth.

The ranks needed replenishing, and the way to ensure that was to keep a steady supply of babies to be discarded by their parents. Silvie had heard some couples left as many as five or six babies on church doorsteps over the years. She wondered how those people slept at night.

Probably very comfortably, kept safe from worry by the hard work of sentries at the gate.

Sometimes she'd wondered if any of the other sentries at the barracks were her siblings. A few had the same complexion and features as her – pale eyelashes and broad hands that went cracked and scaly quickly in the cold – but whether they shared lineage as well as poor luck was irrelevant. Silvie had no way of guessing how important or insignificant family bonds could be. Relatives were something that happened to other people. Kolya would still be Kolya, dear to her and impossibly far away, whether they shared blood or not.

All these thoughts scuffed their way idly though her brain as she lay in bed, waiting desperately for sleep.

It was pouring rain outside: yet another change in the temperature and weather of the city. Having one less Stregone keeping the christallo even was making the climate go wild.

Silvie wondered where the palace servants drank on nights like this, when they couldn't use the roof. Not that she felt comfortable enough around any of them yet to seek out their company. Myles' evenings off were probably few and far between, and as far as Silvie could tell, Azura wasn't close with the rest of the staff.

Silvie wished she had some piecework to distract herself with. If she was going to be up at all hours, she should at least be productive. But all her work for the day was finished, and there was nothing to keep her occupied as she waited out these endless, sleepless stretches of dark.

She wondered what Azura planned to do with herself, if she really was serious about avoiding a life in her father's footsteps. Silvie felt she'd been a little uncharitable with Azura on the subject – after all, Silvie knew better than anybody how frightening it was to face an unknown future when your fate had seemed a foregone conclusion. Just because Azura was abandoning her set future by choice, rather than having it ripped away as Silvie's had been, didn't mean it was any less terrifying. They were more alike than they were different, in some ways.

Accepting she wasn't going to sleep any time soon, Silvie climbed out of bed and lit the lamp. It didn't particularly need doing, but she could check her meagre wardrobe of clothing for anything that needed mending.

She liked being able to wear familiar pieces of clothing, remnants of her old life, even if they were noticeably shabbier than the things worn by other palace servants. She hoped she wouldn't have to wear a uniform – if she did, she'd have to abandon her cloak. Myles wore his red, rather than the palace hues, but perhaps the rules would be different for her. Silvie desperately didn't want to relinquish her yellow.

The snowglobe she'd bought on arrival in Arteria was tucked in amongst the cloth. Silvie shook it, thinking of the ballet. The figure in the globe was like the dancers, caught between one heartbeat and the next as they awaited an unknown future.

She wondered what she should buy with the coin Claudio had given her. Myles had mentioned Lena read romance novels; perhaps Silvie could find out where she got them from. It had been a while since she'd had a new book.

Lena reminded Silvie very much of Kolya, in some ways, and not just because they were about the same age. It disturbed her, because Kolya's story was unhappy even by the standards of the barracks, and Silvie didn't wish similarities to it on anyone.

Lena was a beautiful, pampered young woman, who'd never known anything but the height of luxury. Kolya was the unluckiest of an unlucky caste. But something matched between them, and it left Silvie feeling uneasy and sad.

Perhaps the future would be brighter, to make up for the darkness of the past. It wasn't likely, but Silvie couldn't see any harm in hoping.

Morning saw her battling a mild headache, as it often did when she'd gone several nights in a row without restful sleep. Silvie stifled a yawn as she chopped nettle as small, fine and even as she could for complex tonics.

'Hmm. I've let the elderberry get low, haven't I?' Doctor Corsetti remarked, holding the depleted jar up to the light.

Silvie felt a twist of panic. 'Sorry. That was me,' she answered hurriedly. 'I've already arranged to get more very soon. Sorry.'

Instead of the anger she feared, Doctor Corsetti looked impressed at her initiative, which soothed the churning in her gut. He had yet to be anything but kind to her, but kindness wasn't trustworthy. Kindness could be withdrawn as easily as it was offered, but if he thought she was useful then he'd have a reason to keep her around.

The best things to be, Silvie knew, were invisible and useful. Her height, her cloak and her cane had all worked against her ability to be invisible, at different points in her life, but she could usually make herself useful one way or another.

'Claudio mentioned that the two of you met briefly,' Doctor Corsetti said as he returned the elderberry jar to the shelf. 'He often stops by if he has a spare moment; don't worry about formalities with him unless there's someone else present.'

Between the Little Magdalena and the King, Silvie was starting to suspect that being a lunatic was a prerequisite for being royal in Arteria. She made a small noise of affirmation, utterly baffled that a king would bother to remember her for long enough to mention later.

'Azura told me you were responsible for the pies that were waiting in the kitchen last night. Quite delicious, I must say.'

This was sturdier ground; she knew her baking was good. 'I'm glad you liked them.'

'I've never found particular pleasure in cooking, I confess. Azura's mother never did either, so it's a long time since that kitchen has seen much use. Please feel welcome to commandeer it any time you like.'

Silvie considered telling him that Azura, Lena and Myles had all helped, to portion the credit where it was due, but was uncomfortable admitting that the dowager queen of the realm helped her chop apples.

The workshop door opened and Azura stepped inside without bothering to knock.

'Azura! What a nice surprise!'

'Hey, Dad. I'm here to talk to Silvie, actually,' Azura said, turning to her. 'If the weather's clear tomorrow, we'll go out to Driade Island first thing in the morning, if that's all right with you?'

Silvie nodded. She hoped she'd sleep better before the excursion. She wasn't thrilled at the prospect of being out on the bay again, but there was no getting around the necessity of it.

'I'm pleased you're taking an interest in ingredients and reagents, Azura,' Doctor Corsetti enthused warmly.

Azura scowled. 'I'm not. I'm just helping Silvie, because I know where to find the elderberry. It doesn't mean anything else.'

'Of course not,' Doctor Corsetti replied immediately, eager to keep Azura's mood as even as possible. 'But still, it's good of you to help.'

12. AZURA

AT THE BREAKFAST TABLE IN THE MORNING HER FATHER, FOR ONCE, PUT aside his correspondence and greeted her with a smile. Azura nodded warily in reply, and poured herself some tea.

'Your tutor says you're doing well,' he said. 'At the subjects that interest you, at any rate.'

Azura slumped, exhausted before the day had even had a chance to start. 'There's too much to do it all,' she tried to explain. 'I have to choose what's most important. It's good I know how to prioritise, isn't it?'

Her father's smile thinned into scepticism. 'We've talked about this. You need to try harder.'

'I am trying harder. Can't you tell how hard I'm trying?' She knew she was whining but it wasn't fair. She worked so hard and all he ever saw were the things she didn't do.

'If you stopped wearing those glasses, I'm sure you'd be able to concentrate more easily—'

'Just leave me alone!' Azura snapped. 'You never understand anything!'

'No, I don't! You're a smart girl, Azura, but you seem determined to throw that away. You can't act like a child forever.'

A quiet knock broke the heat of the argument. Azura's father went to answer the door, returning with Silvie in tow. She looked uncomfortable, clearly having heard the argument that she'd interrupted.

'I'm ready to go whenever you are,' she told Azura.

'We have to collect Lena and Myles too,' Azura said, staring down at her tea so she didn't have to look at anybody. Her anger and hurt at her father still simmered below the surface. 'Give me a minute to finish this drink and then we'll go.'

'The island is magically warded, so you'll be alerted to any trace of cadaveri,' Azura's father explained to Silvie. 'There hasn't been any disturbance there for a long time. But you should all keep your guard up, regardless.'

'We will,' Silvie promised.

'We'll be fine,' Azura added, swallowing down the rest of her tea quickly. 'Come on, let's go.'

The water within Arteria was constrained within the city's canals, like a wild animal made docile by years inside a cage. The water of the bay, by contrast, seemed to Azura like a creature that had never been tamed at all but chose to be friendly anyway, like a tiger that deigned to be petted.

It was childish, maybe, but Azura had always felt like the dangerous, chaotic energy of the open water was, well, somehow on her side. A tiger whose claws were sheathed, for now.

The small, quick waves that lapped at their boat were a stormy, steely grey, a shade or two darker than the clouds overhead. The wind was sharp and cold against their cheeks.

'Sorry about the weather,' Azura said to Silvie as she propelled the boat forward by magic, as if she could take any kind of blame for the miserable conditions. 'Once there's a new Stregone it'll become more predictable again.'

'It doesn't bother me,' Silvie replied, pushing windblown hair away from her face. 'I'm used to the cold. In the black wood you can toss hot water into the air and it freezes before it hits the ground. We used to do that for fun – see who could make the best arcs.'

'Really!?' Lena's eyes became very wide, and she snuggled her face lower into the voluminous black scarf around her neck and chin. 'That sounds horrible.'

Silvie looked thoughtful. 'No, not really. It's exhausting, more than anything else. The cold lasts a long time, and it's unrelenting. You begin to forget what being warm was even like.'

Azura, always cold already, shivered as she imagined it: days where the sun was barely present, the night crowding in from both directions, the wet ebony of the trunks and branches that gave the black wood its name, the white snow. The constant prowling of wolves, the constant threat of the cadaveri.

Nobody knew for certain how many mass graves were on the steppe and the mountains beyond the black wood. War had raged there for decades, each surrounding country claiming the land as its own. Eventually, and with poetic irony, the conflict rendered the prize useless to all claimants: that much bloodshed left the lands plagued by legions of cadaveri.

So now the sentries and their wolves kept everyone else safe, or they tried to. And sometimes they suffered terribly for their efforts.

Azura pulled back from the icy precipice of her dark thoughts, instead focusing on the lagoon and the scatter of small islands across its surface. Those little outposts of land made it difficult to tell exactly where Arteria's edges were, where the ocean began.

Azura loved the thought that the boundaries of the city were blurred and hard to mark. Arteria as a whole was such a place of in-betweens, of things that weren't quite one thing or another: canals and roads in equal measure; magic and religion each nursing old wounds from their clashes; corruption policing itself into a state of stable government. It was fitting that its borders should be equally contradictory.

The island they were aiming for had a dark recent history: everyone in Arteria knew someone who'd died in the plague quarantine centre there, or someone who'd spent time recovering there. It was only a few years since the last wave of the epidemic had ripped through the city, and yet nobody talked about it. It was as if everybody had decided to close a door on that part of history, and ignore the room beyond it forever.

Now it was a place for mass graves and memory, and for wild plants to grow riotously over the ruins.

Despite the ominous weather and its grim past, however, the island didn't look the least bit forbidding or haunted as their boat drew close. It was just another small green place, welcoming and still on the wide water of the bay. Azura hoped that people whose loved ones were buried there felt a sense of calm when they looked in its direction.

'I had another fight with Dad about my lessons this morning,' Azura confessed to Lena. 'He doesn't understand how hard it is.'

'I can help you cheat, if you like,' offered Lena. 'I'm sure it wouldn't be too difficult.'

Azura snorted. 'I don't think I could handle the level of disappointment he'd feel if I got caught.'

'You could argue that knowing how to win at any cost is exactly the kind of skill needed for successful palace life,' Lena countered. 'But if you don't want to, that's fine. I just thought I'd offer. Or I could threaten our tutor with consequences if he keeps reporting negative things to your father. People are always frightened at the notion of consequences, the vaguer the better.'

Despite herself and despite the argument that had begun her day, Azura smiled. 'You're slightly terrifying sometimes, you know that, right?'

Lena grinned sharply in reply. 'I do my best.'

13. SILVIE

DRIADE ISLAND WAS RELENTLESSLY ALIVE. BIRDSONGS, BEES, VINES, flowers and drifting pollen motes filled the air. It reminded Silvie of the graveyard near the barracks, where she'd sometimes gone walking when she had a little time to herself. The atmosphere had always been peaceful and lively all at once, just as this place was.

Silvie didn't share the observation with the others, though, because it was likely that some of the dead laid to rest on Driade Island were people they had known. Cheerful comments about the nice mood of the place would probably seem tasteless, or disrespectful. Silvie tried to be respectful when she could, even if she rarely felt especially solemn in her heart of hearts.

She thought it a little unfair that being miserable came so naturally to her when being solemn didn't. Sometimes she felt sad when everyone around her was happy, and yet she could find joy in places like Driade Island, a home for the dead. It was like trying to navigate through life with a broken compass: Silvie could still steer herself by learning other ways to guide her route, but it was all so much more exhausting than if she'd had useful equipment in the first place.

Driade Island's lush life was wild and untended, growing however it wanted through the abandoned rooms of once-grand homes, greenery and thin sunshine overlaying faded finery.

'These buildings were all hospices not so long ago,' Lena said, stepping carefully over a thick tree root that had erupted through a decorative floor. 'This all grew up fast after the plague was over. It looked very different then.'

'You visited the afflicted?' Silvie asked. 'That's a risky appearance for a queen to make.'

Lena shook her head. 'No, Dante and I were quarantined here. It was kept quiet, of course.'

Silvie's eyes widened as she stared at Lena. 'The King had the plague?'

'No, no. Nothing like that. One of my advisors fell ill, so Claudio demanded that Myles and I be sent away for quarantine. I'm sure he was hoping I'd die, and he certainly didn't expect his father to come with me, even though it was the law that husbands had to go if wives were sent, and vice versa.'

'Kings only abide by the laws that suit them,' Silvie pointed out.

'Mm.' Lena continued picking her way over the thick mat of vines underfoot, heading for the broken frame that had once held doors to an outdoor courtyard at the centre of the house they explored.

'It was actually a happy time. We went for long walks a lot. The air's nicer here than in the city. Dante told me all about the history of the lagoon and its islands. He and Myles raced each other at swimming.' Lena made a soft scoffing sound. 'Maybe Claudio hated me because Dante liked my company. He might have been jealous.'

'I had no idea it was so bad for you.' Azura blurted the words out in a rush, clearly overwhelmed with sudden guilt. 'I remember you being sent away, but my father acted like it was all just protocol. I had no idea Claudio demanded it like that, that he wanted you to die.'

Lena laughed at Azura's discomfort, waving it away. 'What? No, don't be silly, it's fine. What would be the point in worrying you? None of us fell ill, so it was like a holiday more than anything. There are elderberries outside this doorway, here, look.'

'Don't touch,' Azura warned, moving towards where she stood. 'The rest of the plant can be poisonous.'

'Sometimes it seems like everything is poisonous,' Lena complained with a frown. 'I'm going to go see if Myles has made lunch yet.'

As Lena walked back the way she'd come, Silvie eased herself onto the ground near the elderberry bush and began to pluck the fruit carefully, mindful not to tear the stems or leaves.

'I could do that. You didn't have to sit down,' Azura said.

'No, it's fine. It really is more potent as an ingredient if the alchemist who'll be using it is the one to pluck it. One of those little witchcraft quirks,' Silvie answered.

Then, remembering her admonishment to herself to be nicer to Azura, she added 'Thank you for offering. You can go hang out with the others if you like.'

'Nah, that's okay. They like being on their own, and they don't exactly get a lot of opportunities. Is it all right with you if I stay here?'

'Of course.'

Silvie worked in silence for a while, collecting the best specimens in her pail. Azura brushed the thick carpeting of dead leaves off part of the courtyard's paving stones, revealing the brightly decorated ceramic patterns.

'Lena was fourteen when King Dante died, right?' Silvie asked, interrupting her task to watch Azura at work.

'Almost fifteen. Her birthday wasn't that long after. Pretty young to wind up a widow for the rest of your life.'

'She can't remarry?'

Azura shook her head. 'Dowager queens can't. I don't think it bothers her all that much now, but maybe it will when she's older. She's different to how she was when he was alive.' Azura stopped sweeping. 'I think she used to be happier, but sadder as well? Now she and Myles, it's like they're both… At first I thought they were calmer, but it's more like–'

'Numb?' Silvie guessed.

Azura gave a small nod. 'Something like that, yeah. King Dante protected Lena from the world a lot. And now she's had to grow up without him there to keep her safe from stuff. He changed the law so Myles was allowed to sleep near her personal suite. Before that, guards weren't allowed past the entrance to her tower, but King Dante knew that Lena would be lonely on her own. He wasn't a kind person, really, but he adored her.'

It all sounded to Silvie like an impossible fairytale that anyone could grow up so loved and sheltered. It made her think of Kolya, whose own childhood was as far from Lena's as a childhood could be.

Silvie didn't let herself think about Kolya's early years, before he became a sentry, if she could help it. Even brushing against the thought of what he'd gone through made her stomach a knot of hot coals. She avoided thinking about it but it burned away regardless, deep down and out of sight like the fires in abandoned mines, never going out.

She sometimes felt like her whole identity was built on top of buried fires, like a village on a volcano. She went through her days pretending there was no risk below the surface, no chance that everything might be engulfed and burned away without warning.

The lingering effects of her injuries were another fire, different in temperature to her fury on Kolya's behalf but no less dangerous. If Silvie let herself think about all the maybes and perhaps and if-onlys around that moment in the woods, she knew she'd fall apart and never put herself back together.

She knew how incredibly lucky she was to be alive at all. It felt like the worst kind of selfishness to wish for more than she'd been given, as if she was scorning this miraculous second chance at life.

But she missed her hearing, the ease of keeping track of the world around her without concentration and frustration, and she missed her balance, being able to walk without a cane to steady her.

She missed her magic. It had never been hers to use on a whim, but that hadn't stopped her daydreaming. Now she didn't even have that.

Driade Island would have been incredible to explore as a wolf. No matter how desperately Silvie tried to suppress the thought, it rose unbidden in her mind. Sometimes she felt she would willingly abandon her humanity if it meant she had some way to retain her wolf-shape. Silvie missed everything about having magic, but the thing she missed most was the way the world had appeared through her wolf-senses.

She couldn't help yearning for those things. The wanting was there no matter how she tried to damp it down. It curled up, hot enough to burn, like steam rising from springs above deep veins of magma.

'Is that enough?'

Silvie blinked, pulling herself back into the present and looking up at Azura. 'Hmm?'

'You stopped again. Do you have enough?'

Silvie checked the pail. 'I think so. Let's go find the others.'

The picnic lunch Myles had spread out for them was a miniature feast of fresh bread, cheese wrapped in red wax, pickles in brine, and ripe fruits.

He and Lena were absorbed in a game of cards as Silvie and Azura approached, their faces as serious as those of seasoned gamblers.

'I fold,' Myles said finally, placing his hand of cards face down on the chequered cloth. Lena gave a close-lipped smile and displayed her own cards, revealing two pairs.

'Don't feel too bad,' she consoled, not sounding the least bit contrite about beating him. Her clothing, heavily embroidered in black on black, rustled as she moved, and the sound mingled with the noise of the wind through the grass. 'You know it's a rare day when anyone can best me at a parlour game. Heaven forbid I should spend my time on anything useful or constructive.'

'Do you two want to play?' Myles asked Silvie and Azura as he collected the deck of cards and began to shuffle them. 'The game will work better with four.'

'No thanks.' Azura's voice was dry. 'I know better than to go against Lena at cards.'

Silvie was tempted, even if it would result in defeat. She had fond memories of playing against Kolya, who was bloodthirsty when it came to cards.

'I don't know Arterian games,' she admitted, 'so I wouldn't be much of an opponent, I'm afraid.'

'Maybe some other time,' Lena replied, gesturing for Myles to put the cards away. 'Let's eat and enjoy the day for now.'

'Dad would be glad to hear you talk about eating,' said Azura. 'He's always being a big worrywart about whether you're dieting too much and stuff like that.'

'Mm.' Lena acknowledged the comment without really replying, picking idly at a dandelion flower growing beside the spread cloth. 'The flowers are impressive this time of year, aren't they? Maybe they grow extra well from the graves beneath the soil.'

'That's a morbid thought,' Azura returned.

'Is it?' Lena sounded surprised. 'I didn't mean it that way.'

'Want me to make you a flower crown? I think I remember the trick of it.'

Lena made a face, prettiness distorting into a grimace for a moment. 'I've had enough of crowns to last a lifetime. And most of the flowers here are poison, anyway.'

Evening had turned the bay to shades of gold and brass by the time they headed back in the boat. Azura propelled them by magic, fast enough that Silvie's seasickness threatened to kick in.

'You didn't even bring oars,' Lena noted, glancing at the dinghy's weather-roughened deck. 'What if we'd needed to get back without magic?'

'Why would we need that?'

'I don't know, genius. You could have been hurt. How were any of us supposed to get help if we couldn't even move the boat?'

Azura grinned and shrugged. 'Oops. Sorry. I guess I didn't think of it.'

Lena snorted. 'For somebody who doesn't like magic very much, you certainly do take it for granted most of the time.'

Azura's smile grew even wider. 'What can I say? My laziness is stronger than my convictions.'

A bevy of retainers were waiting on the dock, drawing towards Lena like filings to a magnet as Myles helped her alight from the little boat. Their postures visibly relaxed as they confirmed that their little queen had avoided harm.

Several of the retainers surrounded Myles, speaking to him in low and hurried tones. His face pinched into a worried frown, and he set off with them towards the palace on foot without a word of explanation to Lena or the girls.

'The plants have completely taken over everything,' Lena told her entourage as the three of them were guided into her waiting carriage.

Silvie hadn't been surprised when they'd travelled the negligible distance from the palace grounds to the docks by carriage rather than by foot that morning; she and Azura had experienced firsthand how easily violence could occur even on Arteria's calmest streets. There was no sense in putting Lena at even more risk than her innocuous outing to the island had already entailed.

Once they were inside the palace grounds, Silvie and Azura headed towards the alchemy workshop, so that Silvie could begin cooking the elderberries into a safe form that could be made into a reagent.

'Are you getting a feel for Arteria? Settling in?' Azura asked, fixing some tea as Silvie worked. 'Would you like a cup?'

'Oh, yes. Thanks,' Silvie answered, glancing over before focusing back on her work. 'And, I think so? I haven't wound up in a canal again, which is a good sign.'

Azura gave a snort. 'That beginning wasn't especially auspicious, I'll agree. But things are going all right? I know my father forgets that other people need to sleep and eat and breathe when he gets absorbed in his work.'

'It's fine. I don't sleep very well anyway, so I prefer having work instead of being left to my own devices,' Silvie admitted. 'Myles showed me where the servants go to drink, up on the roof, and that'd be a trap for me if your father didn't give me so much work, I think. I'd end up going there all the time, and get a bad drinking habit.'

A dark look, maybe jealousy, flickered across Azura's face at the mention of Myles. Silvie wondered if there was more truth to Lena's joking about the pair of them than she'd assumed.

'I could come too,' Azura volunteered in a diffident tone, a faint blush pinking her cheeks. 'I don't go up there much. I don't know, I feel, I don't fit in like you and Myles do. I always feel out of place when I try to hang out with the other servants.'

'You think I fit in? Really?'

'Well, yeah. Obviously.'

Silvie gave a dry, amused little laugh. 'You're wrong. I don't fit in anywhere.'

Azura put down her teacup and crossed the room to a small, dusty wine rack in the corner. Pulling a bottle free, she offered a wide grin to Silvie.

'Come on, let's go now.'

Silvie blinked. 'But the berries…'

'Will be fine until morning. Come on.'

The air on the roof was mild, balmy. Silvie had always known that weather could be exhausting – the seasons were harsh in the north, each offering its own unique pains – but she'd never realised how wearying it could be for weather to be constantly changeable. Having the christallo in the middle of the city had enormous benefit, but it made the weather hideously unpredictable.

Myles was sitting with his back against the parapet, making solid progress on a bottle of dark amber spirits.

'Fancy meeting you here,' he greeted them flatly.

'Everything all right?' Azura asked him, sitting opposite. Silvie eased herself down as well.

Myles' smile was more like a grimace. 'Claudio's sending Lena to Gemelli. He says it's safer there.'

Silvie recognised the name – Gemelli was a small far-southern province, quite a distance from Arteria.

'Lena's furious at herself for thinking she could get away with a day away from the palace. Having me there was just giving her someone to rant to and work herself up again, so I thought she could do with a little while on her own to cool her head and indulge in some proper moping,' he explained.

'I never thought of it like that; a day away as being a day where she couldn't run interference on the plans being made in court,' Azura said, frowning. 'It never occurred to me.'

He gave a bitter little laugh. 'Of course it didn't. Lena shelters you from all the political garbage she deals with. She has to fight for her place every day.'

Myles sighed. He brought the bottle to his lips and swallowed another mouthful. 'And now she's got to go to Gemelli for a week, which gives Claudio an enormous amount of time to plan even worse things for her. I should have stayed here. Not that I could've done a lot, but…' Another drink. 'I just wanted… But I should have been here.'

Silvie shook her head. 'I doubt it would have made any difference. When is she scheduled to go?'

'The day after tomorrow.'

'I hate politics,' Azura groaned, flopping down onto her back. 'This is why I don't want to take over from my father someday. I don't want my life controlled forever by the whims of politics. Ugh.'

'I'll second that ugh,' Myles agreed.

14. AZURA

THEY REMAINED ON THE ROOF SO LATE INTO THE NIGHT THAT when Azura hauled herself out of bed the following morning she felt more than a little seedy. Ignoring the grimy cotton-stuffing feeling inside her skull as much as she was able, she dragged herself to the breakfast table.

The familiar sight of her father with his morning letters was enough to lift her mood slightly, even as he gave her a disapproving look and glanced pointedly at the clock. 'You should already be in your study at this hour. Your tutor will be here in ten minutes. Eat quickly.'

The thought of food made Azura's stomach roil. 'I think I'll stick with tea for now.'

Her father handed her a card as she sat down. 'Lena sent a message; she'll miss the day's lesson. A queen's work is never done, I suppose.'

Azura felt a shade of relief that she wouldn't be seeing Lena or Myles. In all likelihood Myles felt as wretched as Azura did, and she didn't relish the idea of dealing with Lena in a sour mood either.

The first sip of hot tea smoothed Azura's frayed nerves. After the second sip she started to feel human again. 'How's work going? Is Silvie helpful?'

'Terrible. Not Silvie. Yes, she's helpful. But work is terrible,' her father clarified with a sigh. 'There's more and more to do, and fewer and fewer resources to do it with. When I'm low on what I need for alchemy, it's never any trouble at all to arrange fresh supplies to match demand, but when it's people I need...' Doctor Corsetti shook his head.

'There are plenty of foundlings, but sustaining and training them is another matter. We've tried making the older ones pay for more of their own upkeep; we've reduced their rations, made them pay for sundries like medicine. But, understandably, that has led to more of them running off.

And punishing them for desertion is no deterrence when their lives are already such a living hell.'

He sighed. 'I'm sorry. You don't need to worry about all of this. It's nothing to do with you. What's going on in your world, sweetheart? I'm sorry about yesterday morning. That wasn't productive.'

'I don't understand why Lena fights so hard to avoid being sent away from the palace, if life is so miserable for her here,' Azura said, ignoring the apology. She still felt hurt and angry about the argument, and preferred to ignore it than to put it to rest. 'Is it because this is the only life she knows *how* to have, the only one she can remember having?'

Moments when Lena was incomprehensible to her always unsettled Azura. They reminded her of the differences and distance between them.

It was exhausting feeling at odds with Lena; and with Silvie, Myles, her father. She wanted common ground with someone, anyone. It was a lonely, helpless feeling.

'Lena needs to get over herself,' her father said in a pinched voice, making Azura blink in surprise. 'She shouldn't mope about going to Gemelli. It's a gorgeous area, and much safer for her. She'll have a lovely holiday.'

'It's not really a holiday if she has to work, though. She'll have to be involved in all kinds of receptions and things when she visits.'

Her father snorted. 'Royalty don't have to work, they have duties. It's hardly the same thing.'

The distinction probably made perfect sense to him, but to Azura there wasn't much difference. Then again, her father had been worrying over the poor working conditions of the infantry and sentry corps a few minutes earlier. Compared to that, Lena's dismay at having to go away probably seemed a disproportionate reaction to a minor inconvenience.

'Hurry up with that cup of tea. Your tutor's going to be here any minute, and just because you're on your own for this lesson, doesn't mean you can take it easy.'

'I don't take it easy. I know you think I'm a lazy slacker, but I work really hard, Dad. I'm trying my best.'

Her father put his letters aside to give her a thoughtful look. She prickled under the attention. 'I'm telling the truth!'

'I believe you. I was too hard on you yesterday. I'm proud of you, Azura. I know you do your best.'

Azura swallowed down a sudden lump in her throat. 'Well, you know, there's nothing else for me to do, since you never let me go anywhere. Studying is about all I spend my time on.'

'You're right, I have kept you on a short leash. It's only because I love you, but… Would you like to go to Gemelli with Lena, as a holiday? I could pull a few strings, and send Silvie along to help Myles chaperone you.'

Azura stared at him in disbelief. 'Really? Are you serious?! Dad, that would be incredible!' She jumped to her feet, hugging him.

'Yes, all right,' her father said, smiling as he patted her arm. 'Now go to your lessons – and have your tutor write up some work for you to take on the trip!'

Azura had a spring in her step for the rest of the day. The cobwebby hangover mess in her head barely bothered her at all.

Lena's sumptuous travel coach was much larger than the lightweight confection of a carriage she used for journeys within Arteria. It was ornate inside and out, but was surprisingly comfortable to travel in, decked out as it was with an abundance of cushions, and tasty bite-sized foods, and a basket of bright, colourful yarn with knitting needles and crochet hooks stabbed into it, and a chessboard with a balancing spell cast on it to stop the pieces jostling out of place.

As soon as the journey was underway, Lena unfolded the chessboard and began readying the opposing armies.

'I've played these two so often,' she said to Silvie, nodding at Myles and Azura. 'I know all their tactics. I should play against you instead.'

A furrow of worry appeared between Silvie's eyebrows. 'I'm not that good, though.'

'Oh, don't worry about that. I'm not either. I just think it's fun,' Lena assured her. Myles made a scoffing sound.

'Don't believe her. The reason she wants to play against you is because Azura and I both refuse to do it anymore. She's ruthless.'

Lena's smile was like a knife. 'What's the point, otherwise?'

Azura watched as the pair started a game, only half paying attention.

'You're reckless with your queen,' Silvie commented as Lena took another of her pieces. 'Strategy, or personal identification?'

Lena laughed. 'Neither. A piece is only as good as it is useful. Anyway, queens are just pawns underneath. You can make another if it dies.'

The game went on. As far as Azura could tell, Silvie was a competent player, but Azura knew from personal experience that Lena was far more than that. It was only a matter of time.

Azura hoped her father was doing all right. She hoped the powers-that-be wouldn't make him work with the christallo while they were waiting to choose a new Stregoni. It wouldn't be the first time a ring-in was forced to take a temporary place in its maintenance, but it would be the first time Azura's father was the one to do it. She shuddered at the thought.

Without the christallo, magic wouldn't be channelled into a useable form. Everything would fall apart. Other countries had other systems, but each was as intricate and difficult and eerie as the christallo. It was a vitally important element in the prosperity of the country; and Azura's own family's livelihood.

She knew all this, and yet it always seemed as if it was barely under control, even at the best of times, not to mention the price of its power being the random resurrection of cadaveri. All it took was the loss of one wizard or one king to throw it haywire, hurting everything from weather forecasts to the price of tea.

Azura understood the necessity of the christallo, but it made her uneasy to think of it, high in its tower in the palace: a little crystal on a little pedestal keeping the whole kingdom one step away from chaos.

Never any more, or any less, than one step.

She was pulled out of her thoughts by a triumphant cackle from Lena, as Silvie suffered her inevitable defeat.

'Ha! Everyone always forgets – pawns can kill kings too,' Lena gloated.

Lena and Azura read novels for a while after that. Silvie couldn't, because her vertigo made her too woozy to read while the coach was in motion.

'You're not reading either?' she asked Myles.

Azura listened in, because it hardly counted as eavesdropping when they were in a coach cabin together.

'No, I like to keep alert when we're on the open roads. Watchful,' Myles explained. 'There are protection wards on the coach, but you can never be too careful.'

'Understandable. I got a taste of the city's nastier side, just after I arrived,' she said, and began telling him about the canal incident.

Although Azura really wanted to hear how Silvie described the part where she had heroically come to Silvie's rescue, like a dashing fairytale prince, the monotonous movement of the carriage lulled her to sleep before the story got that far.

They arrived at their lodgings, in the guest wing of a local noble's house, long after sunset, too late for them to enjoy anything about being in Gemelli.

Their host had provided a sumptuous feast to greet them. Azura declined all the meat dishes, which earned her a dirty look from Silvie, which in turn made Azura prickle with irritation. Silvie seemed to take it as a personal slight. It sucked that Silvie's life had been so hard, but Azura didn't see what that had to do with *her* making the choice not to eat meat when it was offered.

She felt grimy and antsy after sitting all day; exhausted and keyed up at the same time. She shouldn't have let herself fall asleep in the carriage. She felt embarrassed that she'd done so in front of Silvie, and resented she felt embarrassed about something so dumb and unimportant.

She spent the night cranky and restless, unable to settle in the unfamiliar bed. Not the most auspicious start to a holiday, all things considered.

Azura woke feeling as rotten as she had when she'd gone to bed, with an added dose of guilt about the lessons she was missing. If she was going to feel miserable and crummy, in an utterly beautiful city, she should at least be learning something.

She joined the others in the dining hall and discovered she wasn't alone in her dreary mood. Lena's optimism and Silvie's stoicism were both worn ragged, making it more obvious than usual how much effort it took each of them to be present in the world.

Myles, however, was his usual self. He handed Azura a freshly-poured cup of tea as she sank into her seat.

'You three may well be the saddest things I've ever seen,' he quipped. 'And when I say *ever* I'm including those creepy souvenir figurines all the gift shops sold last year of Lena crying at Dante's funeral.'

That stirred a smirk out of Lena. 'Those weren't sad. They certainly were something, but that something wasn't sad. Did you ever see the full diorama version? It had a little music box of the national anthem attached. It was horrible.'

Azura groaned. 'You are such a weird goblin. You don't have to sound so gleeful about it.'

'It had me and Claudio and all the Stregoni weeping,' Lena went on blithely. 'But if you looked closely, you could tell it had been prepared years earlier, and that the *me* was a repaint of Queen Eve.'

'I've seen figurines like that,' Silvie said. Interest in the subject animated her features, making her ragged exhaustion less obvious. 'The pub I worked in had one. Apparently praying to the Little Magdalena for good fortune could include praying for a good game of tavern darts.'

The idea of people thinking of Lena like that made Azura uncomfortable, but Lena didn't seem bothered.

'She wasn't much older than I am when she died, you know. Eve, I mean. But nobody called her 'Little Eve' or anything like that. She was always Queen of Rivers. Funny, isn't it? Especially since the waterways in Arteria aren't rivers at all, they're canals.'

Azura sipped her tea, though it was still hot enough to burn her mouth. 'I remember her, but only a little. She was quiet, and... sad, I guess? Not that kids can really tell what adults are feeling. But I always thought she seemed sad. She read stories to me.' She frowned. 'I guess she wasn't really an adult, was she? I mean, she was around our age, and I'd never thought of myself that way.'

She caught a glance between Silvie and Myles, and it made her want to crawl under the table. Adulthood only meant anything if you'd ever been a child to start with, and neither of them ever had. They probably thought she was a childish fool. She stared out the window.

The whole of Gemelli was fitted with magical street lamps of beautiful wrought-iron designs. Arteria only had magical lamps indoors, and only in wealthier sections of town.

Gemelli had never needed rebuilding after conflict the way Arteria often had, so the architecture here all dated back to before the cadaveri were a consideration. The whole place was beautiful and quaint, and Azura marvelled at the idea of being in a place designed with aesthetics in mind, rather than as a need for channelling as much magic as possible.

'You know,' Myles said, breaking the air of mopey quiet. 'You three deserve a proper day off. Your appointments don't start until tomorrow morning. Our hosts seem to think it'll take a full day for Lena to recover from the terrible hardship of riding in a coach, even though we made very good time on the roads. And Silvie, I know you have work that Doctor Corsetti wants done while you're here, but I doubt that one day would delay it beyond salvation.'

No mention of Azura, because Azura was already supposed to have the time to herself. Her cheeks burned. Everyone else was busy, she was just lazy.

'I know you don't want to be here,' Myles said, addressing Lena directly. 'But if there's any consolation to be found, it's that you aren't as confined here.'

Lena pursed her lips. 'I suppose that's true.'

'Why don't we each go off on our own, then?' Azura suggested. She prickled at the thought of spending time with anyone. 'Or, well, Myles with Lena, I guess. But that goes without saying.'

Azura had never had an opportunity to wander an unfamiliar city on her own before, and was surprised by how enjoyable it was. She couldn't hold onto her gloomy mood when there were so many things to see, local delicacies to try, and trinkets to buy as gifts. She bought cheap, silly little things for her father, for Myles and Lena, for Silvie.

By the time she returned to the estate, she was herself again, and embarrassed to think how lousy she'd felt when she'd woken up. Low moods were like that, and Azura hated it; hated how unpredictable and unavoidable the darker corners of her brain sometimes were.

As Azura stepped inside the sumptuous foyer of the mansion, the valet at the door bowed a second time to someone following behind her. She turned.

'Guess we've both got good timing,' Azura said, greeting Silvie with a broad grin. Silvie offered a smile of her own in return, less exuberant than Azura's but still carrying genuine warmth.

'Seems like it,' Silvie agreed. 'Oh, could you hold this for a moment?'

She passed the basket to Azura, leaving a hand free to unclasp her cloak while the other stayed on her cane.

Now Azura had a basket in each hand. They were of a similar size, though Silvie's was heavier.

'Buying things?' Azura guessed.

Silvie nodded. 'Yes. It's silly, probably, but it was nice in the carriage yesterday. The four of us. I wanted to find something we could share.' Her cheeks coloured at the confession.

'Hey, if it's silly, then we're both silly,' Azura assured her. 'I bought stuff for everybody too. Things are more fun that way, right?'

Silvie's smile returned, wider now. 'Right.'

After Myles and Lena returned from their own adventures, Silvie showed them all what she'd bought, lifting a white paper bag out of her basket and placing it on the table in the luxurious sitting room of Lena's suite.

Inside the paper bag was an equally pristine white box. Azura sensed faint cooling magic infused into the crisp cardboard and sat up straighter in her chair, surprised.

'You didn't have to do that. This stuff's exp—'

'Cherry cheese!' Lena exclaimed, drowning out Azura's protests. 'Aaah, Silvie, you're the best!'

The box held four portions, each decorated with a delicate pickled flower on top. Azura's mouth watered. She hadn't had cherry cheese very often, despite growing up in a palace.

'You really didn't have to,' she said again, torn between gratitude and guilt as she looked at Silvie. 'This probably costs more than my father pays you in half a year. You shouldn't spend money on people who've got their own.'

Silvie shrugged one shoulder a little and shook her head. 'I wanted to try it, and it seemed dumb to just get enough for myself. The cost isn't the point. I bet you buy things for Lena sometimes, too, right? Why do that?'

Azura's purchases for Lena happened whenever she saw something that she knew would make the girl happy. Unless it was way outside her price range, she never even thought about the cost.

'Okay. I get it,' Azura conceded, smiling in defeat. Silvie gave her a small smile back.

Myles had already retrieved plates and forks from the large mahogany sideboard, setting them down beside the bakery box.

Lena frowned. 'Why only three? There's four.'

Myles shook his head. 'No, I'm good. You girls split the fourth one.'

Lena nodded, accepting the words without further protest. Azura could count on one hand the times she'd seen the two of them disagree about anything, even something as minor as meal portions. Sometimes it was more like they were one person in two parts, Lena-and-Myles, than separate entities.

'It would be nice if you'd come sit with us, though,' Silvie put in quietly.

'You don't have to eat if you don't want to, but I think we'd all like your company.'

Azura damped down a spark of jealousy.

'All right.' He sat with them.

Silvie scooped up a small forkful of the cherry cheese. She inspected it on the end of the sharp silver tines with a thoughtful expression.

'It's funny to me that this is what "cherry flavoured" means in the south,' she mused. 'The girl in the bakery said it's flavoured with the leaves and decorated with a cherry flower that grows here. Where I'm from, only the dark sour berries and the stones of the cherry plant are used.'

She ate the mouthful, savouring the taste before she spoke again. 'My village, or rather the village near the barracks – they'd hate it if they knew a sentry was calling it theirs – is renowned for their cherry brandy. They put it in cakes with cream and chocolate and extra sour cherries. It's very, very different to this, but both are nice in their own way.'

Lena swallowed her own mouthful. 'I've had that kind of cake, the sort they make where you're from. Just the once. I shouldn't even have had it that once, really. I try not to have unfamiliar dishes too often, which is difficult with all the functions I attend. But I can never have much of anything, because people are always gossiping about how much I weigh, or if my skin's breaking out in spots. Sometimes it's easier not to bother; to resist temptation completely than to stop after a little bit.'

Silvie raised an eyebrow. 'It took me quite a few days before I stopped feeling ill about how much food was always left over after meals in the palace,' she confessed. 'I wanted to keep eating and eating until I was sick, so it didn't all go to waste.'

Myles gave a quiet laugh. 'Only a few days? I've been there for years and it still bothers me sometimes.'

Azura put her fork down, her appetite for the treat having faded.

'I used to be assigned kitchen work often, when I was in the infantry,' Myles went on. 'That was punishment duty, and I was constantly in trouble over something or other. But even when I was dealing with an entire unit's worth of portions, I never had to struggle in the same way to stop myself from just gorging on it.'

Silvie nodded enthusiastically. 'No, it's not the same, is it. I often worked in a bakery on my off months, but I knew the food wasn't mine.

At the palace it feels like I could eat until I was sick without getting a beating for it. I wouldn't even be reprimanded. It's weird.'

Despite the grim subject matter, Silvie and Myles were laughing as they talked. Lena stared at them both, looking as out of her depth as Azura felt.

Then Lena grinned. 'I was wrong about Azura and Myles being destined for marriage, clearly. You two should be a match.'

Lena's weird obsession with pairing her with Myles had always rubbed Azura the wrong way, but this new version of the old game bothered her even more.

Myles laughed. 'I'd have to be a very different person for that to happen.'

Silvie's already-fair face went visibly paler at his words. Her fork, mid-air between bites, began trembling.

Azura had no idea what on earth was going on, but Myles noticed Silvie's reaction at the same time that Azura did, and clearly had a better understanding of its meaning.

'That wasn't a threat,' he told Silvie in soft tones. 'I didn't mean... My job means I have to know everything there is to know about anyone who spends any amount of time around Lena, you know? Much more, for instance, than what Doctor Corsetti's files would record about a person. But I didn't mean to frighten you. I didn't mean anything by it. I just thought Lena's dumb joke was funny, considering, you know.'

'Excuse me, my jokes are always funny,' Lena objected, trying to defuse the situation.

Azura stared blankly at all of them.

'I swear to you, I'd never tell a soul about anything in your life unless it was in some way relevant to a threat against Lena, which nothing in your background is,' insisted Myles.

After a second Silvie nodded, still shock-white and anxious. 'I believe you. It was just kind of a surprise to have it joked about.'

'I'm sorry. I screwed up.'

'Okay, what is going on? Tell me,' Lena demanded.

Azura was glad Lena had said it, because Lena could get away with things like that, and Azura was burning to know as well.

'I'm not interested in men,' Silvie said, staring down at her plate, voice flat and quiet. 'I like women.'

A long moment of quiet hung over the table.

'Ugh.' Lena frowned. 'Do you have any idea how much more difficult that makes finding a happy ending for you? With the way people like that get treated, even in Arteria, you've made things so complicated now. I don't even know who I'd pair you up with.'

Irritation flooded through Azura. 'Why are you so obsessed with pairing people up all the time? Do you think my father needs a new wife before he'll be happy, too?'

Lena didn't even blink. 'Yeah, of course. But most of the eligible women in the palace are obsessed with Claudio, and therefore clearly don't deserve your father.'

The answer was so bare and simply given that for a second Azura couldn't do anything but boggle at Lena. Then she started to laugh.

'You're a lunatic.'

'Well, yes, obviously. You knew this already,' Lena replied, still unruffled. 'Anyway, enough about that. We've still got hours and hours left of our day off. What should we do with it?'

Silvie seemed so relieved the topic of conversation had been diverted from her personal life, that Azura didn't want to bring it up again. She *did* want to assure her that while Arteria might not be perfect, it didn't punish people for who they liked, the way a lot of villages still did. And that Silvie didn't have to be afraid of people knowing about that part of her.

'What about the catacombs?' Lena went on, changing the subject further away. 'I went there once when I was little, and they were incredible.'

Of all Gemelli's strange, old-fashioned elements, the catacombs were the most remarkable. Nobody would dream of building a graveyard within easy reach of a metropolis now, and the earlier ones had mostly been destroyed as a precaution against cadaveri.

But Gemelli's officials insisted the catacombs were an important cultural artefact, and worth preserving. From what Azura had heard, it wasn't an empty assertion: the catacombs were said to be an architectural marvel without peer, miles upon miles of underground tunnels full of ornate funerary tableaus.

The catacombs were so singular and unique they'd become a draw for tourists, generating enough income for the city that Gemelli became doubly invested in preserving them.

'I'd really, really rather not,' Myles said, looking grey at the suggestion.

'I've heard they're very safe. The warding magic keeping the remains inert is the strongest example of its kind,' Azura reassured him. 'The city invests enormous amounts of money in making sure it's not dangerous for visitors.'

Lena clasped her hands together in supplication, giving Myles a look so pleading it tipped over into comical.

'You don't have to if it sounds horrible to you, it's all right! You can stay here and double-check all the rooms and menus for the functions tomorrow and be a worrywart about those. I know you love to. I'll stick with Azura and Silvie and won't do anything dangerous, I promise.'

'You and Azura aren't known for your impulse control. That's literally why I'm here in the first place.'

'Yes, but Silvie will be with us this time.'

'I don't actually remember agreeing to this plan,' Silvie said drily, shooting a small grin at Azura in response to Lena's words. When the little queen had her heart set on something, she didn't let anything get in her way.

'I don't know,' Myles reiterated, hesitant. 'I don't like the idea of letting you off on a trip like this without me.'

They exchanged one of their silent looks, unreadable to those around them. Myles broke first, of course.

'Fine, fine. Just don't get into any trouble.'

15. SILVIE

THEY WALKED THROUGH GEMELLI'S CROWDED PRETTY STREETS IN relative anonymity. Lena's actual face wasn't as recognised in Gemelli, as the far-southern style of icons for praying to weren't known for their good likeness.

Silvie's cane still earned its share of looks, but she was used to those and mostly steeled against the tiny sting of them. But at least she wasn't wearing the most noticeable thing about her, as the weather had turned warm enough to leave her yellow cloak in her room.

'It was good of Myles to trust us to look after Lena,' she said.

'I guess.'

Silvie was trying to forgive him for exposing her privacy so casually. She wasn't angry, just hurt. She didn't like people knowing personal things about her, even if it *was* his job to know them. So much of her life was in the control of others. She'd wanted to keep something as hers, and hers alone.

'The next step is for us to actually stay out of trouble,' Azura pointed out with a smirk. 'So his faith in us isn't misplaced.'

'Oh, we're all much more responsible now than when we were younger,' Lena assured her breezily. 'I mean, it's more than a week since the last time you jumped into a canal.'

That made Silvie laugh. 'What are the catacombs like?' she asked Lena.

'The church has a graveyard beside it, which is so different to Arteria. There, even places where bodies are taken to be buried, like Driade Island, don't have any markers to say where each person is or anything. I explored while you were gathering elderberry, and there's big patches of turned earth where corpses have been piled in underneath. But in the Gemelli graveyard, every person has their own stone denoting who they were.

'And the catacombs themselves are incredible, full of so many bones and other cool things, all displayed elegantly. I've always loved the slightly macabre, but the only thing I've ever been allowed to keep in the palace are the items in the mourning hall, and a display of pinned butterflies in Azura's office. But human remains are much more interesting than butterfly ones, don't you think?'

Silvie kept her thoughts to herself. Not about human remains but, rather, her distaste for preserved butterflies. Many households she'd worked in over the years had displayed them, and they'd always made her skin crawl.

At first she'd been puzzled by how repelled she felt because in comparison, like Lena, she wasn't at all bothered by the thought of dead people, and she enjoyed walking in the graveyard beyond the village. But the graveyard was a place to remember, not to preserve. Butterfly displays made her think of jars of water scooped out of a river – motionless inside the glass, devoid of the magic imparted by its movement. A pinned butterfly was as unmagical as stagnant water.

They reached the Gemelli graveyard quickly enough that Silvie's stamina was holding steady. Despite its emptiness the area had a quiet, welcoming air, a sense of calm.

The Gemelli graveyards were famously well-warded and safe. The elderly ward-keeper nodded in acknowledgement as they stepped through the gate.

Guarding those wards for signs of trouble was a necessary job, an honourable one, but Silvie imagined it had also become a very boring one. This man was a wizened figure, shoulders rounded in a hunch beneath his uniform, and he sat on his chair in the guardbox with the stillness of someone who'd spent long years in the same position.

The grass was neatly kept, the paths well-paved. Silvie tipped her face up towards the warmth and light, gaining strength as she absorbed the sun's rays.

'A rare Silvie smile,' Lena quipped, not unkindly. 'Who knew you were as macabre as me?'

'I love being in graveyards,' she admitted. 'I like the calm, and the quiet. Thinking about death in a place like this helps me notice all the life around us: these fat black ants on the edge of the path, the way the water burbles in the creek over there; fish, birds, other people. I don't seem to find any of them half as captivating at other times as I do when I'm in a graveyard.'

She paused, remembering. 'I guess it must be different for a widow, though.'

Lena shrugged, jet jewellery catching light on its facets with the movement. 'My husband's not buried in a graveyard, he's on display in the palace. I mean, I think you're kind of provincial and lame to get soppy about life-in-the-face-of-death like that, but I've never executed anybody for being soppy and provincial.'

Silvie gave a small scoff of amusement. 'There hasn't been capital punishment for decades. You've never had anybody executed for anything.'

'Well, even if I could, I wouldn't do it for the crime of being lame.'

'If Myles was here, he'd tell you not to use lame as an insult. I mean, technically I *am* lame, because I walk unevenly and use a cane, but as you were using it to mean pathetic, I won't take offence.'

'Ugh.' Lena huffed in annoyance. 'You're boring. All three of you. I'll have all of you put to death. Hanged until you suffocate.'

Silvie chuckled. Sometimes Lena reminded her so much of Kolya that it made her heart ache. 'People executed by hanging don't suffocate. The drop breaks their necks immediately.'

'Only if you have a kind hangman. Otherwise you kick and flail on the end of the rope, gasping for air like a fish.'

'I've never seen a fish kick and flail. That sounds quite unique.'

'Gasping like a fish. I didn't say the kicking was like a fish.'

As they moved further into the sprawling grounds, reaching older graves, Silvie noticed a number of the headstones had little bells built into their sides. In times before the rise of ghouls, it had been common practice to attach chains to the toes of people prior to burial, then connecting the chains to bells, so if the person proved to be alive, they could signal for help by ringing the bell.

The appearance of cadaveri had put an abrupt end to the custom.

The entry to the catacombs was inauspicious, just a broad flight of white stone stairs descending into the earth a little distance from the church. The air wafting out of the wide mouth of the tunnel had a strange smell to it – not bad or rotten, but thick with an inert, dense quality.

Silvie was surprised the place had such a strong atmosphere, considering how many tourists must come through. For now, however, the three of them seemed to be the only visitors, and they descended without company.

A few feet past the door, the tunnel widened into a large, well-lit atrium, where magically-enhanced torches crackled merrily in their holders along the edges of the space. A dark marble plinth, close to one of the packed-earth walls, had a tiny glass coffin atop it. Silvie stepped closer, Lena and Azura following her.

Inside the coffin was a stunningly pretty little girl, her face as plump and soft and smooth as any dreaming child's. The glossy dark curls of her hair were tied with a velvet ribbon the colour of summer apricots.

'She was my favourite, when Dante brought me here,' Lena said. 'Her name is Rosalind. People call her the Sleeping Beauty, and it does look like she's waiting to wake up.'

Lena smiled down at the child's body, the flickering light of the torch flames painting gold and shadow over the young queen's face. 'But I think she's so much luckier than Sleeping Beauty. She never has to wake up or marry anybody. She gets to rest forever. That's a perfect fairy tale to me.'

Silvie's memories of fairy tales came from her times working in the village. On cold nights, or freezing thundery days, when there was no possibility of outdoor activity, the workers and servants would huddle around the fireplace for warmth and company. They'd knit socks, hats and scarves to sell to the travelling traders who passed through. The traders took those knitted items to cities like Arteria and Gemelli, where they were bought by people who wanted authentic handmade and rustic things.

Silvie often wondered, as she walked the streets of Arteria, how many of those people were the same ones who glared at her yellow cloak.

To entertain themselves through those chilly hours, she and her fellow workers told stories, frightening and strange and violent tales full of revenge and justice and capricious fate. Fairy tales belonged to the dark. And those stories had often bled into her nightmares, mixing their dragons and princesses with the howling winds and the starving, cold-skinned things among the trees.

Silvie shivered. 'Yeah. Like a fairy tale.'

'You're revolted.' Azura's words weren't a question. 'I can tell.'

Tearing her eyes away from the preserved child, Silvie did her best to give a nonchalant shrug. 'I don't understand why anybody would do that to a little girl.'

'But you like graveyards. How is this different?'

'Graveyards are about wanting the dead to rest in peace. This,' she offered helplessly, 'isn't that.'

'Lena said the girl is called Sleeping Beauty. That sounds pretty restful.'

'No.' The space was large enough for the word to ring with the faintest echo behind it. 'Preserving a body like this, is keeping something that should be let go. It's like the ghouls.'

Silvie didn't know how to explain what she was feeling in the southern tongue and wished she had the language to make Azura understand. She didn't hate death, because that would be like hating the stars or hating winter. Death was too big to hate or to love.

'Making a dead child into this is possibly, probably, her parents' desperate struggle to control something so unfair, so merciless, so huge their hearts had no other way of surviving. This is a testament to a tragedy.'

Lena's gaze was still fixed on little Rosalind. 'Is what they did really so bad?' Her voice was quiet, but the catacombs were designed with quiet voices in mind. 'Is it wrong for her parents to make her look like this to fill just a bit of the deep empty hole inside them? Whatever right you *think* you have to judge them for that, you don't.'

Then Lena shook herself from her serious reverie, giving both of them a tight smile. 'Shall we keep going? Hopefully the next room will be a little less controversial!'

The size of the tunnels varied wildly between the rooms, some more than wide enough for the three to walk beside each other, while others were cramped and claustrophobic.

Silvie had to admit Lena was right – the catacombs were incredible. Some large caverns they passed through had rows of shelves with skulls stacked neatly in their thousands; as carefully arranged as the chips of a fine mosaic.

Other rooms had displays similar to the lonely girl in her coffin near the entrance, but with complete bodies, rather than just empty skulls, laid out in their most beautiful finery and jewels. Surprisingly, a lot of the clothing, though faded, was intact. There were whispers of deeper, richer hues still visible in the folds and creases of the fabric.

It was eerie and unsettling, a strange combination of macabre and celebratory. Silvie didn't like it, exactly, but the intensity was thrilling.

As they went deeper and deeper, the hallways got narrower and the ceilings lower. After a while, the magic torches became less frequent, so Azura lit a small flame in her palm to help them see.

Silvie tried to swallow the usual resentment she felt at how easily magic came to Azura. 'Look, I think we've come far enough,' she said, as they entered another room of stacked skulls. 'This is all incredible and everything, but if we don't turn around soon, my energy's going to run out before we make it back to the estate. Besides, the rooms are starting to feel the same to me.'

Her tone was more demanding and terse than she was usually comfortable expressing, but an uneasy prickle at the back of her neck made politeness harder to perform. It wasn't a premonition, Silvie knew that. She had no magic, no way to sense the subtle shifts of atmosphere that had once alerted her to threats, but even someone psychically null had to feel the close, heavy weight of that space.

Lena and Azura nodded in agreement, despite their clear surprise at Silvie's uncharacteristically sharp tone.

The walk back was a rude awakening. Turns and directions that were obvious and intuitive a little while ago were baffling and unfamiliar, as if the forks and splits in the corridors and the number of exits from rooms had multiplied and changed once they'd been left behind. Iron gates barred entrance into seemingly innocuous tunnels, giving Silvie the disquieting feeling they'd ended up on the wrong side of the barrier, the part of the catacombs that the gates were designed to keep people out of.

'I'm going to, uh…' Azura extinguished the flame in her palm, then reignited it in the shape of a compass needle. 'Not that I think we're lost or anything, but so we don't waste time, you know, this will show us the fastest way.'

Silvie's envy flared hot inside her, but she forced a smile. 'Thanks.'

They moved more quickly and with less hesitancy now, knowing the flame needle would guide them in the right direction. Even so, Silvie's heart remained disquieted. None of the tunnels looked familiar. The rooms they passed through, though similar, didn't appear to be the ones they'd entered by. It might have been the fastest way to the exit, but it was absolutely not the same way they'd come.

Silvie debated whether to mention her feelings, or keep Lena and Azura from undue worry. Before she could decide one way or another, Azura spoke.

'This tunnel isn't part of the catacombs. It's older.'

Lena gave a derisive snort. 'Older than the catacombs? That's crazy. Some of the bodies down here are eight hundred years old.'

'Yes. I know. But this place is older than that.' Azura pointed at the walls. 'These are packed clay with load-bearing crossbeams, not brick and mortar like the other tunnels. They're not properly ventilated. The wood's so old it's basically petrified. And there aren't any lights anymore, are there? Can you remember how long we've been seeing the tunnels by my flame alone?'

Azura stepped closer to one of the wooden support pillars, so the flame in her palm could shed more light on the texture of the grain. 'See how ancient this is?'

Silvie must have seen the fingernail scratches in the wood at the same moment that Azura did, because she barely had time to register what they were before Azura gave a startled gasp and her flame vanished.

The sudden darkness made Lena yelp, and that noise was enough to bring Azura back to herself. The compass reignited in her palm.

The scratches were still there. Though not as shocking as at first sight, they were no less unnerving.

'Silvie, look,' Azura murmured, beckoning her closer.

Silvie stepped forward. 'They get shallower as they go down,' she noted, examining the marks in the ancient wood. 'The person was grasping above their height, perhaps trying to pull themselves towards something. Maybe there was a torch on the wall higher up.'

'Or they were trying to get away from something on the ground.' Azura's voice was grim, which told Silvie they held similar suspicions. 'Look how small the crescents left by their nails are. I think they were quite short.'

'They weren't short,' Silvie corrected her. 'They were young.' She felt ill.

'What are you talking about?' Lena's voice had an annoyed snap to it, the petulance almost covering the wobble of fear in her words. 'Where are we?'

'Somewhere we shouldn't be,' Azura said quietly. 'Come on.'

But the needle in her flame was pointing them further down the unfamiliar tunnel, deeper into a place they hadn't been.

For the first time since they'd stepped into the catacombs, Silvie was afraid. 'I don't think this is a good idea.'

'The magic thinks it's the shortest way out,' Azura replied. 'Let's get out of here as fast as we can.'

Gemelli was historic, and much of that history was beautiful, but the witch trials had been a fact of life here much more than anywhere else.

Even Arteria, pulsing heart of the world, hadn't fallen to superstition and violence in the same way.

But the witch trials were never talked about. History books might make a passing reference, but those were brief and non-specific. Nobody wanted to think too much about the tortures the church had put magic users through, in the days before the christallo's creation made things regulated and orderly; back when only the most powerfully gifted could cast spells at all.

Their gifts hadn't saved them. They'd been hanged and burned and drowned, their trials and executions carried out as public spectacle.

Nowadays, even when people did mention the witch trials, one part was always, always left unspoken. The shame was simply too great to recall the trials of the witch children. Details of them had been hidden away, deemed too terrible and unseemly to mention.

The only reason Silvie knew about them was because she'd grown up in the barracks, where secret lore was passed from one generation of children to the next, without adult interference. If the witch children who died by torture and execution had been born in a later age, their potential would've seen them pressed into sentry service. That affinity, a kinship across time and space, was enough to make sentry children keep the unwritten, buried history alive through their storytelling.

There was no way of knowing how much of it was true, and how much was apocryphal, but it was said some children learned enough about harnessing their magic to take violent retaliation against their torturers.

Silvie had always thought the tales held more truth than not, because they explained the life she'd led. Protecting a country from undead hordes with little more than wolves and foundlings was absurd. But the sentry system kept unloved magical children – the modern heirs of the witch trials' youngest, least-remembered victims – monitored and exhausted.

The long breaks Silvie had been forced to take every year, the months she spent working at bakeries or running errands, hadn't been any kind of generosity on the part of her overseers. Sentry children were perpetually stretched to the absolute limit of their magics, and without the breaks they would simply burn out and die. Better to use them as much as possible over time before they died on duty and were thrown away.

The sentry system was a new way to keep children like Silvie from the havoc they were capable of wreaking. To stop the need to ever repeat the carnage of the witch children's trials.

Or at least stopping the carnage against the adults, who'd been the target of the children's rage. As far as Silvie could tell, unwanted and unloved children who were born with magic still fared about as badly as they always had, with hard lives and early deaths.

Wealthy, loved kids like Azura were a different story, but they always were. Azura would have been in no more danger from the witch trials then than she was of being forced into sentry service now. Money always rewrote the rules.

They reached the end of the tunnel, the space widening out into another room, and Silvie wanted to laugh – inappropriately. If she'd been told a moment before she'd prefer seeing more rows of skulls and gaudy corpses, than what this room held, she wouldn't have believed it. Yet here she was.

Silvie crashed into Azura, who had also stopped in the doorway, whereon her light went out again. In the brief moment of darkness, Silvie prayed she hadn't really seen the horror lurking in the room.

'S-Sorry,' Azura gulped, the flame flaring back to life, again casting its own ominous shadows around them. And then–

As the light reached out to illuminate the shapes within, Sylive broke out in a clammy sweat, but instinctively used her body to bar the view from the girl behind her. 'Lena, don't look.'

While it was clear, from the dust and ruin, nobody had been in this room for centuries, the shape of things stayed clear. And, once seen, the piles of discarded instruments of torture could not be unseen.

Implements of violence and degradation had been shoved into corners like forgotten furniture. There were racks, a Judas cradle, stocks, manacles and whipping triangles. Strangely, Silvie found the plain ordinary woodcutter's saws the most terrifying of all.

The inquisition had been served by the kind of zealots who flayed the skin off their *own* backs to signify the purity of their devotion. So, when it came to pain, they were inventive. The high convex ceiling would have limited any sound escaping the chamber. Instead, it would've pushed the cries and screams back down around the witch children.

Lena, ignoring Silvie's advice, pushed past her and into the room. She hefted a torch down from its bracket on the wall and held the wick to Azura's palm.

'So we don't have to rely on you keeping it together so we can have light,' she said to Azura. 'Come on. I want to see.'

Silvie claimed another torch, more for something to do than from necessity, and held it to Azura's flame. As she waited for the old rope to catch, she did her best to offer Azura a reassuring smile. She was fairly certain the attempt wasn't in the least comforting; or even much of a smile.

Azura's own face was bloodless and stricken.

'Come on, we should stay close to Lena,' Silvie said, guiding Azura deeper into the room.

Silvie wondered if the architects and builders of the catacombs had always known about these rooms and tunnels, but had assumed their own excavations would never expand far enough to meet them. Or whether they hadn't known, but had discovered it as they worked, and decided to keep it secret, by confining visitors to the outer rooms. After all, what could be said about this horror, if the space had become an exhibit, when it reflected a part of history no one wanted to admit? At least none of the catacomb designers had decided to destroy it; to be the one who disturbed and desecrated this testament to the worst and most hidden of eras. But clearly nor had they tried to hide it. It was strange the area hadn't even been cordoned off with a gate or wall.

Another thought occurred to Silvie. What if she, Lena and Azura had somehow found a cavern unknown to anyone involved with the building of the catacombs?

Silvie tightened her grip on the torch, glad of the splintery, tangible texture of it against her palm. A torch was a solid, good, ordinary thing, a small way for her to feel linked to the world beyond this room of horrors.

The seeping misery that permeated the stale air was thicker and colder than canal water, and made her skin prickle into gooseflesh.

'This isn't fair,' she muttered, doing her best to stave off the dark with a flippant tone. 'I don't have magic anymore, but I can still feel the echoes here. That's not fair at all.'

'There's no such thing as fair,' Lena murmured, as she moved closer to the far walls. 'Come over here, both of you, so I have more light to read this.'

Moving deeper into the room revealed strange and awful things that hadn't been visible from the door: small bones, bags of feathers, cryptic writing on bedsheets bundled into corners.

'Look, those used to be a rat king,' Azura said, nodding her chin towards one cluster of dusty bones. 'A rat king forms when a group of rats get their tails tangled together too-tightly knotted and broken to ever pull apart. They can keep on living, but as one creature instead of several.'

'That's like Myles and me,' Lena remarked, glancing at the bones before moving on, towards a portion of the wall with more of the scrabbled scratchings of the kind they'd found on the support beam.

Here there were prayers and pleas in a dozen different scripts. Some marks were dark with a substance that had gone black with age, and which Silvie was absolutely certain was blood. There were tallies, grooves to count off days spent alive and tortures endured. And names, forlorn little marks of proof these children had been here, had once existed.

Yulia. Rosa. Sasha. Kolya.

Silvie swore under her breath, stepping back from the onslaught of misery, whereon Lena made a frustrated noise and grabbed her torch from her, so she held one in each hand.

'If you won't light it up, I will.'

Azura was crying, and that got Silvie's hackles up, replacing dull horror with hot anger. How dare Azura weep? This tragedy wasn't hers.

Silvie knew she wasn't being fair or rational but this hurt so much. One of the children had been called Kolya, for god's sake. Mad as she was, Silvie envied Azura's tears. She wished she was the kind of person who could find solace in weeping.

Lena's attention had honed in on a complex sigil scored deep into the wood of a support beam, the lines more methodical and deliberate than those of any of the other scratches and scrawls.

Sigil magic had been rendered obsolete long ago, replaced by the christallo's more efficient distillation. People didn't need preparation and ritual to make spells work anymore. A sigil that complex would've been a powerful spell even at the time of its creation, and Silvie couldn't begin to imagine how powerful it would be if it was created now, in an age of easy magic.

Lena handed Silvie one of the torches, with a casual imperiousness she rarely displayed. It served to remind Silvie that Lena had been a queen her whole life, had witnessed and endured things Silvie couldn't even imagine.

'Don't touch it,' Azura warned. 'Spells like that are activated when the seal is broken.'

Silvie moved the torch, its halo of light illuminating shadowed places.

'Look, here on the ground. There's scrabbling in the dirt. Someone crawled towards the seal with the last of their energy, dragging themselves forward, but they didn't make it there to set it off.'

Lena didn't move to look where Silvie gestured, her gaze locked on the intricate shape of the sigil. Her beautiful young face was unreadable as she stared. Then she squeezed her eyes shut and shook her head, as if to forcibly dismiss the image from her mind.

Silvie couldn't blame the little long-ago witch for their attempt at revenge, however violent the seal's promise might have proved to be. How could she? It was the church Silvie blamed, all those who'd pushed the witch-children until they were desperate to create mayhem in return.

Azura made a soft choked sound. 'I can't stay in here any longer.' Her face was clammy and pale by the flickering light. 'Come on, we have to keep going. The needle thinks it isn't much further to the way out.'

They'd barely made it into the tunnel before Azura steadied herself against a wall and threw up. Silvie unhooked her waterskin from her belt and handed it over.

'Here. Rinse your mouth out.'

'Wish it was wine.'

'Yeah, of course you do, because you and Myles both have a problem.'

They kept going. The needle-flame in Azura's palm glowed brighter and brighter.

'Sorry I puked,' she said after a little while. 'I know gross smells bother you, Lena. I hope it didn't affect you too much.'

'Mm, it's fine,' Lena answered, distracted and quiet.

The muted response made Azura frown. 'You all right?'

Lena shrugged, looking nonplussed. 'I guess I don't understand why you're both so upset.'

'It might be that you're a little too young to really get it,' Azura answered, which Silvie thought was the most idiotic answer possible. Lena seemed to accept it, though, and gave another shrug as they continued forward.

The narrowness and length of the tunnel meant they couldn't see what lay ahead, only blackness and nothingness.

'If there's another room like that, we turn back. I'm not going through it,' said Azura.

'But if we turn back, we have to go through the one behind us again.'

Azura barked out a startled laugh of horror at Silvie's words. There wasn't anything else for either of them to say.

When they reached the end of the corridor, however, all that awaited them was a blank wall.

Silvie stared at the bricked-up passage, dumbfounded. 'I guess we have to turn back after all.'

'Don't be stupid. Look, here.' Lena handed her torch to Azura and manoeuvred her way between the two older girls, stepping up close to the wall. She tapped a seam between two bricks with her fingertips, then stepped back as the wall swung apart into a wide doorway.

Azura gasped. 'I never would have thought to look for that.'

For a moment, Lena's expression was unreadable. Then she grinned. 'I'm a genius, I guess. Hurry up and go through, anything's better than this.'

The floor of the room on the other side was a foot and a half higher than the bare earth of the tunnel. Azura climbed up first and then reached back, helping Silvie awkwardly hoist herself up as well.

They found themselves, finally, in the very first room they'd entered, where the flight of stairs led back up into the graveyard. Silvie shook with relief, and Azura extinguished the flame-needle in her palm with an exhausted sigh.

Lena, however, kept her grip on the torch, despite the glow of the lamps dotted along the walls. She wore a wary frown.

'What's that noise?'

The sound was quiet enough that none of them had noticed it at first, but now that Lena pointed it out, it was difficult to ignore.

Tup *tup* tup *tup* tup.

For the thousandth time, the millionth, Silvie cursed her single-sided deafness. She would've given anything in that moment for simple clarity, for a sense of direction and location, instead of muffled half-whispers on the edge of her awareness.

Tup *tup* tup *tup* tup.

It wasn't footsteps. Silvie was sure of that much. The little sounds were more like the drum of bored fingers on a desk, or the insistent flapping of a small bird against a windowpane.

'What's...' Azura began, her voice trailing off as she stared, struck dumb, and pointed.

She pointed at the little glass coffin.

At the tiny hands moving inside, beating against the lid.

Tup *tup* tup *tup* tup.

16. AZURA

THE SICKEST PART WAS HOW SWEET THE LITTLE GIRL STILL LOOKED. Cadaveri never looked very human, normally. Their uncanny movements were deeply unlike those of a living person.

But the little girl had been so carefully embalmed – her eyes and mouth sealed neatly shut – she looked more like a child than an abomination. She was both lovely and ghastly, even as she scrabbled and clawed against the thick glass of her casket lid, her pretty burial clothes shifting and rustling, showing glimpses of soft silken colours in the folds of the cloth.

Another noise, a soft shuffling, began somewhere off in the distance, a susurrus in counterpoint to the percussion of tiny fists on glass. Azura thought of the wide and narrow hallways and antechambers they'd walked through, of all the bodies on display.

The shelves of skulls posed no danger, because even if they did reanimate, there'd be no way for them to leverage movement. They didn't even have lower jaws. But the laid-out corpses in their finery were a different story.

Before Azura even had a chance to share her fears, a sudden shuddering made the ground under their feet jerk and tremble. The movement was violent enough to send Silvie sprawling, her stick clattering away across the stone tile.

'Are you hurt?' Azura asked, helping her back to her feet.

'Just scraped my palms. But I think the packed-earth tunnels are collapsing. Look at all the dust.'

The concealed doorway they'd come back through was wreathed in a fine grey-brown cloud.

'That's crazy. They're like a thousand years old! Why fall apart now?' Lena's eyes were wide with terror.

'Whatever power was lying dormant in that room we went through,' Azura managed, her mouth dry, 'it's bringing the old tunnels down.'

'It's very strong magic,' Silvie agreed, 'and strong magic always means a counter-reaction.' She nodded towards Rosalind, still fighting to get free of the small casket. 'And that counter-reaction is always ghouls.'

'I think I can hear them coming,' Azura agreed.

'There's no telling whether this room is sturdy enough to withstand the tremors. We need to get out immediately,' Silvie said, decisive and firm.

Azura knew this was a glimpse of who Silvie had been before: a tactician, who faced down cadaveri regularly with nothing but her clever mind and the borrowed body of a wolf.

Azura, without the benefit of tactics and training, simply wanted to run and hide like a frightened child. She had a sudden flash of memory, a blurry childhood moment curled under sweltering blankets to get away from the sound of her parents shouting at each other.

Another grown-up, this one quiet and sad, had patted her soothingly through the patchwork barrier, telling her to try to sleep. *It will be better in the morning. Everything will be all right.*

It was one of the few memories Azura had of Queen Eve; so grown-up to a tiny child, but not truly a grown-up at all. Azura was already older than Eve ever been. And now, as the first of the cadaveri crawled into view, Azura didn't feel the least bit old enough to deal with this.

'Don't use magic on them,' Silvie warned. 'It makes them stronger, unless it's strong enough to dismember them. That's why the sentries don't fight directly, only through wolves.'

The cadaveri approaching them were so old there was no flesh left. Leathery and skeletal, held together by nothing but the byproduct-magic that had animated them in the first place, they writhed across the floor at a nightmarishly slow and steady pace, getting inexorably closer.

The girls backed towards the stairs leading to the graveyard. Lena swung her torch in an arc, as if to drive the cadaveri back, despite the futility of the gesture. Cadaveri feared nothing and never hesitated. Fire would not stop them.

'The only part that can hurt you is their bite,' Silvie said calmly. 'They aren't strong; they just have endless stamina. If they grab you, you can shake them free. You just have to stay out of range of their mouths. We have to seal the entrance off behind us and alert the authorities.'

'Got it,' Azura confirmed, still envying how cool and collected Silvie was. But she understood they had to make sure the cadaveri were contained, so nobody got hurt before someone could deal with them properly.

'I can seal the entrance with a spell,' she said, 'but it'll take me a couple of minutes. Lena, give the torch to Silvie, she can stand here and hold the light. You go up and wait for us in the graveyard where it's safe.'

'No, I want to hold it,' Lena shot back. She sounded calmer than Azura felt, too. Everyone was helpful in a crisis except her, and they were relying on her for the spell. Great.

Myles was going to murder Azura for letting Lena take such a dangerous role, but since Myles was going to murder Azura anyway, it was a moot point.

'Okay. Silvie, you wait for us up the stairs. Rest while you can. We'll be there in a second.'

17. SILVIE

SILVIE REACHED THE TOP OF THE STAIRCASE, LEAVING AZURA AND LENA to seal the entrance at its foot. She headed to the bench near the creek that ran behind the chapel, her head and body aching, and sank gratefully onto the cool wood.

Night had fallen while they were underground. True night, not the bright city-glow Arteria took on when the sun fell from view. Here the stars were visible, scattered bright and clear overhead.

They'd have to hurry back into town and raise the alarm, which meant it was imperative Silvie regain what stamina she could with this brief opportunity. She rested her elbows on her thighs and covered her face with her palms, doing her best to remember the tricks she'd learned in her earliest childhood for going away for a moment, for making all her thinking and feeling and hurting stop.

A handful of heartbeats later the sprightly tread of Azura's footfalls drew close, with Lena's more nimble, quieter steps behind.

'All done,' Azura told her. 'It'll hold well enough, I think. Even if being so close to a spell made them stronger, the spell is still solid to hold them back until we can get help.'

Silvie's eyes danced with after-images of the press of her palms as she looked up at them. With Lena's torch so close, Silvie couldn't see the stars anymore. The loss of them made something small and sad inside her ache. 'Let's get going.'

They set off back through the graveyard at a brisk walking pace, fast enough that Silvie's mind lurched with vertigo more with every step.

'I can't stop thinking about that room,' Azura admitted quietly.

Silvie reached out and took Azura's hand in her own, squeezing it reassuringly. 'I know. It was... it was a lot. But it's over now.'

'Mm.' Azura did not sound especially comforted, but she kept hold of Silvie's hand, so that was something.

'Honestly, there's no point in thinking about it,' Silvie tried. 'I mean, Myles is going to skin us alive when he hears about everything, so you won't have a chance to be haunted by the memory for much longer.'

Lena's face, visibly ashen even in the low torchlight, twitched into a momentary smile.

Azura snorted. 'Look, I'll be the first to admit that was not as safe as we hoped it would be,' she said, cheerfulness returning to her voice with each word. 'But I don't really think it's our fault we found an ancient secret torture chamber, or that the very act of finding it triggered some kind of—'

Her voice and footsteps froze between one breath and the next. When she spoke again, it was a whisper. 'Did you hear that?'

Silvie strained to hear. Lena was doing the same. But all Silvie could make out was the dead air of almost-quiet, of her weary brain burning energy in an attempt to overcome her limits, and the tiny ringing ghost-noises her dead nerves forced on her like fever dreams.

'There, again!' Azura's voice, still deathly quiet, was harsh with fright.

Lena's inky eyes had gone very round, the torch painting dancing points of gold on the deep grey.

Still, all Silvie could hear was the ringing. She closed her eyes, blocking out her other senses as much as she could.

The ringing now had a shape to it, an uneven rhythm hiding underneath the constant whine of the ear that had withered and died and taken all other noises with it.

The faintest, tiniest ring of a grave bell.

And as Silvie listened, a second bell joined it.

Genuine terror slipped like ice between her shoulder blades.

It made her furious.

How dare they make her feel unsafe here, how dare they resurrect these limbs and jaws whose time was long done? Violate this place of contemplation and calm, of reverence?

How *dare* they?

Silvie had never been religious – people in town would clasp their hands and pray to god and the Little Magdalena that they'd be spared from the ghouls, but Silvie knew that god played no part in it. It was just her and the other sentries, out in the cold, keeping them and their icons safe inside their homes. Where would faith fit into the schema of her life? But graveyards had always been good and safe and kind to her, as rare as they'd become. They represented love and remembering and the weary, cleansing emptiness that came after a long cry.

'Go,' she snapped. 'We have to hurry.'

Running in the dark was agony. Silvie had long ago trained herself out of weeping when she was afraid, but ordinary pain could still make her eyes sting with tears and her chest ache.

She drew again on the childhood trick of going somewhere else in her head as her body endured inescapable things. She thought of the fairytales she'd taught herself to read, fables in which parted lovers journeyed down into the land of the dead to reclaim their other half. Old, old stories, the kind that had stopped being reprinted after the ghouls began to rise.

Those stories always had the same golden rule: don't look behind as you make your way back to the realm of the living. And yet, every time, the lovers broke the rule, too hungry to resist.

To Silvie, this warning came too late. Someone should've offered these words of wisdom to the lover before they set off on their quest to reclaim what was lost. *Don't look back*. The dead cannot return, and turning to focus on them will bring only pain.

Silvie had never liked those stories. But Kolya had loved them, and so Silvie would sit and listen as he stumbled and halted and learned to read them aloud.

Another wave of pain buffeted her, shoving her out of the memory and back into the sharp reality of the present. She knew that if she forced her trembling legs to go on much further, they'd collapse under her.

'We have to slow down,' she choked out, pausing to rest her palms on her thighs and heave for breath, swallowing down bitter bile. 'It will be all right. We have a little time. These corpses will be very old, very weak. They can't climb out very fast.'

Every rule she'd ever had drilled into her was to contain and control the threat as quickly as possible. It made her feel physically ill to think of slowing down, but it would make her physically sick to keep going as well.

Given enough time, ghouls got out. That was what they did. That was why graveyards had fallen so absolutely out of fashion. But they had a little time.

'Okay. We'll go slower,' Azura said, trying to be flippant and casual but failing completely. 'We'll head into town and get the adults. It'll be over soon enough.'

While Silvie was grateful they slowed for her, the kindness also set her teeth on edge. She hated being at the mercy of other people. Helplessness produced a bitter knot inside her, despite knowing this wasn't the time to wallow. They needed to raise the alarm, get help, and get Lena safely back to Myles before they endangered her again and earned further wrath.

'We'll get the adults,' Azura said again, seemingly convinced the mere presence of adults would stop the situation from being a problem.

Silvie noticed Lena was not under the same illusion.

Even now, in pain and nervous and miserable, Silvie still couldn't find any anger in her heart for the young witch who'd drawn that sigil, who'd caused all this, whose spell was so strong even Lena's act of shaking the thought from her mind counted as a breaking of the seal.

Silvie had only rarely faced ghouls as her human self. In fact, she'd seen more with her own eyes in the last few hours than ever before. And now too, the whole world around them seemed built of cracked stone and moss, of lost chances that loomed bigger than fear, as big as the invisible starfield somewhere above them.

As they moved further away from the catacombs, the old gravestones gave way to the newer designs, the ones without bells. The absence of the tiny chimes should've made the atmosphere less eerie, but it did the opposite because they no longer had even a small indicator of imminent danger.

'Are you ready if any of them manage to dig out?' Silvie asked Azura, getting a terse nod in reply.

'Lena, we'll keep them away from you, if we have to face any, but hold onto the torch, okay?' A second terse nod.

They pushed forward through the dark.

The graveyard seemed so much bigger than it had in daylight, rivalling the depths of the canals and the old forests for making Silvie's blood thrum in terror. Her lungs ached for air, her vertigo battered her senses, and every step came with a new stab of agonising discomfort.

She wondered if old bones were twitching inside the mausoleums that they hurried past. Sparks of light pricked at the edges of Silvie's vision, flaring and dying in time with her thundering pulse.

Finally, finally, they reached the graveyard gate. The old ward-keeper wasn't on duty anymore, but his replacement – equally ancient and placid – raised the alarm when they breathlessly recounted the situation; words and events tumbling over one another as they tried to make him understand.

Myles didn't kill them, when it was his turn to hear their story. He took his cue from Lena's bright-eyed excitement as she recounted the events, but Silvie could tell he was barely disguising how aghast he was.

As Myles began coordinating with the Gemelli authorities about the best way to contain the graveyard and catacombs, the three of them were shuffled off to hot baths, warm food and other simple comforts. It was more coddling than Silvie had ever endured before. Even after her wolf had been killed, she hadn't been treated like this. Being royalty-adjacent might have its perks, but she found she didn't like the attention very much. Being cared for was stifling.

By the time she escaped the prolonged fussing, Myles was already back, pacing the width of Lena's palatial sitting room.

'I'm a visiting attendant. They didn't let me help much,' he said by way of greeting, guessing her unspoken question. 'They very politely told me to go look after Lena, instead, even though I'm clearly useless in that role.'

'I'm fine. Stop worrying,' Lena said, emerging from her inner room in a quilted black silk robe over a black nightgown, her long hair a sweep of wet ink down her back. 'Help me comb my hair.'

She'd already handed him the comb and knelt on the floor in front of him before he had a chance to agree. He began running the teeth carefully through the tangled locks without complaint.

Silvie could see Lena understood Myles in a lot of the same ways Kolya had always understood her. Some people needed a task to do, something to focus on so the darkness would be held back for a few more minutes.

'The authorities want to keep the whole incident quiet, of course,' Myles told Lena as he worked. 'So I haven't rescheduled any of your appointments tomorrow. If I did, it'd look suspicious. Be sure not to mention it to any of the dignitaries you meet.'

'But it's the most exciting thing that's happened to me in forever,' Lena complained. 'I can't tell anyone?'

'You can talk to us about it,' Myles answered smoothly. 'You should be flattered the authorities recognise you're mature enough to understand the gravity of the situation, and can trust your silence.'

'Hrmph.' Lena frowned. 'I'm not that easily redirected, you know.'

'I'd never dream you were.' Myles' voice was perfectly polite and entirely insincere. Silvie bit back a smile.

Azura joined them a few minutes later. She was clean, and dressed in fresh clothing, but Silvie could tell she'd washed rather than had a bath, because her boots were still on.

'Can I borrow your knife to cut the laces?' she asked Myles, sheepish. 'My hands are shaking too much to work the knot.'

Myles paused in his ministrations to Lena's hair and handed over his knife. 'Here.'

Azura sat down on one of the ornate armchairs, slicing the laces open on one boot and then the other. She hissed in pain as she eased the boots off her feet. The sore, swollen state of one ankle was obvious even through the fine knit of her sock.

'It was all right when the boot was on – I could grit through it. Now it hurts like murder,' Azura confessed. 'I twisted it when we were running in the graveyard.'

Silvie frowned. Azura hadn't said anything about being injured at the time. Silvie was the one who'd asked them to slow down. Now she felt a wave of shame, realising how much discomfort Azura had endured without complaint.

Silvie examined Azura's boots. The small raised heel had probably made the twisted ankle much worse than it would've been in a flat shoe.

Azura, guessing Silvie's line of thought, went red. 'Don't judge me, we're not all tall. Some of us have to compensate.'

'Even with that heel, you're still shorter than me.'

'My options can't be limited to "being tiny" or "tottering around on higher heels". I wear proper high heels for balls and banquets, so I'm not so miniature compared to everyone, but for walks I use more practical footwear without sacrificing too much height.'

'Yes, well, more practical isn't the same as actually practical,' Silvie noted drily.

Azura gave a snort. 'Yeah, well, I'll stop wearing heels when you stop being tall.'

'Oh, I can help!' Lena leapt to her feet, somehow still possessing abundant energy after the day they'd had. 'Hang on.'

She went into the bathroom of her suite, returning a few moments later with a velvety white hand-towel. She knelt beside Azura and folded the towel in half between her palms. The fabric ballooned out gently, ice cubes clacking against one another inside it. Lena handed the newly-made ice pack to Azura.

'There you go! Ice tricks can be more useful than simply ruining Myles' tea, which is also a good application of the skill, don't get me wrong, but this is even better.'

Silvie was impressed at how much Lena's skills had improved, though a little surprised the girl was comfortable with magic so soon after their ordeal. If anything, Lena was more at ease with it now than when she'd done conjuring tricks in the past.

'Dante could do a lot of things, too. His tricks were all fire ones, but I think ice is nicer. No offence, Azura. I know you're best at fire too. Not that Dante or I were ever allowed to do anything officially, but still.'

'Come back and let me finish your hair,' Myles prompted.

Lena returned to him. 'Will there be any other chances to go sightseeing? I want to explore Gemelli.'

'Maybe,' Myles answered. 'But there's no way I'm letting you out of my sight again.'

'I would've thought what happened was proof that I can manage fine without you.'

'Lena.' The reprimand was sharp, but all she did was giggle, as if what had happened was no more serious than her pranks to turn his tea cold. Her wide yawn halted any immediate retort.

Silvie could see Lena was visibly making an effort to remain upright, swaying a little as Myles braided her newly-combed hair neatly down her back.

'You're practically asleep where you sit,' Myles chided, his voice gentle again. 'Go to bed.'

'I'm not sleepy. I'm fine.'

Silvie saw the moment when deeper comprehension dawned. Lena had realised that, once she turned in for the night, Myles would be able to drop the brave face he was putting on for her benefit.

Silvie felt a sting of sadness that a girl of Lena's age had been forced to learn a lesson that complex, then worried her sadness was patronising. Silvie certainly knew how deeply pity could rankle.

'Maybe I will go to bed,' Lena amended, tone light, standing up in one smooth motion. 'You can all use my sitting room as late as you like. I'm tired enough to sleep through any noise.'

With a little wave, she shut her door behind her with a decisive click.

And then, just as Silvie had expected, Myles' calm, professional manner collapsed. He poured an enormous serve of whiskey and swallowed it in one shot. Silvie didn't even question where the drink had come from. Myles was an organiser and coordinator by nature, and could probably find alcohol at short notice even without his personal reliance on it.

'I intend to get incredibly drunk,' he told them, in case it wasn't obvious. 'You're both welcome to join me, or not, as you see fit. I don't mind.'

Silvie was so exhausted she thought even her chronic insomnia wasn't a match for how tired she felt. But she could see how shaken Myles was, and that he probably wanted the company.

'I'll stay with you,' she said.

Azura nodded. 'Yeah, me too. Pour me one.'

Azura and Myles drank for a while. Silvie had a few sips to be social, but knew she needn't have bothered – Myles and Azura were doing more than their share of getting through the bottle.

The conversation meandered, and Silvie wasn't surprised when Azura brought it around to the sigil Lena had inadvertently set off with a mere thought.

'People don't really need magic that strong for anything now, so nobody learns how to do it. Not that most people could – even if they studied – because the power necessary for a sigil that can be broken just by dismissing the thought of it is incredible.' Azura shrugged. 'To see it in a place like that… I don't want to think about it anymore. I wish I could forget it.'

'You two are accustomed to magic, but I'm not,' Myles reminded them. 'Not anywhere near as much, anyway. This is beyond the limits of my imagination.'

'I've never seen anything like that sigil before either,' Silvie assured him. 'But then I've also never been anywhere like that room before.'

Azura, looking sick and sad, poured herself another shot, swallowed it, and poured another. They were all quiet for a long moment, Azura and Silvie both pushing down the memory of what they'd seen.

'Even after what happened, I still like graveyards,' Silvie confessed, breaking the quiet. 'And I don't care what Lena says about it being trite and provincial, I do find them life-affirming. I felt the same kind of stillness on Driade Island. I liked it.'

'Well, Lena can be a haughty cat about it all she likes,' Myles said with a smirk. 'But a lot of people obiously agree with you, because so many more of them choose island burial over anything else.'

'It got popular quickly,' Azura remarked, sounding surprised at Myles' words. She turned to Silvie, 'It's only been a burial ground for a few years – since it stopped being a quarantine site for the plague. The epidemic ended, but since the soil was so good for digging holes for mass burials, the city kept doing it. Now it's where almost all of the dead go. Nobody ever really liked cremation, but it was the only way anyone was allowed to keep their dead within Arteria proper. The only remains within the city that aren't cremated are the King's. His body's on display in the palace, like that little girl was in the catacombs.' Azura shivered. 'I hate that it's there.'

'It's not actually the King's body at all, you know,' Myles corrected her. 'It's a wax replica. The real body is encased in lead in the base of the coffin display. That's why the guide-ropes for visitors are several feet back, so they can't get close enough to notice.'

Azura's face turned a brilliant pink. 'Well I feel like an idiot. And I had so many nightmares about him rising as a cadaveri inside the palace. I'm so dumb.'

'You should've spoken to your father. Not many people know the real situation, but he does. He could have allayed your fears.'

'I don't like talking to Dad about things like that. I always wind up sounding childish, and then I feel humiliated.'

As the night wore on, Silvie's aching exhaustion became more insistent. She felt dizzy, which was totally unfair given she was the only one not doing their level best to get drunk. The woozy sensation reminded her of the earliest days of her recovery, when she was learning how to walk and eat all over again. She eased herself down onto the comforting solidity of the floor, to lie on her back. With no further to fall, she closed her eyes so the room could spin in darkness as much as it wanted.

'Oh!' Azura blurted, surprise and concern in her tone. 'Can I help?'

'Talking,' Silvie managed to answer. 'Tell me a story. Distract me.'

'Okay.' Azura gave a small embarrassed laugh. 'Um, I can't think of anything. Don't you hate that? It's like with jokes. You hear jokes all the time, but as soon as you want to tell one you go blank.'

'I only remember one joke, but it's the best joke in the world,' Silvie said. She could hear Azura shift, repositioning herself to listen better.

'The best joke in the world, huh? I guess you'd better tell me, then.'

'Okay: which is heavier, a tonne of feathers or a tonne of lead?'

'Uh, that's not how weight works. A tonne's a tonne.'

'Wrong.' Silvie's mouth curled into a smile. 'Try again.'

'I promise they are exactly as heavy as each other.'

'Nope. The tonne of feathers is heavier.'

Azura sighed. 'Okay, why is the tonne of feathers heavier?'

'Because the lead's a tonne, but the feathers include the weight of what you had to do to those birds.'

After a long beat of silence, Azura cackled delightedly. 'That's the best joke in the world.'

'I know, right?' Silvie grinned even wider, her eyes still closed. 'I thought you'd like it, being vegetarian and everything.'

Her grin faded. 'You know, I was never the most athletic person. I fought with magic, not with my body. I was sentry, not infantry. But I was still, technically, a kind of soldier, and required to keep myself in ready condition for whatever might be required of it.

'Now I'm the one who decides what's required of it, and *it* is this new, still-unfamiliar version of my body. More and more, though, I'm realising the things I've lost — my magic, my hearing — were worth losing, in exchange for ownership of myself. Having to learn how to stop myself eating too much, for instance, is a better kind of suffering than never being given enough.'

Neither of the others spoke after she'd finished. Silvie began to worry that she'd said something weird.

Azura, as if sensing that the quiet made Silvie uncomfortable, spoke up. 'That reminds me of a greyhound my father had when I was very young. It had been a racing dog, until it injured its paw and couldn't run anymore. My father felt sorry for it and asked King Dante if he could take it as a pet. It was still good breeding stock, even if it was a useless racer, so the King allowed it. The greyhound had lost its purpose, but gained autonomy, well, as much autonomy as any creature living on the palace grounds ever has.'

Silvie let out an abrupt snort of laughter, and once she'd begun she couldn't stop. 'Are you comparing me to your dog?!'

'No, I was just–' Azura spluttered. 'Look, it was a nice dog, okay. I didn't mean anything bad by it!'

And just like that, the darkness and horror of their ordeal began to fade, and things started to feel all right again.

18. AZURA

WHEN SILVIE WAS ABLE TO SIT UP AGAIN, MYLES HELPED HER BACK TO her room. Azura stayed in Lena's sitting room, staring at her own hands, curling her fingers open and closed in slow movements.

'Mind if I open another bottle?'

She looked up. 'Oh, I didn't hear you come back in. Yes. I'll help you drink it.'

He smiled, sitting opposite her. 'I don't think there's enough of this in the world to help with my nerves tonight. I'm so sorry I wasn't there.'

'It's over now. We made it out,' Azura pointed out, trying to convince herself as much as remind him. Myles passed the bottle over and she took a long swallow.

'I tell you what's weird,' she admitted softly. 'Even during the worst moments, down there, all I could think about was the conversation we all had over the cherry cheese. Stupid, right? There we were, in the worst danger I've ever been in, and I kept thinking about how Silvie likes girls.'

'Does it bother you?'

'Yes. No, not like that. It bothers me because she knows that about herself, and I... I don't know anything. I don't know who I like. If I like anybody. I haven't ever tried to find out.' She knew she was rambling, but couldn't stop. And her hands were shaking. She curled them open and closed, open and closed, as she went on. 'I almost died without knowing; and that's why it bothers me. It seemed so awful and sad, the idea of dying without finding out.'

'Do you want to find out?' Myles asked. 'You can kiss me if you want.'

Azura bit her lip, as all her rambling words left her at once. She nodded.

Myles shifted to sit beside her, setting the bottle out of the way. He was close enough that his breath felt warm against her skin.

Azura closed her eyes.

Myles leant closer and pressed his lips against hers, as careful and thoughtful in this as he was in everything. The taste was sweeter than Azura had expected, a faint hint of sugar under their shared alcohol. Her blood was singing, the thrum of a sustained note humming through her body. She was alive, there in the soft lamplight of a comfortable and safe room, and Myles was there with her. And Lena was safe and Silvie was safe and everything was all right.

Azura's heart gave a low, thrilling swoop, like the winging of a soaring bird. She'd never considered how literal the feeling of butterflies in the stomach could be, but this was like a flutter of wings against the inside of her skin.

In the morning, the chaos of their adventure felt like a dream. Or perhaps it was the morning that felt like a dream, the ordinary routines and reality of waking up and joining the others for breakfast seeming strange and alien after such a remarkable experience.

Lena and Myles were already back to their usual selves, long practiced in the art of smoothing things over to face a new day, no matter what had come before. Being royalty, or a royal attendant, meant never having the luxury of a day off, not when there was work to be done.

Silvie was more frazzled than the others, which was a comfort to Azura knowing she wasn't the only one still finding her feet again. But Silvie looked exhausted, and she had a long, thin scratch on her forehead, a reminder of the peril they'd faced.

Azura reached out without thinking, brushing her thumb over the scratch to push a small burst of energy into the wound, knitting the torn skin back together. In a moment, it was as if the cut had never been there.

Then Azura realised what she'd done and wrenched her hand back as if it burned. 'Oh, shit, sorry. That's just habit.'

Silvie touched the healed place thoughtfully but didn't look angry. 'It's okay. You didn't mean anything by it. You'd do the same thing for someone who had magic of their own, right?'

Azura nodded, although she wasn't sure her answer was entirely honest.

If it had been Lena or Myles or even her father then, sure, she'd have reached out without even giving it a thought. It was one of the weird little perks of a strong gift for magic that Azura didn't mind having, the way she could heal little cuts as easily as wiping a smear of sauce off someone's cheek.

But Azura never initiated or invited even the most casual of touches with anyone else because that ability was also one of the *downsides* of her magical talents. Touching someone meant touching *their* energy, and feeling *their* mood seep into her own. So she avoided it.

But with Silvie it was different. Azura didn't mind touching Silvie at all.

'Myles,' Silvie said, breaking Azura's introspection. 'I want to learn how to fight, now that I've got my cane to account for. All the things I used to know don't apply, and I'm tired of feeling defenceless. If I learn new techniques, I can help to make sure that we're, that Lena is never again in as much danger as last night.'

He smiled, a touch of his exhaustion showing in the wryness of the expression. 'You don't have to sell me on the idea. I'm happy to help you, though it might be a few days before I have any time.'

'Thank you. I appreciate it.'

Azura sipped her tea. Gemelli had nicer tea than Arteria, but she was more accustomed to Arteria's. The experience was odd – to know something was better, but still not like it as much.

'I'm wondering,' she started, giving voice to a worry she'd been mulling all night. 'Lena, do you think there's any chance we were manipulated into going into the catacombs? Did someone perhaps mention it around you, in just the right way, so you'd keep thinking about it without realising it had been suggested? Our progress though could have been manipulated, if some rooms were sealed off and disused tunnels were opened, to lead us deliberately towards that room.'

Azura hated how her voice tripped and stumbled, but she couldn't help it. The very thought of the place made her palms clammy and her heart race.

Lena snorted dismissively. 'If there were any unscrupulous masterminds of that calibre in the government, the country wouldn't be such a mess.'

'You always say that, but–'

'Nobody manipulated me,' Lena snapped, cutting her off, and Azura was surprised to see genuine anger in her face.

'Or if anyone did, it was the ghosts of those witch children, and they're welcome to do whatever the hell they like after what they went through.' Lena's voice was icy.

Then she blinked, her frown softening. 'Sorry. But no, there was no conspiracy. Sometimes things just happen.'

After such a traumatic beginning, the rest of their stay in Gemelli was dull in comparison. Azura was left largely to her own devices, the single tourist, while the others were busy with their work. She was lonely, but Azura had spent more of her life alone than otherwise and had learned not to mind too much. At least being on her own meant she never had to compromise about where to stop for lunch or what sights to go see.

On their last night in the city before heading back to Arteria, as the four of them sat together in Lena's sitting room, Myles revisited the subject of teaching Silvie how to fight

'I've worked out some stances and strikes I think can work to your advantage, Silvie. You've got height in your favour, and you're strong. Those things compensate for your lack of balance quite well, if we can use them properly.'

Silvie gave a sharp, dangerous-looking grin. 'Great. Let's move this furniture out of the way and get started then, shall we?'

Azura and Lena moved to one side as Myles began the lesson. Watching them move together made Azura feel strange, and not with jealousy. Not exactly. Azura was fairly certain she was more of a pacifist than not, despite the deep, hot anger she pushed down inside her. No, she didn't want to learn to fight, and didn't envy Silvie her lesson.

Myles knocked Silvie to the ground again, but she got to her feet immediately, and resumed the stance Myles was teaching her.

'Something's strange,' Lena said quietly to Azura. 'You're being weird.'

'I am not,' Azura whispered.

Lena, unconvinced, gave Azura a long, searching look, and then let out a cackle of laughter.

'You're blushing,' Lena announced, matching Azura's quietness, while tapping a fingertip against her friend's cheek.

'I am not,' Azura repeated, brushing at the spot Lena had touched to find her skin felt blood-hot. Maybe Lena was right. 'Ugh, I hope I'm not getting a fever. Dad gets stressed whenever I'm sick.'

'You don't have a fever, you're blushing. Looks like you've *finally* realised you're in love with Myles. *Finally.*'

Azura glared at Lena. 'If you're going to verbally italicise a word, you don't also need to repeat the word for emphasis.'

'You're not denying it.'

'There's nothing to deny! You're obsessed with pairing people up, so you see what you want to see.'

Lena made a quiet harrumph of disbelief in the back of her throat. 'Whatever you say. You're in denial.'

Azura frowned. 'When I don't deny it, you think it's proof, and when I deny it, you think it's even more proof.'

'And you're still blushing. If it's not Myles you've got a crush on, it must be Silvie. Personally, I don't think I could be in love with another girl, because she'd have to be pretty, otherwise what's the point? But if she *was* pretty then I'd always be worried she was prettier than I was. But since I'm never going to be in love with anybody, I guess it doesn't matter, and we're not even talking about me so it doesn't matter twice. And Silvie bought me cherry cheese, so I like her.'

Azura watched Myles correct the placement of Silvie's elbow as Lena prattled on. Silvie gave him a small grin of thanks, and with her face flushed from exertion and a smile on her lips, she *was* incredibly pretty.

Oh, Azura realised.

19. SILVIE

RETURNING TO ARTERIA WAS A STRANGE NEW GRIEF, BECAUSE SILVIE had to face the fact this was her base now, the place she returned to. A shred of her heart had still expected the journey's end to be the barracks, her old life. She'd had nearly a year there after her injury, which should've been ample time to say her goodbyes to it, and yet it hadn't been enough.

Her new companions made her days lighter, and that was a small respite. But it was bittersweet too, because Silvie would never have met them if she hadn't lost so much. She too often found herself resenting anything that made her feel happy at all, which added to an underlying misery that was so deep and dark and cold, it felt like the black water of the canal closing in over her head. But unlike her rescue from the canal, nobody could dive into this water to pull her back to the surface. She had to sink or swim under her own strength. And Silvie was so tired.

Several days after their return from Gemelli, Silvie was working alone in the records room when the door opened. She looked up, expecting Azura – everyone else knocked before they came in – and blinked in surprise upon seeing Lena.

Silvie smiled a hello. The little queen always brought an effervescent energy into a room when she entered. It was impossible to feel bored or exhausted when she was around.

'Myles is busy examining the central ballroom, where I'll be having my birthday banquet,' Lena explained cheerfully. 'He's ensuring there are no loose slabs on the marble staircase, and that the windows and doors all behave as expected. He always worries things will go awry because he didn't check a hinge. So I'm free!'

'And by "free", I assume you mean wandering the palace when you're meant to be somewhere else?' Silvie said drily.

'Exactly!' Lena chirruped. 'You should take over as my attendant for the day, since he's busy. I'll tell Antonio he has to lend you to me.'

Silvie wondered what it would be like, to have every whim become a command obeyed by everyone; to have such power over the world.

'I have to welcome some delegates this morning, which is going to be boring,' Lena went on. 'But there'll be time for games afterwards. Come on.'

Which is how Silvie, void and former sentry, found herself accompanying Queen Magdalena and King Claudio to a meeting of foreign dignitaries.

Claudio was still dashing and noble with a disarmingly sincere smile, and Silvie didn't trust him one bit. She found it difficult to trust anyone who hadn't grown up in her world, but something in his manner at least made her feel at ease when he was present.

The pair of visiting dignitaries were old but beautifully preserved, their cared-for skin draped in expensive fabrics. Only the very wealthy aged so beautifully. Silvie wished that didn't bother her so much.

'Lena, you're more grown up every time I see you,' Claudio effused warmly, sounding genuinely pleased to see her. Lena gave him a wide, welcoming smile in return.

'We missed your bright presence dearly in court while you were in Gemelli,' he went on, then turned to address the visiting dignitaries. 'Lena is such a help to me, so dutiful and generous with her time. I may not have had a traditional stepmother, but I like to think what I lost in that arena, I gained in having a beloved sister to care for and rely on.'

The dignitaries practically melted at the sweet words.

Lena motioned to include Silvie in the conversation. 'This is my attendant for the day, Silvie–'

'Silvie White, yes, of course.' Claudio turned the full force of his bright smile on her. Silvie blushed at the attention. 'Corsetti's new apprentice. The whole empire is deeply in your debt for your loyal service.' He held the smile for another beat before returning to his guests.

'Miss White, a wounded veteran from our sentry corps, lost her magic in the line of duty. It's wonderful she still flourishes despite her difficulties.'

The visiting dignitaries offered kind, bland murmurs of sympathy, which rankled Silvie. She knew her poisonous fury accomplished nothing, did nothing but harm her, but knowing it wasn't enough to stop the bitter flood. She loathed pity, loathed the lip-service kindness that didn't care a whit about her or how she felt or what she'd gone through.

Lena, Claudio, and the dignitaries sat down and began to speak. Silvie took her place on a chair in the corner of the room, hoping she wasn't expected to help the servants who were bringing in refreshments. Myles probably would have been, but Silvie knew absolutely nothing about courtly manners. She'd make a dozen mistakes if she even tried.

'Do let us know if you need anything, Silvie,' Claudio offered, with another charming grin. She gave a polite nod in return, hoping it wasn't considered rude to be so casual with a king.

Silvie had never seen Lena in this context before, and was struck by how the girl seemed simultaneously younger and older than her private self. She was sweet and guileless, utterly the innocent sheltered little queen, while at the same time polished and well-mannered, and sophisticated in her conversational skills. It was unnerving to watch how effortlessly she switched from one persona to another.

After they'd eaten and chatted for a while, one of the dignitaries presented Lena with a small, extravagantly-wrapped gift.

'A cameo pendant, an ancient artefact previously on display at our national museum. A little jewel for a little jewel,' he said, grinning at his own quip.

Lena gave a placid, pleased smile, and deftly unwrapped the gift.

'There's a provenance letter, detailing its origins,' the same dignitary went on. 'In case you want to know about your new little bauble.'

Lena gave another pretty smile. 'Thank you so much. This is beautiful.'

Claudio began to speak again, diverting the diplomat's attention. Silvie watched Lena's face as she read over the letter, recognising the look of someone who had learned perfect control over their expression.

Kolya hadn't yet learned the trick of it, the last time she'd seen him, probably because he hadn't been in the corps from the beginning of his life. Silvie herself had certainly learned the skill by the time she was Lena's age, though she had less cause for it these days than when she'd been a sentry.

Silvie missed the mask, a little. It had given an easy anonymity, her real self hidden away where nobody could touch it. She wasn't sure she'd actually liked her real self very much back then, now she was too exhausted to try to hide it, and with that change came blessing and curse alike.

'If you'll all excuse me, I'm feeling a little tired,' Lena announced. She slipped the fine gold chain and pendant over her head. 'Thank you again so much for the gift. I love it, truly.'

With a bow of farewell to the dignitaries and the king, Lena left the room. Silvie followed. When they reached the stairs leading up to the queen's tower, Lena let out a long sigh of relief. 'You got to see Claudio's good side. He's always at his best when he's in public,' she told Silvie, a smirk twisting her lip. 'But in my experience, that's true of most people. There are very, very few people I've met I'd trust in the dark.'

They climbed the stairs slowly, but even so, Silvie had to concentrate on keeping her balance. She let Lena carry the conversation.

'Claudio has to spend more time than anyone with the christallo, though, so maybe I should be kinder about his horrible personality,' Lena conceded. 'I've heard that magic, really, really strong magic, speaks back to you in the voice of the most secret part of your being. You have to grapple with the worst version of who you are, when it's at its most powerful.'

'That sounds daunting.' Silvie tried not to shiver.

Lena shrugged. 'Doesn't sound so bad to me. I've changed my mind. Claudio's awful, he doesn't get a pass just because of the christallo. He's all nice and friendly when other people are around, but he's not like that at all.'

They reached the top of the stairs, which opened onto a wide, sumptuous sitting room. 'Myles is allowed in here, but not in any of the other rooms on this level. He sleeps outside the door to my private room.' Lena nodded towards one of the doors. 'Dante made it a law he can't go any further than that, on pain of death. This main room is for entertaining official guests, though they don't often come up here. It's mostly just Azura, when I beg her to play chess with me.'

Silvie sat down in one of the beautifully made armchairs and looked around. The room was decorated for someone much younger than Lena, with bright, simple hues chosen by adults on behalf of a child.

'There used to be a skeleton in here. I don't remember it, but Dante told me about it. It was a river dolphin for the River Queen, suspended over there.' Lena pointed to a corner, now empty save for a small writing desk and chair. 'The skeleton was rare enough to be a royal gift, because there aren't any more river dolphins. They all died out when people began channelling magic, and the telluric currents upset their habitat.

'Dante had it moved to the hall of mourning when this tower became mine, because he liked it so much. He used to tell me the folk tale that went with it: a man took his daughter out on the river in a boat and wanted to have his way with her, but she jumped over the side and was transformed into the first of the river dolphins.'

Lena wrapped her hand around the pendant at her throat. 'It's funny, isn't it? There are so many stories like that, of women turning into dolphins, into trees, into gorgons with snakes for hair. And so many different things just to escape. But the truth is you become nothing.'

For a moment she was still, staring far away from the room around them, then she shook herself and smiled at Silvie. 'People say there are ghosts in the mourning hall, but I've never seen any. A ghost dolphin would be something remarkable, wouldn't it?'

Silvie thought of the night of King Dante's death, the night she'd nearly died herself. Had *she* been a ghost, in that strange moment? Had some other ghost called her there?

'I keep meaning to do something with this room,' Lena chattered on, her usual vivacity returning. 'I really only think of my inner room as mine, since that's where I keep the things that are important to me. My sitting rooms and dressing rooms aren't mine in the same way. That probably sounds stupid.'

Silvie had lived in barracks and shared bedrooms for the vast majority of her life. She knew far more about not feeling a claim on a space than she did about ownership. 'Not at all.'

'Maybe I should have it painted green,' Lena went on. 'I like green. When Dante and I were quarantined on Driade Island we had a green house, with wrought iron shutters – the kind they make in Gemelli. It was nice. I wanted to get them in here, but the window frames are the wrong shape.'

Silvie glanced at the closest of the windows, its glass panes far too broad for shutters. Two tiny x marks carved into the wood of the frame caught her eye, and she peered at them, curious.

'Oh, you found the kisses?' Lena asked. 'I think the old queen put them there. Queen Eve. Like a mark of solidarity for whoever came next.'

'That's quite touching.'

'Not really,' replied Lena dismissively. 'The future's an abyss. We can't see into it, and it can stare back at us all it likes, but it can't touch us. Eve left the marks there for me so I'd know she was thinking of me, sending love, but what good does that do me? I can't send the past any kind of reply. For all she knew, I might hate her. The past can't be our friend, or our ally. Except…' Lena glanced at the wastepaper basket beside the desk.

Silvie could see empty ink bottles inside, and paper torn to confetti scraps. Whatever had been written on it was destroyed completely.

'Anyway!' Lena interrupted herself brightly. 'Shall we play chess? Sit down, I'll get the table.'

Lena won the first round, but she didn't win it easily.

'I think you could learn to be a really good player if you wanted,' she noted, moving a knight forward to begin the second match. 'Much better than Azura.'

'That's not surprising. I was taught strategy from a young age,' Silvie pointed out, repositioning a pawn.

'No, it's not just that. Azura's too soft for this game.' Lena moved one of her own pawns.

Silvie shifted a bishop. 'I almost envy that softness.'

'You wish you were more wistful?' Lena pressed another pawn into the field.

'Yeah.' Silvie nodded. 'It sounds silly, but I do.'

Lena moved her other knight. 'I guess I understand. Azura's not as sheltered as you think, though. She's not soft because of the life she's got, she's soft despite it. There's a big difference.'

Silvie stared down at the board, puzzling over her next move. She pushed a pawn forward. 'What do you mean?'

'Paolina Corsetti, Azura's mother, was Queen Eve's handmaid. They were as close as Myles and I are, or nearly so. Paolina nursed Eve throughout the illness that took her life. Anyone I've been able to bribe into telling me about those days has told me the same thing: Paolina and Antonio – Doctor Corsetti – often had screaming arguments, with Paolina imploring her husband to see how rotten the palace had become, how complicit they'd become in evil.'

Silvie wondered what could be so awful to cause fights between Azura's parents, but didn't want to interupt the story.

Lena moved a bishop. 'When Eve died, part of Paolina died along with her. Only a few weeks later, Dante put out the proclamation about his next arranged marriage with the youngest daughter in a foreign royal line, the Princess Guji. That was me. Dante changed my name when I came to live here, because he thought mine was ugly. He hated ugly things. So I became Magdalena. I think he named Eve, as well, but I don't know what her old name was.'

Silvie moved one of her castles as Lena continued to speak. 'Anyway, the thought of watching another little girl grow up and die young as a political puppet was more than Paolina could stand. Antonio knew her grief was bigger than whatever love remained in their marriage, so gave her leave to go. But told her, in no uncertain terms, she could not take Azura with her. Doctor Corsetti was not going to deny his daughter the life he'd worked so hard to give her, out of sentimentality for a dead queen.'

'So she left Azura behind?' Silvie said, as neutrally as she could.

Lena gave her a sharp look anyway. 'You left Kolya.'

The words stung like a whip, and Silvie physically recoiled from the pain of them. 'It's not that simple, I–'

'Nothing is *ever* simple. Like Azura's mother, she– If someone knows a terrible thing, they should do whatever they *can* to change things. But if they can't then, for their own sanity, they must leave. Even if it means breaking their own heart, leaving their family. The whole *it's not that simple* sounds like Claudio and his reasons why a thing is too hard or impossible or *just not sensible, Lena*. As if he could only ever do the easy stuff.'

Silvie realised Claudio's apparent unreliability in meeting Lena's expecations was the reason for her intense dislike of him.

Lena's expression had screwed up into genuine anger before smoothing out again. She gave Silvie a rueful smile. 'Ignore me. Of course you had no say in leaving Kolya. It wasn't right to make the comparison.'

Silvie lost that game, and the one after it, but the methodical routine of the battle, the framework around the ruthless strategy of the competition, was pleasant. She couldn't remember the last time she'd had such simple, ordinary fun.

Silvie was only beginning to understand what it meant to grow up as she had – not merely the specific circumstances and events of it, but the mindset behind everything. Silvie knew it wasn't the specific things, because when she looked at Lena, she saw a mirror of herself. And Kolya. They were three of a kind in a fundamental, terrible way, because they'd been forced to learn how to be good soldiers.

One might have been called a queen, the others a sentry, but the heart of it was the same: they'd been taught to follow orders, and to be malleable to whatever those who gave the orders demanded they become at any given moment. They'd had to train and train and train, until their backs were straight and their manners perfect; until their magic was so honed and the wolf went so deep that, in Silvie's case, it took half of her with it when it was ripped away.

They'd grown up knowing their only worth lay in how well they could play their role, and that those who'd come before them had perished young. Silvie didn't feel sympathy for Lena, exactly; she didn't even feel sorry for herself. It was just recognition, acknowledgment.

Lena fiddled with her new pendant as she contemplated the board, jumping a knight into the fray as her opening for a new game. 'I wonder who the girl in the cameo was,' she mused. 'She could be a goddess. A genie. The curator who wrote the provenance note for it said she was probably a slave-girl dancer, owned by the jewellery carver, and used as a model. Or maybe a famous harem girl. But nobody knows for certain. Only she knows her real history, and she isn't telling any of us. She's as mute as the witch-children from that room, now.'

'What's your choice for her?' Silvie asked, trying to keep the talk away from what they'd seen in the catacombs. She pushed a pawn forward.

'Hmm. I don't know.' Lena moved a pawn. 'I think I want her story to ambiguous; to be everything and nothing. Although, perhaps I do think she was a harem girl, trapped in her room with a eunuch guarding the door, all her thoughts on the sultan who might call any time. She knew she should love him, that *was* her purpose, but I think she hated him too.'

That's dark, Silvie thought, as she moved her bishop. It also occured to her how similar Lena and Kolya were when it came to playing. He simply hadn't known any games when they'd first met; while Lena, skilled in every genteel pastime, didn't how to *play* when she engaged in them.

They fell quiet for a while, engrossed in the battle on the board, concentrating hard on move and counter-move to chatter idly. And then...

Silvie slid a pawn one square forward. 'Checkmate.'

Lena stared at the board, then gave Silvie a shocked grin. 'Nobody's been able to beat me for years.'

'You don't vary the placement of your king. It's the only reason I won.'

'I didn't realise I was so easy to read.'

She didn't look pleased, but Silvie chalked that up to the petulance of a spoiled queen losing at a game she typically won. With a little sting of homesickness, it reminded Silvie of Kolya, as Lena so often did.

You left Kolya.

It wasn't until Silvie had left Lena's quarters that it occurred to her what Lena had said. At the time, the sting in the truth of it had blinded her to fact of it, but now she gave it a second thought. Lena knew about Kolya. How many of Silvie's secrets did Lena and Myles know? Did she have any left?

On her way back to her room, Silvie had her second royal interruption of the day when the King caught up with her in the hallway and offered her a candied fig.

'Part of the trove of gifts presented by my earlier visitors,' he explained, holding the blue and white china jar out to her. 'It's absurd, really. Jewellery for the queen and sweeties for her stepson, when our ages make a mockery of the correct order of things.'

Silvie's mouth twitched in a smile. 'Seems to me like yours is the better prize.' She accepted one of the figs, biting into the candy-rich flesh of it.

'I've escaped my entourage again. I hope you don't mind aiding and abetting a fugitive,' Claudio said with a sheepish grin, falling into step beside her. 'I've only been King for a year, and I'm still getting settled in the role. My apologies.'

'I don't mind,' Silvie assured him. 'And I'm certain you're managing. Lena said you were at your most charming during the meeting earlier.'

He gave a quiet snort. 'I'm sure she didn't intend that to be a compliment. I did mean it honestly, you know, when I said she was like a sister to me. And I'm sure you had enough of those in the sentry barracks to know how deeply a sibling can loathe you at times.'

'You know, then? How she talks about you?'

'Oh, yes.' Claudio laughed. 'She tells everyone I'm horrible. I try not to take it personally. I'm sure I'd be a little contrary just like her, if I'd lived her life.' An edge to his tone belied the breeziness of his dismissal, but Silvie didn't remark on it.

As they turned a corner he hurried forward, beckoning for her to follow. 'Here, let me show you a secret.' He led her over to several small potted trees arranged against the wall, their leaves and branches carefully pruned into a graceful shape to obscure the window behind them.

'The plants are here to discourage anyone lingering at the view,' Claudio told her. 'Come see.'

Several storeys below was a small sandstone courtyard, the pale rock making the dark stains splashed across it stark and obvious. The scene was instantly familiar to Silvie, a twin of one she'd visited periodically throughout her childhood.

The ghoul tied by a length of rope to the scarred post in the courtyard's centre was new enough to ooze. In life he'd been a man in late middle age, rangy and thin. Now his body was bloated beneath the tight leathery casing of his skin, which was carved open down to the bone on one thigh.

The wound would have been enough to incapacitate a living man, but it was nothing to a ghoul.

The awful scene was common enough in the village she'd worked. The poor and sickly paid for nursing through their final weeks by donating themselves to the barracks after death. Silvie had spent her earliest years learning how to use her wolf to tear them apart until they were harmless.

'I didn't know you had these here,' she said quietly.

'Corsetti doesn't like to think on it, so I'm not surprised he didn't mention it to you.'

It made sense. Palace guards needed cadaveri training more than anyone.

'One way or another, we're all bodies that serve the realm,' Claudio noted cheerfully. Silvie didn't reply.

Down in the courtyard, a second figure came into view, this one living. Myles wore a shirt and trousers very similar to his typical attire, all fine fabric and clean, well-tailored lines. It was only because Silvie's upbringing was similar to his that she recognised them as his day-off clothes: cuffs a little too high on the ankle and wrist, the edge of the once-crisp collar worn soft, small tears mended with careful but uncertain stitches. His uniform had been neatly kept for a long time, that much was obvious, but even the most careful keeping couldn't last forever.

He ran at the ghoul with swift directness, not at all the style of combat Silvie expected him to use. The thin blade in his hand stabbed forward in a series of quickfire jabs, driving deep into the ghoul's rancid flesh.

Claudio clicked his tongue in disapproval. 'Play-lessons from my father taught him to move like that. I learned the same tricks. Father loved the Gemelli style; he thought it was elegant and savage. My swordmaster was furious when he noticed I'd begun to copy it. It's useless against cadaveri – what does a corpse care about a few pinpricks?'

'He knows it's useless,' Silvie said. 'He's playing.' Her eyes were locked on Myles as he avoided each clumsy lunge of his rotting opponent. 'Infantry do that, sometimes. Seek out the fun while doing their duty. I was the same with my wolf.'

Myles made another sudden strike, breaking the ghoul's jaw with the pommel of his weapon. Silvie nodded. 'See? He was always in control.'

'Hmm.' Claudio's eyes were narrowed as he watched Myles rebalance his stance. 'He's hard to get the measure of, don't you think? I've been puzzled by him for a long time.'

'You could ask for a proper demonstration, instead of lurking up here,' Silvie offered drily. 'He's not a bad teacher.'

'I don't want to learn the things he'd show readily. I need to know the tricks he hides.' Claudio's murmur didn't seem meant for Silvie at all, his attention entirely captured by the figure below. 'Understanding a friend is no preparation for facing a foe.'

The words sent a chill down Silvie's back. She cleared her throat, breaking Claudio's daze and lifting the pall of the moment. 'It's good to see Lena's protector takes his role so seriously.'

'Protection is the least of what he gives her,' Claudio replied. 'An aide-de-camp like him is a prize beyond measure for any noble. That's why I'm so grateful for Corsetti. He's been a confidante and helpmeet far beyond the bounds of duty this past year, as I tried to gain my footing in the role of King. He and his daughter have a bright future within these glittering walls.'

Silvie couldn't help but glance at the splatter of black, thickened blood sliding down the wall beside the increasingly maimed figure tethered to the pole. It didn't look all that glittering to her.

'It's highly dangerous to have a cadaveri within the palace grounds. Any benefit to training with it has to be outweighed by that,' she said, nodding at the ghoul.

'There are wards on the edges of the courtyard and throughout the rest of the palace; the same kind that are placed on the plague island, to stop the mass graves rising. The strongest possible.'

Silvie gave a snort, despite the fact that snorting at the king was probably a whipping offence under most circumstances. 'Those could be broken easily enough, if someone wanted them broken. Magic is even easier to destroy than it is to create, and this close to the christallo it's extremely easy to create. The very existence of that island is tempting fate.'

'I agree with you. But the majority of my subjects hate the notion of burning their dead. They consider it a desecration. I have to follow the will of the realm.'

'But that, down there, that's not desecration?' Silvie retorted, nodding towards Myles, who'd reduced his opponent to little more than twitching gore.

Claudio chuckled, shrugging one shoulder. 'Don't ask me to find logic in sentiment.'

20. Azura

In the mid-morning, after her morning lessons were done, Azura sat in her grandfather's office, knees curled up to her chest atop the springy cushion of an overstuffed armchair. The one advantage to being small was she could still fit into the places that had been refuges when she was young.

She wished her problems had retained the simplicity of childhood too.

It felt as if everything was slipping out of her grasp, and the harder she gripped, the slipperier life became. She'd been scolded by every one of her tutors for failing to keep up with her studies, with more than one of them threatening to tell her father about her lack of progress.

Azura felt like a ghost in her own life, like a paper doll in front of a paper backdrop, never truly a part of the image.

In the past, when she'd heard people talking about emotional pain, Azura had thought it was how people used language to describe feeling angry or sad or helpless, all the emotions she'd felt before. But lately she'd begun to feel a new kind of pain, like something was broken or torn inside her. She didn't know if this phantom sensation was something slowly knitting together, or if the wound was in a constant state of reopening with every new movement.

She ached for something she didn't have a name for. And it really was an ache, as bare and simple as any physical injury.

A pair of dappled brown sparrows alighted on the windowsill, pecking at the crumbs Azura spread to lure them close. They chirped, small sounds as bright as the overbearing sunlight flooding the morning air. The sky was gloriously blue and clear above Arteria.

And here she was feeling miserable. It felt like she was rejecting a pretty gift from the universe. It was one thing to wallow on a rainy day, but this perfect weather should be celebrated.

With a sigh, she unfolded herself and left the study. There was no point trying to catch up with her studies now. The damage was done; she was already a failure, so why bother?

Silvie was in the kitchen, herbs in neat piles on the cutting board, a small pot bubbling merrily on the stove.

'What horrible experiment does my father have you working on now?' Azura asked, peering at the mixture, as Silvie added a minty-smelling pinch of dried leaves to it.

Pure magic had always come so easily to Azura that physical witchcraft felt stodgy and boring by comparison, more like the chore of cooking than anything interesting. But when Silvie brewed potions – or baked food, for that matter – it wasn't a chore. She made it worthy and important, through the care she imparted the task.

'Headache tonics. It's my own recipe, but Doctor Corsetti thinks there's a market for it. I'm doing it in here because the ventilation's better than in the workshop. It can get a little pungent as it steeps.'

'Headache? I thought Dad already made those. Little brown glass bottles, gold wax over the cork.'

Silvie nodded. 'Yes. This is a much stronger recipe, though. More like a narcotic, to be honest, but not especially harmful if taken in moderation. I developed it because I needed something to keep my own migraines at bay while still being able to function through the day.'

'If your headaches cause so much pain that you need a tonic that strong, you should ask Dad for help. He'd find a way to accommodate you. Give you breaks.'

Silvie's posture stiffened. 'I've already been given more than my fair share of help,' she replied, the words chilly.

'Help doesn't work like that.'

'Doesn't it?' Silvie's voice was even colder now, and she wouldn't look at Azura.

Azura slumped back to her study, feeling even worse, and wondered what her father was like as an employer. Was it Silvie's own hangups that stopped her asking for help, or did the compassion in the dynamic between master and apprentice have a limit?

Azura flicked through the pages of her textbook without reading. She knew how everything would go: her tutor would report her failures to her father, who'd look disappointed but not actually mete out any kind of discipline for the infraction. Which was worse than any punishment.

She knew she shouldn't take her father's endless forgiveness for granted, especially when Silvie was so starved of the same compassion, but Azura couldn't help it. She suspected, in her heart of hearts, she wasn't a very good person.

She certainly didn't know how to relate to the stubborn drive that fuelled Silvie's every movement. Azura had never tried hard at anything, so could only dimly understand the frustration and futility Silvie faced every day.

Even discounting the migraines, Azura knew if she was in Silvie's position, she'd reach for the narcotic tonics at every opportunity. Anything to stop her from feeling, even a little. Anything to dull the edges, make herself numb. Make the pain of that burning, yearning lack easier to tolerate.

She curled up in her grandfather's chair again. The sparrows were long gone, leaving nothing but hot blue stillness and hard sunlight outside.

Azura knew she should feel more changed by what they'd gone through in the catacombs. Maybe it was too soon to tell. Maybe the waves were still settling.

She was glad they were alive, that much she knew for sure. And there was a new and fierce desire for closeness with both Lena and Silvie, and that was something she couldn't remember ever feeling about anybody before. Even so, it was a weird, private emotion she didn't want to share with them, or with anyone for that matter. The sentiment was her business, not theirs, even if it was directed towards them.

But, aside from that, Azura didn't feel any different. She hadn't found some new everlasting well of respect and gratitude for the simple realities of her life, the way that characters in books did after a dangerous adventure.

For the first few hours after they made it back into Gemelli, sure, her whole heart had been singing with elation at being alive. Colours were more vivid, food tasted better, laughter more precious.

But now she was home to all the tedious everyday things – worrying about studies, and trying to ignore the stink of the canals, and the way Lena wanted attention all the time, and how she kept trying to have a civil conversation with Silvie but they always wound up having stupid, pointless arguments – it felt like nothing untoward had happened to them all.

She didn't know why those arguments kept happening, no matter how she tried to avoid them. She was tired and sad and exhausted and cross, exactly how she used to feel before the strange, horrible encounter in the catacombs.

Maybe the sharp delight of being alive was also like pain. The human mind couldn't properly hold onto it for any length of time without the clarity of the sensation fading into vague, dim memory.

Despite their moment of tension earlier in the day, Azura couldn't help but be pleased when she went up to the palace roof in the late evening and found Silvie there, alone in a little pocket of dimness overseeing the glittering lights of the city spread out around them.

It looked as if Silvie was painted in shades of silver and grey against the darkness, the white streaks in her hair glittering in the wash of night, the rest a ghostly pale grey, her skin soft and unearthly, near-luminescent. She was like a marble statue, a creature outside of time, meant for some other more graceful, more ancient world.

She was beautiful, but it was a remote, cold beauty, one Azura suddenly felt too clumsy to even imagine drawing near to.

Silvie turned, looking at Lena's tower for a long moment. With the golden candle-glow visible in the high windows, and the silvery ghostliness on Silvie's features, it made Azura think of the moon contemplating a distant sun.

'I guess Myles is too busy to come by tonight,' Silvie remarked, acknowledging Azura's presence.

'He'll make the effort if he can, since he tries to avoid drinking near Lena, and–'

'He likes to drink.'

'I don't think like is the right word.' Azura shook her head. 'I think he needs to. I doubt he knows how to go without. He would never interfere with his duties, because Lena is always, *always* his priority, even when it's to the detriment of his own wellbeing. By his own admission he can't sleep without it.'

'Mmm.' Silvie was silent for a beat, a thoughtful expression on her face. 'Headaches and vertigo are blessings, in their way. They make the aftermath of heavy drinking so bad I don't do it much. If it was the only way to sleep, though...'

Azura frowned. 'You're still not sleeping?'

'It will get better eventually.' Her tone suggested she didn't really believe that, but telling herself otherwise would be unbearable.

'Are you doing okay, though? You don't get too worn out? I know you don't want to ask my dad for help, but–'

'Azura, I'm fine. Honestly. Not all of us are vegetarians. Some of us get enough iron and protein to keep our energy levels up, even with a little insomnia.'

Azura snorted in amusement, despite herself. 'You make *vegetarian* sound like such a dirty word.'

Silvie gave a small chuckle.

'I'm not sleeping super-well myself,' Azura admitted. 'Most nights I have to read for hours before I can drift off.'

'What do you read?'

A faint blush of embarrassment heated her cheeks. She hoped the lighting was too low for Silvie to notice. 'It's dumb. Lately I've returned to a book I really loved as a kid. I wanted something comforting and familiar, after... after the stuff in Gemelli. I was obsessed with it when I was younger. And, this probably sounds incredibly silly, I had such a crush on the hero. I was madly, sincerely in love with a fictional character.'

As Azura had expected her to, Silvie laughed, but there was nothing mocking in the sound.

'Come on, Azura, did you really think I'd find that silly?' Silvie asked, her voice warm. 'It didn't occur to you, growing up the way I did, that I'd need the perfect escape only found in fictional worlds? Believe me, I rushed headlong into novels whenever I had the chance. I've had fictional romances capable of ending the world with their intensity.'

Silvie gave another laugh, one of the unbridled ones Azura had come to love. 'If you want to talk about shameful confessions, how's this: those book-crushes I had were one of the reasons it took me so long to realise I only like girls. I got crushes on boy characters, and then couldn't understand why I didn't feel the same way about the real boys I knew. Especially while I found the girls so much more interesting.'

Azura laughed. 'I do like boys, I think, but even I find fictional ones more interesting.'

A breeze stirred their hair. It was coming in from over the bay, so the air was fresh and salt-laced, not dank and gross like the smell from inland over the canals.

Azura made her thumb and forefinger into a circle and blew through it, conjuring bubbles into existence. 'I don't do air magic often,' she explained, as they floated away on the light wind. 'But I've always liked bubbles.'

Silvie smiled. 'I used to blow ones like that, using soapy water.'

'Why didn't you make them with magic, like I did? It's a simple spell. Even Lena could do that one.'

Silvie shrugged. 'My magic was never mine to use, even when I had it. I wasn't allowed to do frivolous things with it.'

'Oh, I'm sorry.'

Silvie waved a hand. 'It's fine. I always liked making them the ordinary way, anyway. Frozen soap bubbles are pretty. They pop easily, so they aren't pretty for long, but watching them freeze is so lovely, for those few seconds while it lasts. Kolya – he was another sentry – and I used to make them when we were younger.'

Silvie gave a soft smile as she stared out over the lights. It was clear to Azura she was actually in her mind's eye, in the past.

'I miss him,' she was saying. 'I knew I would, but didn't know it would be this much. When we were children, when he first came to the barracks... He didn't get put there as an infant, the way I did. So he was a little older, but he didn't know how to play. We never had much in the way of recreational time, but whenever the others got a chance to play, like children, he'd hang back.

'I used to take him to the playground at night, when the village kids weren't around to bully us. We'd go on the swings. We had to keep our gloves and cloaks on when we did, so the cold of the metal didn't hurt us. We'd swing and swing there in the night. It was as if we were suspended there, high up in the air, even though it only lasted for a moment.'

Silvie gave a dry, sad little chuckle. 'And now, I can't go on swings. A few months after I lost my magic, Kolya took me back to the park. He saw how sad I was, like he'd been when he was small, and wanted to return my favour. But my vertigo made it impossible. I only pumped my legs a few times before the movement of the swing made me so dizzy I had to stop.'

She drew in a shaky breath. 'It's a stupid thing to be sad about, you know, when there are so many important things I lost. But not being able to use a swing anymore feels like such a loss.'

'I hope I get to meet him someday,' Azura said.

Silvie shook her head, expression turning wistful and lost. 'Even I probably won't ever see him again. He'd like the palace, though. He'd love having so much to eat. I know he'd pester Myles to teach him how to fight, and plead to hear as many stories about the infantry as possible. Kolya deals better with men than with women, as a general rule, because things happened to him that made him not trust women very much.'

'He trusted you, though,' Azura said. 'It sounds like the two of you were very close.'

'Hmm,' Silvie agreed. 'It's probably because he knew I'm not attracted to men, so I was safe.'

Yet again, Azura was pierced with the icy knowledge of how sheltered her life had been.

'I miss the person I used to be so much.' Silvie said. 'Not as much as I miss Kolya, oddly enough. You'd think I'd miss myself more than someone else. But it feels like I'm *in* a whole other person's life now. So maybe I don't let myself miss the old me and her old life. I don't allow myself to feel it, like how Lena doesn't allow herself sadness.'

Azura gave a start of surprise. 'Lena feels everything at full volume, what are you talking about? She's constantly in the heights of delight or the depths of misery. I don't know anyone else as melodramatic as Lena.'

Silvie shrugged one shoulder. 'Putting on a show isn't the same as what we feel though, is it? Nobody really knows what anyone else is thinking.'

Azura bristled. 'What makes you think you know whether Lena's sad or not?'

Another shrug. 'Just a feeling. Recognition, maybe. I'm glad she has you and Myles.'

Azura settled at that. Lena was fine. Silvie didn't know what she was talking about.

'It was especially clever of Doctor Corsetti to hire Myles as Lena's personal attendant, even though he's younger and scrappier than anyone the court would want filling the role. Your father could see Lena needed someone closer to her own age if there was ever going to be any trust between them. He's very smart.'

'You make him sound so calculating.'

Silvie hesitated. 'No, I think there's a kindness to it. He seems like a warm, decent man, but he's shrewd. He'd have to be, to thrive in a place like this.'

She gave Azura a crooked smile. 'I mean, I know you don't think his role is a coveted position, but most people would consider it to be. When it came to getting Lena a bodyguard to keep her in check, Doctor Corsetti was smart enough to see a friend would have more chance of success than a guardian. With me, well, he needed an apprentice because you weren't interested in the job, right? Isn't it interesting he chose someone whom nobody would ever consider fit to possibly take over the role someday?'

Azura said nothing.

Silvie gave a bitter huff of amusement, staring down at her hands. 'I used to have dreams I could still be a witch but, since coming to Arteria, I know it's a dream I'll have to give up some day; when I can bear to accept the reality of it.'

She looked at Azura again. 'But, I was perfect for this job for that reason. Doctor Corsetti found a way to have someone around to help him, someone whose very existence would reinforce *to you* how temporary they were. And how temporary the abandonment of your destiny would have to be. Because, in the end, I'd never truly be able to take over the role. You'll have to do it one day.'

'No. You're just cynical. Dad's a good person. He chose Myles and you because you both needed a place in the world.'

Silvie's smile was surprisingly soft. 'I'm not saying he isn't a good person, and, yes, perhaps I am being too cynical. You know your father best.'

'Dad's great,' Azura insisted stubbornly. 'You just don't want to be vulnerable, to trust anyone to catch you if you fall.'

'That's fair,' Silvie agreed. 'Maybe I'll never quite learn the trick. But I am getting better at letting people help me up, when I fall. I let you aid me a bunch of times in the catacombs.'

'Ugh, let's not talk about that.' Azura shuddered. She made the circle with her forefinger and thumb again, blowing a fresh torrent of bubbles out over the sprawling view of the city.

'When I was very young, I thought crystal balls were made of bubbles.' Silvie's voice was as soft. 'I'd never seen a picture of the christallo, so I thought it was probably the same, except larger. I had a recurring nightmare where I was trapped inside it.'

'I thought you had to shake them,' Azura confessed. 'Crystal balls, I mean. I thought they were like snow globes, and the little scene you *wanted* to see would appear inside when you shook them.'

'Child-logic is so funny.' Silvie's gaze followed the remaining bubbles across the sky. Then she looked at Azura. 'Children expect the world to make sense, to all fit together in a way that's neat and good.'

'And when you're a kid, adults all seem so wise and clever,' Azura said. 'So sure about everything. It isn't until you stop being super young yourself, you realise little kids are way surer about things than adults.'

Silvie shook her head. 'I've heard adults say things like that a lot, but it never sounds true to me. I think if you want the things you're supposed to want, and love the things you're supposed to love, it's as simple as anything to be an adult. The problems only come if you aren't what you're supposed to be. Like us.'

Silvie's final words were no more pointed than the rest, but Azura felt as if her heart had worked its way up into her throat. She felt exposed, like her most secret self was laid bare. It was so silly and yet absolutely simple and clear. Silvie knew they were two of a kind, and Azura knew it too.

'Would…' Azura cleared her throat. 'Lena's birthday banquet is coming up. Would you like… would you like to go together? With me, I mean.'

Even in the dark, Azura could see Silvie's grin was one of the disarmingly bright, guileless ones she liked so, so much.

'Yeah,' Silvie told her. 'I would.'

21. SILVIE

As they walked down from the roof together, Silvie felt awkward and giddy after Azura's invitation. Judging by the quiet between them and the blush on Azura's cheeks, visible once they were back indoors, she wasn't alone in her sudden shyness.

To distract herself, Silvie concentrated her surroundings.

The palace of Arteria, renowned for its sumptuousness, often exceeded its own reputation. Even Silvie's cynical eye couldn't deny it was beautiful and luxurious, from the dazzlingly ornate embroidery and tapestries to the delicate carvings on door frames and windowsills. There was a feast for the eyes in every direction.

Yet Silvie felt a faint sense of rot below all the luxury, of mould just out of sight. It stood to reason, heavy fabrics and expensive wood were subject to the same vagaries of existing atop a canal system in a humid climate as the materials of poverty were.

So many things in the village near the barracks were dilapidated, but with such constant, violent cold in the air, any kind of damp was treated as an immediate and serious health risk. Even though it was worn, everything stayed sealed and dry.

Arteria, especially its palace, was as unlike Silvie's old world as it was possible to be. She wasn't sure she'd ever grow accustomed to it.

Having avoided conversation with irrelevant thoughts, Silvie realised in another minute she and Azura would reach the point where they'd have to say goodnight and part ways. She baulked at the idea, not wanting to break the evening's evanescent spell, to end the fragile sweetness blooming between them.

What if, the next time they met, it was nowhere to be found? What if this warm, happy connection was a one-off, never to be repeated?

'Do you want to come and see my grandfather's study?' Azura asked, interrupting Silvie's increasingly desperate thoughts. 'It's where I do my lessons, and I really should do some work on them before I go to sleep. I'm behind on my independent study, and it's just going to get worse the longer I leave it.'

Silvie grinned. 'I'd like that.'

The decor in the study reminded Silvie of the officers' quarters at the barracks. Visiting overseers would come to the outpost and take turns at running it. They always thought they could prove how clever they were by making it more cost-efficient through spending reform (they couldn't, the budget was as lean as it could possibly be). Others thought to distinguish themselves through exemplary military leadership (they couldn't, nobody cared about the work the sentries did, except when it went wrong). Or they used the rotation to get as far away from Arteria as they could (until, inevitably, they realised they didn't want to be that far from anywhere).

These reasons, however they varied in the particulars, were always about the visiting overseers' ambitions and desires, never about what they could do for the sentries they commanded. So, to Silvie, the pale fabrics and dark wood of the study's aesthetic had long been synonymous with pompous old men who acted like their bad mood was not only someone else's fault, but should be someone else's problem as well.

Silvie never paid much attention to the overseers. She got in trouble more than some sentries, less than others, but it wasn't as if there was any threat of punishment real enough to keep anyone in line. Misbehaving sentries couldn't be made to go hungry, or be deprived of other luxuries, since they had so little to begin with, and needed to eat in order to be capable of doing their work. They had nothing, so there was nothing for the overseers to threaten them with.

Thinking of those ridiculous, stuffy men from her old life, Silvie wondered what that same breed of bureaucrat did with their time in Arteria. What flimsy achievements did they dream up in order to big-note themselves? What were their pet political causes? What were the real problems of the city these men failed to acknowledge, because there was no glory in them; only difficult choices and hard work?

The answer to the last question, at least, was obvious to Silvie.

'It must cost a lot, to feed the city,' she noted. 'There isn't any farmable land within its boundaries, and no stockyards.'

'Mm.' Azura nodded. 'I had to study that stuff in economics. The only thing Arteria farms is magic. Tithing and taxes are very high. Anyone who doesn't live inside the palace complex has a tough time of it. To be perfectly frank, I'm terrified of what the future holds for me if–' She stopped herself. 'When I don't take up my father's role. If I renounce my future, where will I go? What will I do? This is the only life I know.'

'Well,' Silvie said, trying to keep her tone light without being mocking. 'Some of whatever your life becomes wouldn't be as hard for you as it would for other people. You won't, for instance, lament your sudden lack of good food, since you don't appreciate the food you have now anyway.'

Azura gave her an annoyed glare. 'The way you're so mean about what I eat says a lot more about you than about me, you know.'

Silvie bit back half a dozen retorts. Maybe Azura had a point. Silvie hadn't thought about it from her own perspective. 'Explain it to me, then. I'd like to understand why you turn down good meat when it's offered.'

Azura was quiet, almost taken aback by Silvie's request.

'Well,' Azura started. 'I thought about it for a long time. I'd never liked eating meat. I mean, I liked the taste, but not the fact it came from animals. And I know you probably want to say something catty like "it must be nice, to be able to turn down food just because you don't like it" or whatever, but I'm not *obligated* to accept something simply because I'm lucky enough to have it available to me. Whether I eat it or not has no bearing on whether others, elsewhere, have it. Or not.'

She paused, inviting Silvie to break the moment of civility, but Silvie held her tongue.

'Anyway, that was the background, not the turning point,' Azura went on, obviously realising Silvie wasn't taking the bait.

'I stopped eating meat because…' She paused, the memory enough to make her visibly pale. 'I had to kill a rabid fox once. I did it as humanely as I could, by snapping its neck with magic. But since then I've never, ever wanted to be responsible for another creature's death. Not for anything.'

Azura frowned, as something had just occurred to her. 'Now that I think about it, it's also when I decided I didn't want my father's role. I don't want to make magic the centre of my life when it allowed me do something like that. I didn't want the… that power.'

Silvie shrugged. 'You think you committed some great cosmic wrong that requires a lifetime of atonement? Trust me, the universe doesn't put a black mark on your soul to taint you forever because you kill something, least of all a rabid fox. In the grand scheme, it doesn't matter at all.'

'But that's *exactly* why,' Azura snapped, eyes flashing. 'It's because it was so easy; and so small. The universe didn't even blink.'

A troubled frown pinched her pretty features. 'Life only has value if we treat it like it does. So, I do. I know I'm weird, but it's how I feel. I don't want anything to die because of me.'

Silvie was astonished by her own response, by the curious thing she was thinking even while Azura *was* being weird... Silvie just wanted to kiss her.

'Well, I didn't think anybody would ever like me,' she admitted, changing the subject completely. 'Or want to take me to a banquet, or anything like that.'

Azura gave her a surprised look. 'Really? I thought it was legal for girls and girls or boys and boys to be together in the corps now.'

'It's not illegal, but that's not the same as accepted,' Silvie replied. 'And it's not because I was a sentry that I felt like that. I tried not to care about believing no one would like me that way, the same way I now try not to care about needing a cane. I figured some things about me were too different, too horrible for anyone to want to be with me. That it was never going to be on the cards. I've tried to be pragmatic about it.' She did her best to laugh off the darkness of her words. 'You know: I need a walking cane, I'm deaf in one ear, I like girls, I'll die alone. No biggie.'

Azura kissed her.

Silvie froze.

Azura's lips were soft and warm, the ghost of sweet wine in their taste. Illogically, ridiculously, Silvie's immediate thought was: *Oh, hello. I know you.*

Silvie parted her own lips a little to kiss her back, not at all certain what she was doing but simply following her instincts. Azura gave a small hum of happiness, tongue darting out to lick at the slightly open seam of Silvie's mouth. The strange, pleasant tickle of the sensation made Silvie open her mouth wider, drawing Azura's tongue in and sucking at it lightly.

Azura's hand was holding Silvie's hip now, resting there gently, careful not to move her even the slightest bit off balance. Silvie had no idea how she was managing to stay upright at all; her head was whirling with a dizziness she'd never felt before. It was as if the whole messy jumble of the world had turned sideways, the picture coming clear, everything making sense even though she didn't have the words to explain this newfound clarity. It just was. The two of them just were.

When Azura pulled back her eyes were dark, her breathing rough. Kissing had brought a flush of blood to the delicate skin of her lower lip, and for one wild moment Silvie understood the ghouls, a little, because something painful and sharp and hungry low in her belly wanted to taste that vivid, living red, to suck that lower lip between her own.

'Oh, okay,' was all she managed to say.

22. AZURA

THE WEATHER WASN'T ESPECIALLY SPECTACULAR THE NEXT MORNING, BUT TO Azura it was a peerlessly pretty day. She didn't have any lessons ahead, and there was a spring in her step as she got ready to go out, a happy song thrumming in her ribcage. She leaned out the window, breathing in the dank air as if it was a fresh spring wind.

'Nice to see you so cheerful, for a change,' her father remarked, joining her by the window. 'You're dressed up – going somewhere?'

'Yeah, I was going to go buy a dress for the birthday banquet.'

'Really? You don't often go into the city on your own during the day.' Her father tousled Azura's curls as he spoke. 'You're a moody little night owl.'

It was a true enough observation, but Azura felt embarrassed her father knew her so well.

She did like to go for walks at night to collect her thoughts, that much was true. The palace – even its quieter corners, like her study or the rooftop – were never still enough for Azura to really think. And yet, somehow, the glittering city at night, full of scents and noise and bustle, offered peace whenever she sought it.

'Most of the market stalls selling clothes aren't open at night,' Azura told her father. 'I think Silvie would feel a little weird if I got something tailored, so I'm going to find something off the rack.'

'Silvie? I didn't realise she was going. Although I suppose Lena enjoys her company, so it's lucky the queen can invite who she likes, even at the last minute, no matter how finalised the guest list is.'

Azura chuckled. 'No, no. I'm taking Silvie. She'll be going as my date.'

Her father was quiet, his hand lifted away from her hair. 'You know, sweetheart, just because Lena wants to make a point with her invitations doesn't mean you should encourage her. When you're her advisor someday, you'll need to be a more tempering influence on her whims than when the two of you were children.'

Azura looked at her father in bafflement. 'This has nothing to do with what Lena wants.'

'Oh, my contrary little girl. Is this because I took an apprentice?'

'Uh, I guess? Since that's who I'm going on a date with, then technically–'

'So this is a way at getting back at me, for paying attention to her instead of you?'

Azura was struck speechless. Finally she managed a reply. 'You think I'm going to the banquet with Silvie because I want to punish you? You think of that as your punishment, to have a daughter who likes girls?'

'Azura, you know I didn't mean it like that. I just think it's a silly way to prove whatever it is you're on about.'

A shocked laugh burst from Azura's throat before she realised it was coming.

'Don't be stubborn, sweetheart. You're always doing silly things that put you at a disadvantage for no good reason. Like those glasses you wear, even though your eyes are fixed.'

A chilly rage dissolved her earlier muteness. 'They didn't need fixing. I wasn't some machine that needed repair.'

'I still don't understand why you're angry about it. It was an improvement. You can see now.'

'I could see then! That's what my glasses did for me! Like how Silvie's cane lets her walk! I was fine the way I was. You act like it's pitiful or shameful that she needs a cane but it isn't, it's just a part of who she is. And there's nothing wrong with who she is, she's perfect and I really, really like her, and I'm taking her to the banquet!'

Her father's frown grew deeper, an irritated edge sharpening the corners. 'This is an immature way to try to hurt me, Azura. I hope you see that before you do something you'll regret. Even if you do like Silvie's company, then, well, perhaps if things were different...'

Weariness washed over Azura like a heavy wave. *Perhaps if things were different.* She was so tired of people finding excuses to forsake happiness, to accept lack as inevitable.

'I'm not you.' Azura's voice was cold. 'Who I love is always going to be more important to me than pleasing the palace.'

Her father gasped, flinching as if Azura had struck him. Azura left the room, slamming the door behind her.

Azura went for a long walk. She bought a pair of pretty but stupidly impractical high-heeled boots of soft black canvas.

Azura loved Arteria. She'd never lived anywhere else, but even without the experience of comparison she knew Arteria was dear to her, but she hated how trapped she felt by her life. She hated that her lack of other experiences meant she couldn't imagine what the alternatives might be. Sadness acted like blinkers, narrowing her view of the future to the barest strip of light.

And now, all around her in the stink of the air itself, Azura couldn't help but notice the poverty that infected Arteria. She hated how much suffering the city held, how many hungry, unhappy people did their best to eke out survival in its cramped, narrow streets. She hated that it was kept secure by the sacrifice of children, far away in the distant cold.

Azura also knew hatred did nothing by itself. Anger was only useful if paired with intelligence, or creativity, or sufficient compassion. Azura didn't have enough of any of those to change things. She was just caught up in it, like a butterfly in a bell jar, beating hopeless wings against the glass while the air ran out.

Azura hoped Lena and Myles might be around in the evening, but wasn't surprised when she didn't see either of them; the preparations for the birthday banquet were in full swing after all. Azura's father and Silvie were in his workshop until late, and she was glad she didn't have to experience whatever the atmosphere in that room was like right now.

She ate in the dining hall, making small talk with a few of the palace staff and, after dinner, joined some of them on the roof to drink for a while. Her life was so insular she realised she didn't really know any of them well. On any other day that might have felt liberating as her lack of close bonds meant it should be easy to leave her life behind, if she ever worked up the strength to sever the ties to the future laid out for her. Tonight it made her feel sad, because it also meant so few people knew her. Even those who were supposed to know her best, like her own father, didn't see the real her. Or chose not to.

It didn't feel like it was only one day since she'd been up there with Silvie, and had asked her to the banquet. Despite her father's reaction, Azura wouldn't take back the invitation for anything in the world.

She sat up there long after the others had gone to bed, feeling sorry for herself, breathing in the briny bay wind. The queen's tower lights were still on, even at such a late hour. She hoped Lena and Myles were getting enough rest.

'I thought I'd find you here.'

Azura turned at the sound of Silvie's voice, and gave her an exhausted smile. 'I'm not exactly an unpredictable person.'

Silvie eased herself down beside Azura. 'Doctor Corsetti was in a bad mood today. Did something happen?'

'Yeah. I told him I was taking you to the birthday banquet. He didn't take it well.'

'Mm.' Silvie didn't look surprised.

'I got angry,' Azura confessed. 'He was cross, but I was the one who got angry. He loves the *idea* of me more than the real me.'

'I doubt it's that simple,' Silvie said. 'Your father loves you very much, and part of his reaction might be the realisation your life is going to be more difficult than he hoped it would be. Nobody wants the people they love to face hardship. Blending in is always easier.'

'No, I think he's actually disappointed in me, that I'm not who he wanted me to be.'

'It's not your job to be what he, or anyone else, wants you to be. You just have to be. Even if it makes your father disappointed, or uncomfortable, or angry, or sad. No matter how much you love him, you can't betray who you are for his sake, because who you are isn't up to him.'

Silvie took a deep breath. Her face held the bare and open, wonderful expression that declared that, somewhere along the line, she had stopped bothering to dissemble and second-guess the world. She had simply decided to deal with it head-on. Azura envied her for that, though she knew the lesson was hard-won.

'Maybe it's different for me because I never had parents,' Silvie went on. 'I had people whose opinions meant a lot to me, who I didn't want to disappoint, but I learned early on if I looked for support from a source that wasn't offering it, I was going to get really miserable really fast.'

'I just wish...' Azura tried to find the right words. 'I wish I wanted the things he wants me to want.'

'Well,' said Silvie. 'For whatever it's worth, I'm glad you don't.'

23. SILVIE

ON THE DAY OF THE BANQUET, AS AFTERNOON EDGED TOWARDS A RAINY evening, Silvie began to dress up.

She'd made a trek to the markets the day before – staying well away from the edges of any canals – and found a pretty dress within her budget. She'd never had a pretty dress before, or owned anything in the deep wine-red shade of cotton she'd chosen, and she loved it.

She wore her usual sturdy boots with the dress, even though the hem was too high to hide them. A floor-length gown would be no use, because she'd trip on it, or it would get in the way of her cane. Silvie hated how her attempt at finery was spoiled by necessity, but it couldn't be helped.

She picked up her comb from its place on her bedside table beside her snow globe. It had been a while since she'd shaken the globe, and its snow lay dormant, the frozen moment tranquil in its iciness.

She'd bought a deep red lipstick as well, to match her dress. Silvie had only worn makeup a few times. The girls she'd stayed with in the boarding houses and some of the other sentries used it, and occasionally offered to help her try it out.

The results had never really pleased her, back then. When she'd put black on her lashes and red on her cheeks and lips, she *looked* like a different person, and that person gave the impression of being more vivid and interesting than the person she really was underneath. But it was an uncomfortable mask.

Tonight, however, the same look enchanted her. Maybe it was because, as her body didn't feel like home anymore, the result was now wrong on purpose. Silvie was built entirely of intent, of deliberate creation. She'd given herself lips of this shade, made her lashes a feathery dark sweep, and the transformation gave her the same feeling her cloak did. She was surprised to find she liked it.

A sudden rush of vertigo dragged her down into its undertow. No warning, just the sudden swirling, sucking pull of it, making the world a rolling, veering mess around her.

Silvie sat on the edge of her bed with a jolt, then crawled across the soft surface of the blanket so she could lie down.

Everything was spinning, and all she could do was hang on. It was a bad attack, the kind that forced her to triage her entire existence from moment to moment: her makeup didn't matter, her hair didn't matter, the banquet didn't matter, all that mattered was staying very, very still, her knuckles clutch-white as they gripped her bedding.

Silvie didn't know how long she lay there with her head roiling. Forever. The eternal hideous now of her pain made every second endless.

She didn't realise she wasn't alone until she felt a touch on her arm. She started in surprise and looked up. Azura.

'Sorry. I knocked, and said your name, but I think you were lying on your good ear.' Azura explained.

Silvie nodded. 'Right, yeah. Sorry. Vertigo.'

Azura gave her a sympathetic smile. 'I figured. What can I get you?'

'Would it be tacky if I said "the sweet release of death".' Silvie closed her eyes again. Azura chuckled. Silvie shivered, chills prickling her skin to gooseflesh.

'Let me get you a, oh wait, you're lying on your blanket. Um, here.'

Silvie could hear fumbling, and then the familiar weight of her cloak was draped over her. She immediately felt a little better. 'Thank you.'

'Too bad I don't have a joke book, to help distract you,' Azura quipped. 'We could make a whole kit of things, for times when you feel like this. We'll put a joke book in there, and things for making tea, and painkiller tonics. Things to make you feel better.'

Silvie burrowed deeper under her cloak, eyes still shut. 'I'm sorry. I've ruined everything.'

'Nah. We'll just be fashionably late. No big deal. The King will give some speech about how great Lena is, and she'll give out some knighthoods. We aren't missing much.'

Time slipped away from Silvie, for a while everything narrowed to one breath and then the next and then the next. She was vaguely aware the rain had set in and was pounding against the window. She hated feeling imprisoned in her body, trapped in a cage bearing down from all sides.

And then, as randomly as it had hit her, the vertigo receded. The relief was so profound Silvie wanted to weep. She sat up gingerly, readjusting her cloak to rest over her shoulders, the weight of it providing more comfort than warmth.

And then she got her first look at Azura's outfit and simply stared in wonder. She was dressed in a sleek suit, black with red accents. Like Silvie, she wore boots, but Azura's were shapely and femme and stylish – and had a significant heel on them.

'You look gorgeous.'

'I should have put a feather in my buttonhole, to match the fancy cane Lena gave you.'

'Sorry I'm in my boots. I know they kind of ruin the look.' Silvie eased herself off the bed. She still felt awful, but at least she could move now.

'I like them. You look tough, and beautiful.'

Silvie blushed, and then felt embarrassed about blushing which made her blush deepen. She felt nervous and vulnerable and stupidly happy. She realised she must really like Azura because there was no way she'd endure the awkward absurdity of romance for anyone else.

'I think I need to keep my cloak on,' Silvie confessed. 'I'm sorry, I know I look stupid.'

Azura smiled softly. 'You really do look beautiful. There's nobody else I'd want with me but you, and the walking stick and sentry cloak are part of you.'

'Well, the stick's looking appropriate for the occasion, anyway,' Silvie said, gesturing to the impractical silver and ebony contraption. 'But if I wear the cloak to the banquet, people will talk. They'll already be thinking I shouldn't be there, and it'll–'

'You've always had to give things up so others can have them,' Azura said gently, lacing Silvie's fingers with her own. 'Just this once, let yourself be selfish. If the cloak makes you feel better, then stop caring about what other people think you owe them, okay?'

Silvie's face flushed. She nodded. 'Okay.'

They walked hand in hand to the ballroom. The warmth and energy steadied Silvie's nerves, but her pulse still gave anxious little stutters whenever she thought about things too much. She suspected Azura felt the same. They didn't let go of each other.

Rounding another corner led them to a long corridor. Silvie leaned against a recessed alcove in the wall that had probably housed a statue at some point. Outside the windows, the rain had become a storm.

'Are you all right? Do you need to rest?' Azura asked, a line of worry on her forehead.

Silvie smiled at her. 'No, I just wanted to do this,' she said, pulling Azura in close enough to kiss.

'Mm. I guess that's reasonable.' Azura had a smile in her voice, pressing back in against Silvie's mouth after speaking. Her lips felt searingly hot against Silvie's own, soft and slick, and one of her hands came up to rest against the curve of Silvie's jaw. The pads of Azura's fingertips ghosted against the hollow behind her soundless ear, and Silvie felt like every nerve in her body was alive and fizzing.

Time stopped mattering as they stood there together, a far more pleasant way for minutes to cease being important than the earlier bout of vertigo. Silvie felt as if they could go on as they were forever, but eventually, regretfully, she eased Azura a few inches back.

The seafoam-green of her irises was a thin rim around her large pupils, and her cheeks were painted with a high flush. She was so beautiful Silvie's heart gave a little flip.

'We should keep going,' she managed to say, voice low. 'We don't want to miss the whole party.'

'Don't we?' Azura gave a wicked little smirk. 'Okay, let's keep going.'

As they drew closer to the ballroom, it became clear the people hurrying up and down the corridor either side of them weren't simply moving with the bustle keeping an event running smoothly.

Azura's hand tightened in her own. 'Something's wrong.'

Silvie nodded in agreement. They picked up their pace, heading towards the heart of the commotion.

Panic was rising in the crowd gathered in front of the closed ornate doors of the ballroom, as everyone reacted to the screams and frantic pounding coming from within.

The girls pushed their way through to the front, Azura's grip on Silvie's hand now white-knuckle tight.

'The food's been poisoned!' a voice wailed from the other side.

Thumps and thuds punctuated the screams and pleas for help as people inside threw themselves against the doors.

'The dead are already rising! Ghouls are loose in here! Save us!'

'The doors have been magically sealed shut,' Azura said. 'It's like the spell I used to keep the cadaveri from coming out of the catacombs, but much much stronger.'

Silvie glanced in horror at Azura. 'With every cadaveri that rises from the poisoned people in that room there will be attacks, which will result in even more cadaveri. We should get away from here,' Silvie said, trying to pull her friend away but she wouldn't budge.

'Lena?! Myles?!' Azura called, loud and sharp enough to override the other raised voices. 'Dad?!'

'I'm out here,' Doctor Corsetti said, as he pushed through the crowd behind them. The throng was growing rapidly in size and volume. He caught Azura in a relieved embrace. 'Lena asked me to write a short speech for her, so I was running late—'

'And Lena's not in there either.' King Claudio's voice was sharp.

The crowd fell quiet as realisation spread their monarch was in their midst.

'Antonio, take two of my guard to help you collect as many healing tonics and salves as you can carry back here. They'll be needed when we get these doors opened. You two,' he jerked his chin at Silvie and Azura, 'follow me. Everyone else, stay back or move to other areas of the building. Armed forces are on their way here.'

He set off towards the eastern wings of the palace, with Azura and Silvie hurrying to keep up with his long strides.

'The accolades don't begin until the banquet's done,' Claudio said, over his shoulder. 'None of Lena's precious artisans or dancers have been admitted yet. The only people trapped in the ballroom are the higher nobility and the Stregoni.'

The King stopped, as they'd reached a branch in the corridor, and faced them. 'I was also supposed to be in there by now.'

'What are you saying?' Silvie asked, trying to ignore Azura's painfully tight grip on her hand.

'It was Lena who sealed the doors,' Claudio stated, as if it was obvious. He pointed down the hall. 'You two check her rooms, I'll check the christallo.'

'Wait, what's—' Azura began, but the King was already striding away from them in the other direction.

'Come on. This way,' Silvie said. 'You might have to help me climb the stairs.'

Silvie hadn't been to Lena's tower since the two of them had played chess together. The outer sitting room was still sumptuous and impersonal, a space bearing close to no stamp of its occupant. This time, however, the doors to Lena's inner quarters were thrown open.

And inside was chaos.

Broken objects and torn furnishings were tossed every which way around the room. The windows were wide open, a strong gale and heavy rain forcing its way inside through wildly flapping curtains. Part of an internal wall now revealed a steep, narrow flight of hidden stairs heading down.

'That's how Lena knew how to find the invisible catch in the catacomb walls,' Silvie said quietly, as too many things Lena had alluded to, now made sense. 'She'd seen architecture like it before.'

'But where does it go?' Azura asked, confused. 'This room's supposed to be absolutely safe. Myles was stationed outside at night so nobody could get in...' She trailed off as realisation dawned.

Silvie didn't want to be the one to help Azura understand the truth of it, but there was no point trying to protect her now.

'He was there to prevent Lena from getting out,' she corrected, squeezing Azura's hand with her own. 'Because if she fled, then Myles would be forced to stop her, which would be torture for them both. Remember what she said? They're like the rat-king bones. They wanted to be one being, because it's much harder to hurt one than to hurt two.'

'The stairs go to the old King's rooms, don't they? For when other loving kings and adult queens visited each others chambers,' Azura said in a wavering voice, as the horror took shape in her mind. 'But she was a child. She was only two when she came to the palace. Are you saying– Did he– He treated her like a *wife*? All that time he pretended he regarded her as a daughter, and... The court would have been horrified, Silvie. Disgusted. I... I never knew–'

'Of course you didn't know,' Silvie said softly. As if anything could soften this for Azura. 'Lena protected you. King Dante probably told her if you found out and said anything, you'd be executed for daring to voice such wicked treason about him. She and Myles had to carry this alone.'

Azura choked on a sob. 'How are you so calm about this?'

'I'm horrified,' Silvie assured her. 'I'm just not surprised. The more I got to know them, the more I suspected something was awry. And she reminds me of Kolya.'

For a few seconds, Azura didn't move. She stared at the opening to the flight of stairs without saying a word. Then she pulled her hand away from Silvie's and, as she'd done in the packed-earth tunnel, braced against the wall and threw up.

Silvie's eye caught a dark smear of fresh wet ink on the carpet. It was unmistakably a man's shoe print, made by the type of elegant, hardy sole that Myles wore.

That chilled Silvie almost as much as the room's other revelations. It was the most dangerous thing they'd seen; more than the sealed ballroom or the hidden door.

Myles entering Lena's room was an offence punishable by death. To ignore the law so blatantly made it clear the pair didn't care if they lived through this; and that a chance at freedom made them capable of anything. *If* that's what this was all about.

Silvie led Azura back into the outer sitting area, hoping to calm the worst of her distress. She noticed the wastepaper basket in the corner had been knocked over, spilling several empty ink pots and torn paper across the floor. Unlike the last time she was here, however, the paper wasn't shredded as finely, and they could both see what had been written on the pages.

'This sigil is like the one in the catacombs,' Azura said, sharing Silvie's horror at the the symbol scribbled over and over and over. The mark had been powerful enough when simply dismissed from Lena's thoughts, as she'd done in the catacombs. Silvie could only imagine the strength it would gain from being repeatedly formed and then broken through the physical act of ripping the design to pieces.

'Replicating it like this wouldn't just strengthen its power in general,' Silvie said. 'It would increase its hold over Lena, as well. The – *whatever* was waiting in that room in the catacombs found the scars in Lena's heart and festered beneath them.'

An inky footprint on one of the pieces of paper was a match for the stain on the bedroom floor.

A sudden dagger of lightning made Silvie and Azura turn towards the window. The accompanying thunder sent out its deep bass rumble a few seconds later. They could feel it in their bones.

High in the tower, they had a clear view across the bay to the darkest of the churning clouds. The epicentre of this furious storm was directly above Driade Island.

24. AZURA

'It'll be faster if we walk to the docks than if we try to take a carriage,' Silvie said, already making her way as swiftly as she was able towards the stairs that let down from the tower. And the main stairs, not that obscene little secret flight hidden in the wall. 'Neither of us knows enough about horses to harness them, and they're likely spooked in this weather anyway.'

'Will you be okay?'

Silvie smiled thinly. 'I'll be fine. I'll have to be.'

Claudio met them as they reached the last few palace steps. He wore his sword belt, longer blade and dagger both present in their sheaths. As was so often the case, he was unaccompanied by guards.

'The christallo's gone, like I expected,' he told them bluntly. 'She's missing, isn't she? That little viper. She seemed so earnest and happy, planning for this party. I thought for sure her plots were on hold until afterward. She outsmarted me.'

His words made Azura's hammering heart judder in fear. There was nothing nice or charming about Claudio anymore. He seemed ruthless and bloody-minded, and would clearly show no mercy for Lena.

Silvie, meanwhile, ignored him and didn't break pace, intent only on reaching the docks. Azura and Claudio fell into step beside her.

'What do you mean, outsmarted you?' Azura asked him.

'She's been working to destroy Arteria for years. I've kept her from the worst of her meddling, but she managed to slip this one past me. I have to stop her before she does any more damage.'

'But why? Why would she do that?' Azura asked.

'I don't care.' His face was hard. 'Come on, we don't have much time.'

Oh, Azura thought. You don't care, but you *do* know. Because now that she knew the truth, she wondered why Claudio had not protected Lena from his own father. He must have known. It's no wonder Lena hated him so much.

The rain had grown heavy enough that the streets were mostly empty. Azura's high-heeled boots threatened to slip out from under her on the slick, uneven terrain of the cobbles, and Silvie had Lena's fancy cane to contend with, but going back for more practical options would take time they didn't have.

Azura's teeth chattered in the unexpected chill of the downpour, her fancy suit no match for the icy rain. Silvie at least had her sentry cloak over her party clothes, and Claudio seemed to hardly feel the cold at all. To Azura, the storm felt unnaturally freezing.

At the docks, the bay was as disturbed as the rest of their surroundings, the water churning and choppy. The upside was that nobody was around to stop them from climbing into a small boat moored at one of the jetties.

'It's got oars at the ready. Good,' Silvie said.

The words made Azura shudder, because they reminded her there was no guarantee they'd be able to use magic to get back. They might have to destroy the christallo. Or she might die, leaving the others stranded.

The thought was terrifying, but terror gave Azura a clarity that strengthened her resolve. They pushed forward, across the wildness of the bay, towards the island.

The storm was a barrage of hail and snow. Azura thought of Lena's chilled cups of tea, of ice packs for sore ankles. The stolen, and now unbound, power of the christallo had turned the little queen's ice-conjuring tricks into a magic capable of great harm.

At the island, Azura helped Silvie out of the boat and the three of them pulled it onto the shore, high enough it wouldn't be swept off by the violent tides. Azura held out her palm, conjuring up her compass-needle, the magical flame immune to the rain lashing them.

'Lena's this way, I think,' she told her companions. The arrow swung from side to side erratically, the magic in the air too unbound for a steady read. 'The magic's completely crazy. I... I think the Stregoni must be dead.'

They pushed against the brunt of the wind, crossing the wide grassy lawn where Azura and Silvie had once shared a picnic lunch with a little queen and her attendant. Azura pinched her own arm hard enough to bruise, to check the whole situation wasn't some nightmare. Nothing made sense and everything was horrible.

'You can't stop her. I won't let you.'

It was Myles.

The rain had darkened the scarlet of his infantry coat to something sinister, rust or old blood. He was swaying slightly as he stood barring their way.

Azura had seen Myles drunk before but never like this, the glitter in his eyes as bright and hard as needles. No amount of alcohol could ever be enough to numb the pain scrawled across his face. It was like the ceiling of that chamber beyond the catacombs, a void without end.

'She's right. The whole world needs to burn down,' he went on, his voice quiet enough the storm almost swamped it.

'Someone needs to be the villain, and if she wants to be the villain, I'll follow her into hell.'

'But–' Azura started to say.

Claudio pushed past her and charged Myles, the steel of his unsheathed sword a sudden line of brilliant silver in the hazy dark as he slashed. Myles dodged the strike and weaved to the left, instincts sharp despite his drunken state.

They clashed and clashed again, ducking and feinting between the thick tangle of wet tree trunks. Silvie and Azura followed the duel as it moved to higher ground, kept at a distance by the swing of Claudio's sword and the nimble darting strikes of Myles' dagger.

Claudio didn't make a sound when Myles drew first blood, an arc of red splashing down from the meat of his thigh. He simply adjusted his weight and redoubled his press forward, driving Myles back.

Azura could see this was a dirty fight. This was a raw clash of blood and muscle and survival.

Myles struck again for Claudio's leg, this second swipe blocked more successfully than the first. Claudio used the moment to butt his head into Myles' mouth, splitting his lip open and forcing him to stumble back. Myles lost his footing for a moment on the uneven ground and Claudio pressed the advantage, forcing Myles back a step and then another.

The icy wind was an impediment to both men, the wildness of the storm present all around in the whipping of dark branches and the slick shift of leaves underfoot. It was nothing like the temperate climate both men had trained in. None of the palace-bred finesse the combatants had learned was present. Nothing here bore any semblance to structured training.

Claudio's next strike surprised them all, coming out of nowhere with the cleverness of an unexpected checkmate. Silvie shouted a warning but it was already too late. The rain splotches on the scarlet of Myles' jacket were joined by a gush of crimson as his face was sliced with a deep cut from forehead to chin, wounding his eye.

He cried out in pain, stumbled back and fell to the sodden ground.

Silvie and Azura moved forward, trying to halt Claudio's attack by grabbing at his sword arm, but the King bore down on his opponent from the other side, his newly-drawn dagger finding its home deep in Myles' heart. His eyes, blinded and seeing alike, went wide with surprise as the hilt met his chest. They remained open, as the little magic he'd ever had left him in death, the violet of his hair bleaching to white in an instant.

Azura was aware she was crying, sobbing, but knew her feelings were the least important thing in the world right now.

Claudio straightened and wiped his sword on his thigh, not bothering to retrieve the dagger. This, too, was entirely unimportant.

All Azura could do was stare at Myles. Real death was nothing like the graceful collapse of a ballet dancer.

Claudio set off again, his previous run reduced to a limp thanks to the wound on his thigh.

Silvie pulled hard at Azura's arm, breaking her daze. 'Come on, we have to get there before him. They'll kill each other. We have to talk her down.'

Azura knew that would be impossible. With Myles gone, any hope they had to bring Lena's plans to a peaceful end was gone. But they couldn't let Claudio take her too, to end her like... like it didn't even matter.

They overtook the King in a moment, as the compass flame in Azura's palm led them one direction and then another, through the thick trees and into a partially-cleared area near the remains of the old quarantine cottages. The ground was turning quickly to muck, and ice was forming a silvery rime on the branches and grass. Even with his injured leg, Claudio couldn't be far behind.

And then, there she was.

Lena stood in the clearing, her face tilted up into the freezing rain. She was dressed in her black silk party dress, a confection of lace and sparkles, though she'd clearly never intended to be present at her birthday banquet.

'Lena!' Azura yelled. Silvie grabbed her arm, as if to stop her from making a sound, but it was too late.

Lena looked over at them, muzzy confusion on her face.

'Azura? Silvie?' Her voice was distant, distracted. 'What are you doing here? Where's Myles?'

'We've come to…' Azura paused, conscious of how inadequate and silly her words were, while also being the truth. 'We've come to save you.'

The sound Lena made might have started as a laugh, but by the time it emerged from behind her teeth it was a harsh, broken sound. It was like staring at an echo of those long-ago witch-children, her small, vulnerable form infused with a rage larger than the world.

It was also like looking at the zealots who'd killed those children, and who'd flayed the skin of their own backs in the name of holiness.

Lena's eyes bore the glimmer of an open wound.

'You little snake!' Claudio broke free of the trees with a furious shout, sword still in hand, the blood he'd wiped from its blade a smear on his thigh.

'*You*,' she snarled, the word full of venom. 'Nobody else in the kingdom could have stood up to Dante. Nobody else could have saved me from your father. But you pretended you didn't know, even after I begged you! After Myles pleaded. Myles–'

Lena looked at the gore smeared on Claudio's trousers. The little queen's face drained grey as realisation slammed into her.

The scream that ripped free of her throat was like a tear in the world.

The sky cracked with it, lightning flared a hard dagger of light stinking of ozone. The ground trembled beneath their feet, and split open in long jagged gashes.

25. SILVIE

A LIFETIME OF TRAINING KICKED IN, GIVING SILVIE DISTANCE AND clarity from the agony of the moment. Newly open ground over a mass grave while magic was going haywire was a recipe for things to get very, very bad.

'We need to get out of here,' she said to Azura, unsure if her friend registered the words at all. Horrified disbelief had already curdled into fury in Lena's small form, and Azura's gaze was locked on the sight before them.

Even Claudio hesitated at the evidence of Lena's power.

The girl clasped her hands together in front of her and closed her eyes, gathering strength. Within a second, frost condensed in the air, making the world shimmer with cold white.

She pushed her hands out, as if to shove Claudio back, and the force of the icy blast threw him away like a rag doll hurled by an angry child. He slammed into the trunk of an ancient, gnarled tree with an audible crack. He dropped to the ground, as still as Myles had been.

'It's just us, now,' Azura said quietly, the shock of the second murder enough to break her stupor from the first.

'Ghouls are going to rise. You protect her. I'll find the christallo,' Silvie replied. She grabbed Azura by the arm and pulled her into a hard, swift kiss before pulling away.

26. AZURA

Lena made no move to stop Silvie's exit. She turned her face back up to the pelting rain.

'I'm going to lay ruin to it. All of it. I'll give them what they deserve. I'm going to raise every single last cadaveri on this corpse-choked island. They'll find their way underwater and over to the mainland. With all the magic gone haywire, nobody will be able to fight them off.'

'You'll kill everyone. That's not revenge, it's a massacre,' Azura pleaded. 'Lena, this isn't right.'

'I. Don't. Care.' Her venom returned as she snapped at Azura, eyes flashing with her old fire. And then she closed her eyes and dropped her face, shoulders slumped.

Azura had never seen Lena with anything less than elegant posture, but now she was like a broken doll.

'I know why the ghouls try to bite people. It's because there's a hole inside them so big it's going to swallow them if they don't feed it. But it's never going to be full. They aren't even hungry. They don't feel anything.'

She gave a raw laugh, nothing like her usual chuckle, and when she spoke again there was an unfamiliar lilt to her words.

'Do you know how they proved the children were witches? They tortured the smallest ones, and that was enough. They were so very young, and though they'd hidden their power so carefully, the pain was enough to unleash it.

'The older ones though could endure the agony for longer, so the church chose a different tactic. They tortured their parents in front of them. Killed them slowly, hideously. Sooner or later, the children broke, either to save their parents, or to give them more merciful deaths.'

Another fractured laugh, mirthless and terrible. Lena spoke again in the same strange intonation. 'That's what the old King did to the little queen and her boy, you know. He made the boy sit outside and listen. If the boy resisted then the King took it out on the girl. When she struggled, he took it out on the boy. Love is the cruellest weapon. The little queen learned that, just as the children in the catacombs learned that.'

The being that still looked like Lena, but was no longer her, glanced in the direction Silvie had gone. 'It could've been her, if she still had her magic. It could have been you, if you understood your own rage better. But neither of you were quite right. The little queen, though... we were so glad when she broke our seal. She was already perfect.'

Azura's eyes narrowed. 'If she is so perfect, why not let her be in charge?'

The raw, wild laughter had a mocking edge this time. 'You think this is against her will? You think she doesn't want this even more than we do? Fine. Ask her yourself.'

Lena's posture shifted and straightened, her expression familiar again. 'Remember the rumours about the christallo,' Lena said to Azura, 'that it speaks as your secret self? The witch-children spoke as mine. They knew we were the same. Otherwise, how do you explain the fact that Eugenio died before we even went to the catacombs?'

Azura took a half-step backwards, as if the words had physically knocked into her. 'What?'

'He was my control test. His power was about the middle-point among the Stregoni, so his death was a way for me to see how much control each individual magician had over the christallo.'

'But you liked him!'

'I don't like anything. I don't hate anything. I'm empty.'

'Bullshit. You gave my dad a useless errand, to keep him out of the ballroom tonight. You didn't have it in you to kill him, because you're still capable of love.'

Lena's mouth curled into a humourless grin. 'Maybe I just needed to give *you* the motivation to kill me. Maybe the witch-children think you'd be a better choice than me after all. Want to save your father, and Silvie, and everyone? They're not dead yet but they will be soon enough, as long as I'm alive. But you can end this, break the spell. Wanna be the new heroine the sentries pray to? Just kill me. Save it all.'

27. SILVIE

WITH THE DEAD RISING, LENA WOULD HAVE FOUND SOMEWHERE SAFE to stash the christallo, out of harm's way.

Silvie searched her memories of every conversation with Lena about her past, and every scrap of chatter, for a clue as to where she might have hidden it.

A green house. That was it. Silvie needed to find a pretty green house with wrought-iron shutters. Her progress was hampered by the stupid, fancy, flimsy cane Lena had given her. It made movement difficult and dangerous. The little queen hadn't accounted for all the variables, but she'd covered enough. If Silvie hadn't been in dire peril, and worried about Azura, she might have been impressed.

Some of the houses were too ruined to be certain of their colour, but most had enough remaining of their cheerful shades, to be identifiable despite years of neglect and the dark violence of the storm.

She didn't let herself think about how defenceless Azura was, tasked with protecting Lena from the horde that would soon rise. There was no point dwelling on that. All Silvie could do was accomplish the task she'd set herself: take out the christallo, and cut off the source of the rising ghouls at the root. There was a very real possibility she'd be responsible for unbinding all the tamed magic in the country by doing so, but there was no other way. None Silvie was willing to consider anyway. This night had seen enough death already.

The snowstorm was stronger around one house, the intensity of the maelstrom almost obscuring the merry green of its half-collapsed walls. It was a terrible parody of a snow globe, a memory sealed in a swirling storm.

Silvie slammed her shoulder against the door to force it open, and stumbled inside gracelessly.

Energy crackled thick in the air, sending little shocks skittering across Silvie's skin. There was snow inside, too, and ice, so much ice. Crystals of it grew off the christallo in all directions, increasing its size, feeding the pulsing, restless, magical hunger that sought to infest the dead. Every dimension inside the little house was off, distorted by the strength of the energy.

Silvie could feel the hate and anger of the witch-children all around her, too. Even without magic, she could feel it, crackling like lightning in the air, infused in every gleaming edge and facet of the icy christallo.

As Silvie's vertigo reeled she shut her eyes to stop herself vomiting, and took a careful step forward, then another. The dizziness was making every movement a misery, but without sight she could at least limit its dimensions. Gingerly, she slid her feet across the frozen floor. One step, another. There, she should be close enough.

Silvie swung the stupid, flimsy cane against the christallo with all her might, striking it hard with the beak of the silver bird handle. She felt the ice crack. The impact shuddered down her arms and through her whole body, rattling her like a child's toy. She bit her tongue, tasted blood.

Silvie couldn't sense magic anymore, but like anyone alive she knew the inkblot tendrils of entropy when she felt them; the seeping hopeless dark that spread and could not be contained. It rushed at triple speed through her, up, up the silver bird and lacquered wood of the walking stick, over her white-knuckled hands, into her nose and mouth and eyes and ears, deaf and whole alike.

It spoke with her own voice inside her head, because the dark had always sounded like that. Her cruellest, least kind tones, reserved for nobody except herself.

'You dare to stand against this ending? You?' the power asked her, contempt in every soundless syllable. 'Broken, unmagical, useless Silvie, who left her only family behind with nothing but a hand-me-down coat? Whose kiss poisoned a father's love for his daughter? It isn't even a stand, is it, when all it takes is the smallest shift to–'

The walking stick jerked in her grasp, throwing her off balance. The ice was hard under her hands and knees, making her gasp from the sting of its impact. She spat out blood from her bitten tongue as she tried to dampen the wave of nausea from the fall.

'You're no saviour. You know you're not. You're nothing.'

Teeth chattering, fingertips and feet too cold to hurt anymore, Silvie stood as steadily as she was able, clutching at the walking stick again.

'I'm someone who likes the sunlight in graveyards,' she told the cruellest voice inside herself, struggling to make the words defiant and meaningful. That lasted about four seconds, and then she stumbled to the side again and rolled her ankle hard underneath her. The jolt of pain made her swear loudly, but the curse was immediately lost in the roar of the room.

'Pathetic,' her own snide voice replied inside her head.

No. It wasn't coming from inside her head. At first she thought it was, but now she had her bearings.

It was speaking into her deaf ear.

She needed to keep it talking. Keep all that darkness and anger and hate focused on her, on the lonely little spirit of one sad teenage girl.

The wind roared louder. Ice stung her eyes, forcing her to squeeze them even tighter shut. It reminded her of the nights she spent in boarding houses and barracks, telling fairytales while storms raged outside.

She took one careful step forward before the power knocked her to her hands and knees again, several feet back from where she'd stood. The voice in her dead nerves laughed.

'Why bother? Just give up.'

She thought of Azura, of her thick dark hair and beautiful eyes, of her dorky unselfconscious laugh at Silvie's favourite joke.

Silvie crawled toward the christallo.

The laughter in her left ear was so serrated with contempt it was hard to concentrate on the sounds in her right. She was so very tired. Discerning specific sounds from the cacophony, in crowded markets and noisy rooms, made her weary at the best of times and right now there were no threads of conversation for her to untangle, no background hum she could disregard.

There was just her in the chaos, trying to find her way. But she kept crawling forward, because if this is what it came down to, nothing at the end but her and the looming dark…

Well, she'd been there before.

And she hadn't given up last time, so she might as well keep trying now.

'You could have your magic back,' the voice in her left ear said, and though it still sounded like her own worst inner voice, the tone had changed. It sounded like it was bargaining. 'You could have your ear back. You'd never have to use a cane again.'

'That's your big sales pitch? You're not going to offer me kingdoms or riches or anything?' Now Silvie was the one with contempt in her words. Her hands slipped out from under her and she went down hard on her elbow, but she kept crawling forward.

The howling wind was louder now, which meant she was close to the centre of the room again.

'Those are all there for the taking, with my help. You could have a life unfathomably better than the one you have now. You already know that,' the wheedling voice of power promised. 'But I could make *you* better, too. All the magic in the country would be yours to control. Think of what you could do. You could run in a wolf's thoughts every day. Azura would love you forever, with a devotion no human heart can manage unaided.'

She was back at the base of the stand. It was so cold to the touch Silvie wondered if the deep sting in her nerves was from the temperature or if her skin was sticking to the metal and being torn away.

'Is that what you offered the Stregoni? Lena? Did you offer them love and freedom and the return of lost things? The promise of no more loss to come?' Silvie asked.

She had to keep it talking. It was easy enough; she didn't have to fake any of the longing in her words. Her heart ached to be weak. To give in and let it take her over, to accept the hollow promises. Wise, kind rulers had fallen for less, and the voice was right – who was she to defy it? An apprentice who liked sunlight in graveyards, whose balance was bad and whose magic was gone.

She was standing now, braced against the pedestal. The wind felt hard enough to bruise as it pummelled and shoved her, trying to drive her away.

'Silvie. Silvie, let me fix you,' the voice crooned.

Silvie opened her eyes. She could see her little tattoo, the mark of the wolf that Kolya had helped her put there.

She balled her fist and punched forward.

28. AZURA

THE DEAD WERE RISING. TERROR HELD AZURA IN PLACE AS HIDEOUS rotting hands came up through the fissures in the earth, pushing through the tangle of tree roots and dirt to scrabble for purchase on the rain-drenched ground.

'Lena, we have to get away from here. We have to stop this, please!'

Azura's words sounded trite and flat even to herself. Words like that weren't going to mean anything when things had already fallen apart so utterly. When Myles was already dead.

Lena offered no response, her eyes brittle and blank as she looked at her. Azura knew what a sight she must be, in the suit she'd chosen for the birthday banquet; an awkward, nervous kid playing at dapper dress-ups, now ruined in the rain and mud and wind of the storm.

Lena was equally bedraggled, her shoes gone and stockings torn to almost nothing, her exquisite dress shredded to a mess of dark silk and gemstones and lace.

None of that mattered now.

The cadaveri, clawing up from the ground below, scratched and scrabbled at Lena's legs; their cracked nails and exposed bones scraped weeping lines of red into the flesh of her calves. They were trying to drag her beneath the muddy earth as they climbed free of it.

Hands and hands and more hands, from the tiniest baby bones to the remains of tall strong brawlers, a mass grave's worth of the mindless driven to devour, were striving to consume the halo of energy radiating from Lena, who stood above the chaos with a passive, vacant look on her face. She was barely aware of where she was.

A tree limb cracked and crashed to the ground beside Azura, close enough to impact the soles of her feet. It broke her frozen terror. She grabbed the branch which was much heavier than expected, soaked as it was with the ice in the air. She evaporated the extra weight without thinking about it, then lit the end into a crackling flame.

Azura took a deep breath to stave off the sadness of knowing Myles was beyond anyone's help, and the fact Silvie's own desperate fight, hunting down the christallo, meant she was also on her own.

Azura couldn't help them. They couldn't help her. There was just her, and her tiny flame, against the waking nightmare of so many dead rising between her and Lena. When grasping bony hands tried to wrench the stick from Azura's grip, paying no mind to the fire at its tip, she had to stop herself from vomiting at the smell of burning rot.

'Lena, please! Come this way, come over to me,' Azura shouted into the wind.

'I want it all to stop.' Lena's voice was barely audible. She stumbled, staggered and almost went down as the cadaveri arms grabbed and clawed and pulled. They would soon be free enough from the dirt to bite as well as scratch.

Shuddering at the thought, Azura scrambled closer, grabbed Lena's arm and hauled her against her own body. She expected Lena to shove and struggle, but the smaller girl was as passive and limp as a ragdoll.

'I want it to stop. I just want it all to stop.'

'It's going to be all right,' Azura promised. More empty words, helpless and meaningless but all she could think of. 'I promise, it's–'

The platitudes were a mistake. It was like a spark had caught on dry kindling – Lena was suddenly flailing in Azura's arms.

'You promise?' she howled. 'Liar! Liar! Nothing will ever be all right ever again!'

Azura held on as best she could, caught up in a hurricane of anger harder to bear than the whirlwind of magic around them. And she was still trying to beat off the cadaveri with the flaming branch.

The rage, radiating off Lena like a furnace, brought its own pain but Azura couldn't tell how much was Lena's own and how much came from the witch-children. Maybe it didn't matter.

'Just kill me! Do it already!' Lena fought harder, scratching her nails against Azura's cheek and throat, causing long stinging welts.

'The witch-children died. They can't want you to die as well,' Azura said.

Lena snarled at her. 'How can you know anything about what they want? About what I want? You don't know what it's like. You don't know anything.'

Lena tried to twist out of her grip but Azura clung even tighter, splaying one hand against Lena's back, as she fought to keep their balance. It was like trying to save a drowning person whose movements dragged and tired their rescuer, dooming two instead of one.

Lena punched and kicked and screamed. But she was small and light, and Azura managed to keep her close, holding on for dear life. Both their lives.

Please, Silvie, please…

'If you're so frightened, kill me yourself!' Lena shouted. 'That'll save you. That'll save everyone. Just destroy me!'

Azura slapped her, hard.

'Have you forgotten who was there with you when you jumped in the canal?' Azura demanded. 'Why you needed Myles in the first place? I'll never be your conscience. I'd let the whole world burn before I sacrifice you to save it. What would be the point in saving it, if you're lost?'

A huge hand, purple and green and bloated, wrenched Lena's ankle so hard the two of them nearly fell. Azura held the fire to it, afraid the flame would hurt Lena as well, but if it burned her, Lena gave no sign, her teeth already bared in a feral grimace.

'What's the point of saving it anyway? It's horrible. It's all horrible. Everything is cruel and dark and awful, and it deserves to fall to pieces.'

'Yes, probably!' Azura agreed, words ripped from her by the wind. 'So let's make it better!'

With a final shattering crack of thunder, the gale stopped. The sudden stillness was eerie, as if time itself had ceased.

The grasping hands went limp, merely dead flesh and bone once more.

For a moment, there was nothing.

Then Lena drew a deep and ragged breath, gave a howl of thwarted rage, and began to sob.

Azura wasn't sure the little queen was able to breathe properly through the enormity of the pain. The screaming had been easier to listen than Lena's weeping, which was the sound of a grief large enough to swallow a soul.

The snowstorm evaporated around them, leaving the air thick and damp with humidity.

With the immediate danger gone it was hard to know how long they stood there, Lena lost in her pain, Azura holding her.

'I want to die,' Lena gulped. 'I want everything to die. I want it to stop.'

'I've got you. It's okay.'

'It's not. You're a liar.'

'She's not lying. She just doesn't get it.'

Lena went prey-still in Azura's arms at the sound of Silvie's voice. 'Get what?'

'How it feels when people treat you as a thing they own.'

Silvie stood before them, leaning heavily on her cane with one hand, the other hand wrapped in her cloak, its mustard yellow stained to such a wet red it was almost black. Her hair was tangled with twigs and leaves, one of her eyes had begun to swell shut, and a long cut on her cheekbone was bleeding a sluggish trickle down her jawline.

'It sucks,' Silvie said simply. 'Maybe it's never going to be all right. But it's better than death.'

'It's not.' Lena was still buried in against Azura's shoulder, clinging to her now, burrowed in so tightly Azura could feel her mouth move for every syllable.

'Take her to the boat.' Silvie didn't look at Azura as she addressed her. 'Don't go the way we came. Go another way. I'm going to—'

Her expression was closed-off, even more distant and shuttered than when Azura first met her.

Azura felt a slice of cold fear down her back. Something was very wrong.

'What are—' Azura started to ask. Silvie still wouldn't look at her as she cut her off.

'I'll join you soon. I need to close his eyes.'

29. SILVIE

WHEN THE OTHERS WERE GONE, SILVIE UNWRAPPED THE RAGGED yellow cloak from around her arm. Shards of the christallo were embedded between her knuckles. Her blood gleamed oddly in the refracted light.

She dropped the remains of the cloak. It was of no use anymore.

Claudio was still alive, although barely. It seemed unfair to Silvie, that Myles barely had a moment to understand his life was over, while Claudio was still clinging to life, long enough to be rescued, to get a second chance.

It wasn't fair. But none of it had ever been fair. Silvie understood Lena's rage in a way Azura never would.

'Please,' Claudio gasped, his commanding self-assuredness gone. 'Silvie, please. Help me.'

'I'm sorry,' she told him, kneeling beside him. 'I can't.'

'You can. Your hand, you can... There's enough power in... I'll give you anything. I'll make you my queen. The whole kingdom will be yours.'

'I'm sorry,' she said again, reaching out to place her hand on his heaving chest. His breathing grew more even, as she took away his pain, then stopped. He was still.

Silvie knew Azura would have saved him. Azura was a good person. Silvie wasn't.

Her pain was agony beyond agony. But Silvie had known that was the price of clinging to the christallo's power for long enough to accomplish what she had to do.

She'd known from the moment he fell that Claudio wasn't dead, because Silvie had seen a lot of death. And she'd known from that same moment there was no way both he and Lena could come out of this alive.

There was only one resolution Silvie found acceptable.

She could already feel her third finger was never going to be quite right again, could feel the deep and profound wound left by letting the shard stay embedded there instead of wrenching it free. The cost of a little borrowed magic in her bloodstream, kept for long enough to kill a king.

She didn't regret it. She'd never been the kind to regret things. Silvie didn't care that she and Azura had saved Arteria. She'd never been welcome there. Her place was always going to be outside the gate.

Silvie had suffered too much in her life to believe suffering had any transformative grace to it. It didn't make her stronger, or more noble, or braver, or kinder. But it did make her who she was.

Her footsteps were shaky as she stumbled over the uneven ground, the twisted roots and the nightmarish remains of ghouls under her feet. The ornamental cane was almost useless for actual support, but it was all she had, so she made do.

She reached Myles' body, crouched beside him and closed his eyes.

She'd changed her mind about endings, now.

Silvie had no white fan to hold aloft, to let those dancers know their fate. She didn't even have a yellow cloak anymore. All she had was the last crackles of a dying age, shards deep in her flesh like a dagger in her heart.

And perhaps one other thing.

Silvie closed her eyes and reached into the dark, into the void that lived on her left shoulder at every moment.

A year ago, something had wrenched her across the world and shown her the grief and misery of two girls very like herself. For a long time, Silvie had wondered why she'd been given that vision, what it could mean.

Now she thought she understood. The witch-children of the catacombs had died so horribly their rage had lingered and haunted, clinging to a new vessel who could carry out their will. They'd left their sigil behind, a bridge into the future.

Silvie thought of a windowsill in a high tower, of two small crosses in the wood.

The queen's decision on the ending trumps all else.

'Queen Eve. Your spirit found mine when my wolf died that night, when the magic was at its most chaotic,' Silvie said softly into the dark. 'And you knew I'd care about them more than about any kingdom. That's what pulled me across the world, when I was halfway to being dead myself.'

She gulped back a sob. Her whole body hurt so much. She could feel every broken bone in her hand.

'The christallo's almost spent, but there's a little left. If I go to Lena and Azura now, everything will go back to normal, eventually. Spell-casters will coax the magic back into line, using this little shard that's left to build it all back up again. The ghouls will rise as always, the sentries will die as always.'

She flexed her fingers. The pain gave her clarity, gave her focus.

'But I want something else to happen instead. Whatever's left of you, let me have it.' She let out a broken little laugh. 'I've got all the power left in the kingdom, and I don't know if it'll be enough. I need your help.'

There was no sense of another presence, or of any strength being lent to her. She'd have to trust to hope.

Not her strongest skill, but she would make do with what she had.

She looked down at Myles. Even with his eyes closed, there was no illusion of sleep. His white hair made him look older, but he was still so young. They were all so young. Silvie couldn't remember the last time she hadn't felt very, very old.

She pulled the dagger free from his body and threw it aside, forgotten, then placed her ruined hand over the wound it left behind. The torn flesh was already cooler than the painful fever-heat crawling up her arm.

'They're waiting,' she told him quietly. 'You have to help build what comes next. We need you there with us, alive. So you can't go yet.'

And she dumped all the magic left in Arteria into the broken heart of a changeling child.

About the Author

Mary Borselino is a writer and translation editor of Japanese games who lives in Melbourne.

Mary's books include the YA punk vampire series *The Wolf House*; the queer horror novel *The Devil's Mixtape*; and the YA speculative fiction *Thrive* (Clan Destine Press).

Acknowledgements

The Hollow Witch was written with the support of Writers Victoria, who were kind enough to include me in their Writeability and Publishability Fellowships. I especially want to thank Jax Brown, Scot Gardner and Shivaun Plozza for their feedback and guidance.

My heartfelt thanks to Lindy Cameron and Narrelle Harris for believing in this book, giving it a home at Clan Destine Press, and a superb editorial hand – you made this book what it is today.

A sincere thank you to Simone Dorra for translating the novel into German.

Thank you to Maria Borsellino, Lauren E. Mitchell, Asajii Reynolds and Tabby Wright for reassuring me the book was good when I didn't believe it.

I never could have written this novel without the love and care of the people I lived with while working on it – thank you to Maria Borsellino, Eris Barnes, and Lisa Reeve for letting me sit on the couch typing for endless hours instead of being social. Thanks to Gally and Glinda for important dog duties.

Thank you to Sitara Jaronson for listening to my endless angst and offering sensible words of support.

Thank you to Verity Mathews and Belinda Rule for allowing me to ramble at brunch, and to Audrey, Erin, Erinna and Gracie for Discord chatter.

Thank you to AkirouArt for the beautiful cover artwork, and to Clara Stone at AuthorTree for the German cover design.

Deep appreciation and thanks to C.S. Pacat and Jess Walton for providing quotes about the book – you believed in my words when even I didn't!